SCHOOLED
IN DEATH

SCHOOLED
IN DEATH

Wendy Milton

Typeset by Sunset Publishing Services Pty Ltd
Cover design by Patrick Hawkins © 2019
www.patrickhawkins.com.au
Printed by Lightning Source

PawPrint Publishing
PO Box 415, Rozelle, 2039
www.wendymilton.com

ISBN 978-0-6482487-2-9

ONE

Slowly, almost reverently, she shook the lipstick from its silver casing. Taking a deep breath she began, steadying herself as she leaned forward, a frown of concentration on her face. Her hair fell slightly forward, but she brushed it back. She didn't rush. She paid particular attention to the Cupid's bow, and then stood back to examine her handiwork. The flower she had brought didn't quite match the pink of the lipstick, but no matter.

At 7.40 a.m. on Monday, 23rd May, 1975, two girls were seated on the wooden bench on the verandah of Edwards House, regarding with mild curiosity the plump figure of the bursar as she descended the steps of the headmaster's cottage. Why was Miss Hancock clinging to the railing? Why was her bosom quivering like a blancmange? The sun was reflecting off her glasses as she turned this way and that until, with a little shriek, she turned and hauled herself back up the steps into the office, daunted by the indifference of the autumn morning.

It didn't occur to Mary Grimes and Josie St John to ask if she needed help. Miss Hancock must have been at least fifty, and the thought of strong emotion attaching itself to anyone so old was disgusting.

'Do you think Radish tried it on with her?' said Mary, squinting over the border of hydrangeas surrounding the verandah and trying to penetrate the darkness of the doorway across the sunlit yard. Josie giggled at the prospect of Miss Hancock being groped by Mr Radcliffe. 'Maybe she walked in on him while he was . . . you know.'

'And then went back for another look?' asked the incredulous Mary.

The girls dissolved into laughter, and were still laughing when Mildred Obermeyer, better known as Matron, came to remind them that they had very little time to shower and get ready for breakfast.

So it was that they missed the police car that sped up the drive and screeched to a halt in a cloud of gravel and dust at the bottom of the steps that were the scene of Miss Hancock's agitation. They were unable to describe for their friends the relative heights and builds of the young policemen who took the steps two at a time and disappeared into the office. Even worse, they were confined to their bedrooms, and later to the hall when the ambulance arrived to convey their headmaster to the morgue.

Miss Hancock was gabbling almost incoherently into the moist receiver, clutching it like a lifeline. 'Oh, Mrs Graham!' were the only intelligible words Constables Lockyer and Fraser heard as they passed her office and entered the study, the door to which was ajar. There were no signs of a struggle. At his desk, leaning back in his chair (an ornately carved, gothic affair) was Horace Radcliffe. The headmaster's eyes were open, staring with surprise and disbelief at a person or persons unknown. He'd been dead for some time.

It wasn't the ghastly pallor of the headmaster's face that surprised them, for they'd seen death before. It was what had happened to the headmaster *after* death. His tie was fastened around his head at a rakish angle, and behind his left ear was a wilted hibiscus. As if in protest at this indignity, the headmaster's lips were pulled back from his teeth, giving his mouth the appearance of a snarl. Around his mouth was a lavishly drawn smile in bright-pink lipstick, its exaggerated curves extending onto his cheeks and the points of the Cupid's bow peaking to his nostrils. It looked for all the world, said Constable Fraser, like an end-of-term prank.

TWO

At his last public appearance, a late-summer day five weeks earlier, death had been the last thing on the headmaster's mind. Open Day at Eldersley was something of a social event for a school that played host to the daughters of the rich and famous. Horace Radcliffe was resplendent in full military regalia, including brown leather gloves, swagger stick and colourful decorations. The officer's cap that concealed his thinning hair was extremely flattering. He surveyed with satisfaction the setting for his speech and nodded and smiled paternalistically, extending his right hand to those fathers whose social pedigree or bank balance warranted such familiarity.

Around him there was much activity, the culmination of weeks of planning. On the verandahs around the quadrangle, chairs were arranged for parents and VIPs (very important parents), who were arriving in larger numbers than expected. Extra chairs were being fetched from the hall. The larger than expected turnout was a satisfying indication for the headmaster of his popularity and influence.

On the dais were chairs for Gilbert Fairweather, executive director of the firm that managed the school, the headmaster, the mayor, the lady mayoress and the archdeacon. A microphone promised speeches, and a bouquet of flowers for the lady mayoress was wilting in a nearby classroom, like the spirits of the nervous child nominated to present it. Two divisions of the Girls' Service Training Unit (GSTU) were waiting to give a demonstration of precision marching.

As the official party moved to the dais, a hush fell. The headmaster, swagger stick tucked beneath his left armpit, took the microphone. His voice was rich and melodic.

'Ladies and gentlemen, visiting dignitaries, members of staff, girls . . . *the school is the place!*' He paused. 'It is the place where the care previously administered in the home now rests. It is the place where the responsibility for guiding and counselling youth now lies. It is the place where the traditions of loyalty to a group, to a community, to one's country and one's race, are upheld. It is the place, the *only* place, that will shape the future of Australia.'

The tenet of the headmaster's speech was that society was going to the dogs. He cited drugs, free love and reduced standards in schools, including the move away from prescriptive teaching. He cited social service payments to the indolent, attempts at rehabilitation in a justice system that favoured the criminal over the victim, and grants of public money to half-witted attempts at artistic expression. He cited condemnation of military service as ignoble and unnecessary, and a government prepared to scorn those cherished traditions such as the national anthem, the flag and the honours system, that were responsible for Australia's existence.

Why, he asked, were traditional social values declining? The question was rhetorical. They were being sacrificed, he said, on the altar of materialism, fanned by the flames of technology. Labour-saving devices had created a dangerous amount of leisure for society's traditional homemakers, women, who were abandoning their kitchens and plunging headlong into the workforce, leaving the guidance and care of their offspring to social welfare agencies. The government, instead of tackling the need to reduce the desire for material goods, was encouraging this trend by setting up state-controlled kindergartens. Why could not social welfare payments be made to mothers who stayed at home to bring up their children? If it were up to him, it would be *illegal* for mothers of young children to go to work at all! The executive director glanced nervously at the sea of female faces.

The trend was fuelled, the headmaster went on, by cheap birth-control methods that made it possible for women to delay reproduction. What happened when children *did* intrude? Working mums, anxious to earn the extra income needed to maintain their automated homes, turned to welfare agencies and preschools to avoid the inconvenience of rearing them. This, he warned, would have dire effects on a generation growing up starved of a normal family atmosphere and of the maternal influence in early life.

Having despatched the traditional homemakers, the headmaster turned his attention to the church. It was, he said, no longer providing effective pastoral care for individuals in a world that had become cynical of religion. It was little more than a social welfare agency for groups in the community, or for groups in someone *else*'s community (here there was a small ripple of laughter). The executive director shifted uncomfortably in his chair, glancing at the archdeacon's face, which had heightened in colour.

The school was the place, the headmaster repeated. The school would pick up where women, the family and the church had left off. The school would arrest social decay by producing great leaders of men. The school would uphold family values, discipline, censorship. The school would not jettison prescriptive teaching. The school would guide children – guard them from those dark, totalitarian ideologies that promised them a society in which the world's wealth was shared on a more equitable basis. The school would thwart totalitarianism's stated aim of overrunning the world by military action and by stealth through the ranks of the naïve, the less educated and the less intelligent.

At a signal from the headmaster, the GSTU erupted onto the quadrangle to the strains of the Colonel Bogey March, slouch hats tilted at identical angles. They marched proudly, eyes to the front, shoulders back, heads erect. Even those parents whose feathers had been ruffled by the headmaster's anti-feminist views were sufficiently appeased by his talk of old-world values, discipline, capitalism and elitism. The embodiment of these values was their daughters' military display. The key to securing them was money.

THREE

Detective Sergeant Haines was dozing when the phone rang. He rolled over and looked at the clock. God, it was nearly eight-thirty. Why did he have that last whisky? His mouth was dry and he was still wearing yesterday's shirt, underpants and socks. He'd had the foresight to remove his trousers, which were hanging over the back of the chair. He hauled himself out of bed and snatched at the receiver.

'Haines. No, I was just doing my morning exercises. Where? Jesus Christ, Fraser! You should have rung me earlier. Ah . . . I was probably in the shower. Give me twenty minutes. Don't let them touch anything.' In the bathroom he drank deeply from the tap, cleaned his teeth and examined his reflection. His eyes were blood-shot. He threw water over his face and torso, and wiped himself hurriedly with the towel. The floor was awash. Then he changed his socks and underpants, and put on his last clean shirt. Within minutes he was in his car, heading towards Eldersley College.

As Edward Haines was walking towards his car, Amy Graham was replacing the telephone receiver and enjoying the silence into which the waves of Miss Hancock's hysteria were receding. The headmaster of Eldersley was dead? Lipstick? Flower? She thought of the many public figures compromised by death, but immediately dismissed the thought that Horace Radcliffe could have been leading anything other than the puritanical, passionless life he appeared to lead. She hadn't liked the man, but the very reasons she disliked him made it impossible for him to have been involved in anything indelicate.

She recovered her car keys from the dresser and drove towards the college that had employed her all those years ago. As the grounds came into view, she could see Mr O'Flaherty leaning on his broom, watched closely by his Jack Russell, Ira. Mr O'Flaherty assumed the responsibility of Eldersley's ambassador-cum-outdoor-receptionist, doffing his cap to parents and passing the time of day with staff. Although his official role was to maintain the buildings and grounds, it was the social aspects of the job that appealed to him. This view was not shared by Ira, who was always glad when his master stopped hanging about on street corners and got down to the serious business of rooting around in gardens, emptying rubbish bins, destroying pigeon nests and, if they were very lucky, despatching the odd rat.

Amy greeted Mr O'Flaherty, who seemed oblivious to the events unfolding at the top of the long driveway. In front of the headmaster's cottage, three police cars and an ambulance were blocking further entry. She could see men moving about inside the cottage. Girls were being directed towards the hall, though they would rather have stayed to find out what was going on. A rumour was spreading that the headmaster's cottage had been broken into and that Miss Hancock had been raped, a rumour fuelled no doubt by the testimony of Mary Grimes and Josie St John who'd decided, belatedly, that their early-morning observations might have been useful.

Amy approached one of the constables and asked for Detective Sergeant Haines.

'He's around, ma'am. Just arrived.'

'I'd be grateful if you could let him know that Amy Graham is here. I'll be on the verandah.'

'He's pretty busy right now, ma'am, but I'll see what I can do.'

When Haines got the message, he wished he'd had a shave and a proper shower. He extricated himself from the scene inside the headmaster's study, smoothed his hair and crossed the yard to where Amy Graham was standing. He walked self-consciously, aware that she was observing him. Twenty years earlier, minus his paunch, he'd crossed a dance floor and swept her into his arms for a jazz waltz. She didn't look any different now, he thought, though the signs of age were there in the form of lines around her inquisitive eyes. She was still slim, shapely and delicate, like a piece of fine china.

''Morning, Amy. How's things?'

'Not very well, apparently. Laetitia rang me. Was it a heart attack?'

'Not sure. If it was, someone mucked around with the body afterwards. Have to be an autopsy. What was he like, this bloke? Hadn't been headmaster long, had he?'

'About eighteen months. I suppose you're aware that there have been changes?'

'I was told the Church had handed over the college to some company. Has it been sold?'

Amy gave a wry smile. 'Sold out, some would say. It wasn't making money. It's been leased to a company called Pastoral Enterprises – a family company, I believe. The Church still owns the buildings and grounds, but Mr Fairweather of Pastoral Enterprises runs the school as a business. He's a sort of . . . educational entrepreneur.' Amy dropped her voice confidentially at the word 'entrepreneur', giving the impression that it was something shameful.

Haines, who prided himself on being a no-nonsense sort of bloke, didn't have time for games. 'And Radcliffe was *his* man?'

'Yes. Mr Fairweather appointed him.'

'Does this mean there were a few disappointed hopes amongst the locals?'

'More than a few,' Amy acknowledged. 'I can think of two who would gladly have taken the helm when Mrs Bridges retired, and undoubtedly there were other staff who nursed aspirations. Ambition is a common cause of dissent, don't you agree, Edward?'

Haines experienced a brief thrill as she spoke his name. 'He was having trouble with the staff? Is that what you're telling me?'

'I'm not quite sure whether he was having trouble with them or they were having trouble with him,' Amy replied. 'I do know that he was directing his attention towards certain staff. He made it clear at the last board meeting that he wasn't satisfied with the calibre of some of them . . . Yes, "calibre" was the word he used,' she assured Haines in response to his quizzical look. 'He even hinted that he was conducting some sort of investigation. Nothing specific, of course.'

'No names?'

'Definitely not. Do you think he was . . .?'

'No one can be certain of that yet, Amy. Scientific squad will have to decide. All I can say is that I wouldn't have chosen to be found like that. He was conservative?'

'Oh goodness, yes. I'm certain he expected everyone to take him very seriously.'

'And what was your opinion of him?'

She hesitated. 'He was a little . . . inflexible,' she said carefully. 'Would it be possible for me to see the body?'

Haines shrugged. 'If you must. He's certainly inflexible now.' He turned, and Amy Graham followed him back across the yard, up the steps and into the coolness of the headmaster's office, where the government medical officer, a tall, broad-shouldered man in his late fifties, had just completed his examination. Mervyn Jamieson looked up as Haines and Amy walked in. Amy had the distinct feeling that he disapproved of her being there. 'I'll try not to be in your way, Mr . . .?' Haines was left with no choice but to make the introduction.

'Not a problem, I assure you, Mrs Graham,' Jamieson responded gallantly.

'You're not local, Dr Jamieson?'

'No. Quite a coincidence really, me being on the scene. I was at the hospital . . . sudden infant death syndrome. They called you in late last night, I believe?' This last was directed at Haines, who nodded. 'Very sad. So when the sergeant here rang the hospital, I was just about to head off. As chance would have it, I was chatting to the nurse who took the call. I'm stationed in Goulburn normally. Yes, the headmaster was very lucky to have caught me.'

Haines snorted, and Amy, smiling politely, detached herself and stood by the window. Nothing in the office seemed out of place. She turned her attention to the corpse, which reminded her of a vandalised waxwork. She studied it for some time before becoming aware that Haines was addressing her. 'I'm sorry. Did you say something?'

'I just wanted to make sure you were all right.'

'Perfectly, thank you. I was just wondering why . . . well . . .' She glanced apologetically at Jamieson. 'It's his hands. Have you noticed how the fingers of his right hand are different from the fingers of his left? It's probably nothing, but to see one hand so firmly clenched and the other so open and . . . well, relaxed. It seems strange.'

Jamieson flashed her a practised smile, taking the opportunity to observe her more closely. Up-market. Expensively dressed but not ostentatious. Must have been a stunner in her day, and still easy on the eyes, particularly in this light. 'No offence, Mrs Graham. The fingers of his right hand appear to have been released from rigor. Needless to say, this information is confidential.' This remark was directed at Haines.

'Mrs Graham's discretion can be relied on,' said Haines. And you can pull your head in, he thought, peeved at Jamieson's tone and the fact that he'd not previously mentioned the corpse's hands. 'Have you been able to estimate a time of death?' he asked abruptly.

'I'd say somewhere between Friday night and Sunday morning. I'll do a complete post-mortem when I get him back to Goulburn. Tomorrow morning, first thing. Interested?'

'Just send me the report.'

'As you wish. Delighted to have met you, Mrs Graham.'

'Oh . . . yes. Goodbye, Dr Jamieson.'

A photographer's white light illuminated the corpse upon which Amy's attention was riveted, displacing the dim, scholarly atmosphere. She moved closer to the desk, peering at Horace Radcliffe's waxen visage. They were impatient for her to leave.

'Just a couple of minutes, please?' As Haines left the study, she removed a handkerchief from her handbag and waved it briefly in the direction of the hapless photographer. 'May I? A tiny sample of the lipstick?' It was done. She smiled sweetly at the photographer, held a finger to her lips and hurried after Haines.

FOUR

Matron surveyed the scene in front of the headmaster's cottage from her room on the upper storey of Edwards House. The boarders had been sent to the hall and would remain there for the next hour at least, or until lessons were resumed. Staff had been rostered to supervise them. The remaining staff members were on the ground floor, exchanging versions of events.

She saw Mrs Graham descend the steps and pick her way through the throng of vehicles. Would she be able to tell them anything? Miss Hancock was reaching her use-by date as a source of information. But if Amy Graham suspected anything, she'd probably keep it to herself; the woman was infuriatingly circumspect.

Matron turned from the window and glanced complacently at her reflection in the dressing table mirror. She straightened her shoulders, tugged gently at the peaks of her white blouse and brushed a speck of lint from her navy skirt. She examined her rear view and reflected with satisfaction that no seams or bulges were apparent. Her hair, pulled tightly into a vintage french roll, had ceased to struggle. She glanced around the austere little room, as she did habitually before leaving it. Nothing was out of place. The only concessions to vanity – a hairbrush, comb and a lipstick – were neatly aligned on the dressing table.

Amy Graham and Haines entered Edwards House just as

Matron's legs, in their support hose and sensible shoes, appeared around the bend in the stairs.

Amy's hand fell lightly on Haines's arm. 'Mildred, this is Detective Sergeant Haines. Sergeant, this is Mildred Obermeyer who looks after the boarders and the administration of the residential block. I'm sure she won't mind if you call her Matron. Most people do.' Matron nodded her assent, shook Haines's hand, and the usual greetings were exchanged. 'Sergeant Haines would like to talk to the staff,' Amy continued. 'In fact, I believe he'll want to interview staff over the next few days. Perhaps,' she added, turning to Haines for confirmation, 'he'll also want to talk to you about the boarders? I'll leave that to you to discuss.'

The three continued into the staffroom, where a dishevelled, puffy-eyed Miss Hancock roused herself from her isolation and misery with: 'Oh, Mrs Graham . . .' The attention of Matron and the staff focused on Haines, whom Amy briefly and efficiently introduced. Leaving the sergeant to those who would undoubtedly find themselves under his scrutiny, Amy beckoned to Miss Hancock and steered her in the direction of the kitchen where, she knew, a large black kettle would be simmering on the stove.

'Nothing like a cup of tea, Laetitia, to settle the nerves.' She busied herself with cups and saucers, chatting to the emotionally exhausted bursar as if nothing had happened, hoping that hot, sugared tea and a semblance of normality might restore the latter's speech and render her capable of recounting, for Edward Haines, the morning's events. No point in rushing.

She turned her thoughts to what Miss Hancock enjoyed most: crochet work, African violets, and black-and-white movies starring Katherine Hepburn and Spencer Tracey. 'I nearly rang you last week,' she lied. 'There was the prettiest pattern for a woollen throwover in one of the magazines in the library. You know the sort of thing – squarish in three of four different colours, with a lovely scalloped edge. I thought it would look nice on the back of my old leather lounge, but of course I don't have your expertise with a crochet hook. I was going to ask whether you'd take it on. It would mean months of work, but as you know I'm quite comfortable and cost isn't an issue. You do still do all that lovely work, don't you?'

Miss Hancock, relieved to discover someone willing to discuss something other than the horrible scene in the headmaster's study, blinked appreciatively and eyed the steaming cup of tea Amy placed in front of her. She lifted it carefully from its saucer, her ringless hands embracing the bowl and her eyes closing as the heat penetrated her palms and the smell of Darjeeling wafted across her nostrils.

She sighed, opening her eyes, and an involuntary shudder made her replace the cup. 'There are some that are done in squares and sewn together, but I've seen quite a few that are done in rows,' she offered, sliding into the familiar subject like a hunted animal into a hole. Amy's persistent interest warmed her, like the tea. The colour returned to her face. She chattered mindlessly about tiny garments fashioned for her niece's children, her grandmother's precious pattern for bed socks, and the double-bed quilt it had taken her almost twelve months to complete. She promised to look for Amy's throw-over amongst the magazines in the library, and offered to propagate a leaf from one of her most recently acquired African violets for Amy to keep on a warm window sill, preferably on the eastern side of her cottage.

'They burn, you see. But they're hardy, you know. I've never actually had one die . . .' She paused, the word hanging in the air between them like a sentence. She removed her glasses and tried to polish them on her damp handkerchief, gazing at Amy with myopic, desolate eyes. 'He is quite dead, isn't he?'

'I'm afraid so, Laetitia. Do you want to talk about it now, or will

I come to see you tomorrow? I suppose the sergeant will want to see you, too,' she said casually. 'He could interview you here – or at home, if that's best for you.'

'There's nothing to talk about.' Hysteria threatened to engulf her once more, but Amy's hand covered hers and the moment passed. 'I was going to make him some tea. I went in . . .'

'And found him like that?'

'Yes.' She shuddered. 'His eyes . . .'

'He hadn't complained about being ill?'

'No. Apart from his asthma, he was a very healthy man. He jogged, you know, and he had one of those juice machines. He told me he had carrot juice every morning.'

'He was asthmatic?'

'Yes. He had one of those . . . you know . . .' Miss Hancock held up her index finger and thumb, pumping the former, the thumb just touching her lips.

'An inhaler or ventilator?'

'Yes. I don't think he liked people to know he used it, though. I saw him using it once and he seemed annoyed. He kept it in the drawer of his desk.'

'Was there anything else he took? Medication?'

'No. I'm sure he didn't need anything else, and I never saw him take so much as an aspirin. He was a very healthy man.' A tear rolled down her cheek. 'I'd like to go home. Do you think I could go home?'

'I think it could be managed. I'll drive you myself, but I'll have to let the sergeant know first. Where are your things?'

'In the office.' Several more tears formed and fell, forcing her to remove her glasses. 'I can't go back in there,' she moaned.

'I'll get them for you,' said Amy soothingly. Why don't you just stay here and have another cup of tea. I'll be as quick as I can.'

Haines was no longer in the staffroom, and the staff had gone to the hall to fetch their classes. Matron was seated on the wooden bench on the verandah, from which the two boarders had witnessed the morning's drama. 'I've left the bursar in the kitchen, Mildred. I hope you don't mind. I'm just off to fetch her things, and then I'll run her home.'

'That's very good of you. It saves calling her a taxi.'

There was something in Matron's manner that made Amy hesitate. She sat down. 'You're taking all of this very well, Mildred, but I know they employed you because of your strength in a crisis. Someone has to remain calm.'

'Perhaps it didn't come as so much of a shock to me,' she replied, fixing Amy with a knowing stare.

'Really?' Amy didn't rush. Matron loved to savour information. 'I should have realised that you might know more than everyone else. There's not much you miss, knowing the girls as you do. And, of course, you have the best vantage point in Edwards House for keeping an eye on things.'

Matron turned her gaze to the cottage. 'He was being threatened.'

'And he didn't he go to the police?'

'No.'

'Did he have any idea who was threatening him?'

'No. He thought it might be one of the girls. That's why he told me. He wanted me to find out where the letters were coming from, and he trusted me to be discreet.'

'He chose wisely. I'm sure if he'd confided in any other member of staff, it would have been trumpeted all over the school. Did you discover anything?'

'No time. He only asked me a week ago, and now he's dead.'

'Do you have any suspicions?' Matron pursed her lips and would not be drawn. If she knew nothing, there was at least some value in pretending to know something. 'When did you last see him?'

'Friday evening. He came into the kitchen for some carrots. Most of the time he bought his own food – organic food, he said, from a market garden. He ate salads and juices and nuts. There's a kitchen in the cottage.'

'And you didn't see him Saturday at all?'

Matron paused. Her timing was superb. This was the question she'd been waiting for. 'No. But I know he was there at two a.m., because he had a visitor. I saw the shadows against the curtains. The lights were on in the cottage. There were definitely two of them.'

Amy felt instinctively that this was the end. She rose. 'Would you mind very much, Mildred, if I tell Sergeant Haines? He'll probably need to go over it with you. Or would you like to arrange that?' Matron shook her head. 'I'll mention it when I get poor Laetitia's things, then. Take care.'

As Amy hurried towards the cottage, Matron felt satisfied that her news would make that overweight sergeant sit up and take notice. But she was puzzled by Amy's parting words: 'Take care' was such a strange expression to use. Did Mrs Graham anticipate danger to herself or the boarders? Matron dismissed the thought and smiled in anticipation of Haines's surprise. Serves him right for devoting his attention to the academic staff. She could tell him a thing or two about those educated posers.

Matron, in all fairness, had revealed to Amy everything she knew – or everything she *thought* she knew – about events leading up to the headmaster's death. At the back of her mind, however, was a vital piece of information about which one person at the school had every reason to worry.

FIVE

When Amy reached the cottage, a uniformed officer prevented her re-entry. Haines roused himself and met her at the front door, nodding to the constable on duty. He jerked his head in the direction of Edwards House.

'They're a queer lot. I'll start interviewing tomorrow. What have you done with our bursar?'

'She's in the kitchen. I've promised to take her home, if that's all right. I've come to get her things. She knows you'll need to talk to her, but perhaps you might get more out of her if you went to her flat? She'll be there tomorrow. I've written her address.' She handed Haines a piece of paper.

'Do you think she knows anything?'

'She told me Horace Radcliffe was an asthmatic. He used an inhaler that he kept in the top drawer of his desk.'

'Nothing there now. I'll get the men to search the grounds. Did she say anything else?'

'Only that she was going to make him some tea.'

Haines glanced at the small sink. 'Two cups and saucers, both washed. We'll do a check anyway. I'll get Fraser to bag them.'

'And I have some other information, Edward. Matron says the headmaster was receiving threatening letters. He suspected one of the girls.'

'Why didn't she tell *me*?'

'Well . . . you haven't started interviews yet.'

'That's not the point! The woman stood beside me and said nothing about threatening letters. What else did she tell you?' He could see from Amy's face that there was more.

'She said the headmaster had a visitor in the early hours of Sunday morning. She saw the shadows of two people against the curtains at about two a.m. She sees quite a lot from that room of hers.'

'So it seems. Let me know if she fingers anyone in the next twenty-four hours, will you?' Amy smiled apologetically and gathered up Miss Hancock's handbag and coat. 'Before you go, who did the office work? Did the bursar type his letters?'

'No. There's a secretary, Brenda Stokes, who comes in three days a week. She may be able to shed light on the letters.'

'And his appointments, though I can't imagine she'd know who was visiting him at two a.m. on Sunday morning. The visitor none of us expects, I suppose.'

'You're becoming morbid, Edward.'

'Just old, Amy.'

Miss Hancock unlocked her front door and beckoned Amy into the tiled entry. Something herbal tickled Amy's sinuses before sidling past and making its escape. She smothered a cough. 'What a lovely scent. What is it, Laetitia? Something you burn, like an oil?'

'Yes. It's a mixture of juniper, jojoba and lavender.' She coloured slightly. 'It's for warding off negative feelings. It's sort of calming and . . . well, it's supposed to make you feel good about yourself.' She gave a nervous laugh and unlocked the sliding glass door that led to the tiny enclosed garden, waving a magazine in an attempt to restore some negative karma for her guest. 'I'll just get rid of this,' she said, removing a small ceramic receptacle containing the remnants of the morning's oleaginous offering.

Amy watched as she deposited it next to a madonna lily on a green plastic table with matching chairs. Miss Hancock, she thought, turning her attention to the lounge room and adjacent kitchen, was the victim of galloping consumerism. Every knick-knack imaginable had been crowded into the small flat, with little concession to taste or style.

A sideboard, on which photographs vied with painted figurines and china plates, caught her attention. She left her chair for a closer look. Most of the photographs were of Miss Hancock at school events, but there was a portrait of the headmaster that she'd seen in the local newspaper. Miss Hancock must have paid to have it printed and framed. Another, smaller photograph, probably taken at the same time but never published, showed Horace Radcliffe surrounded by his staff, including Miss Hancock. The latter stood at his elbow, beaming not into the camera lens but at its object, Horace Radcliffe, with rapt adoration.

Why had she never noticed it? To be sure, Laetitia was always fussing over the headmaster and plying him with cups of tea that more often than not went cold on his desk, but Amy always attributed this to general fussiness. That it was motivated by anything other than respect and sycophancy had never occurred to her. She returned to her seat just as Miss Hancock emerged from the kitchen with a plate of Iced Vo-vos and two cups on a tray, completely unaware that in those few unsupervised moments her visitor had wandered into her private life.

Amy removed a biscuit from the plate and placed it on her saucer as Miss Hancock returned to the kitchenette to make tea. 'Thank you, Laetitia. I'm sure Mr Radcliffe appreciated the way you looked after him, though I can't imagine a sweet biscuit ever passing his lips.'

'No,' replied Miss Hancock, speaking through the hatch that separated the kitchen from the lounge. 'He didn't eat cake, either, because I used to bake things I thought he would like, until he told me . . . He said I wasn't to waste my time because sugars and fats were things he preferred to avoid.' She paused. 'He said it was important to eat macro . . . macro something . . .'

'Macrobiotic food?' Amy offered.

'Yes, that was it. I didn't know what that was, but I got a book from the library.'

'Any success?'

'I made him lentil soup, and he seemed to like that. But he still told me not to bother. I don't think he enjoyed eating.'

'He was a self-sufficient man,' said Amy. 'There was probably little he enjoyed, because enjoyment is close to indulgence and he was too disciplined to indulge. A true ascetic.' Miss Hancock returned and poured two cups of tea.

'An asthmatic?'

'No. An ascetic. Someone who withdraws from life and sensual pleasure.'

'Oh.'

'I wonder if he was ever married?' Amy pondered. I pity his poor wife if he were. There'd be no pleasing him, and that can be very destructive to a woman who really cares . . . and hurtful, too.' She glanced slyly at Miss Hancock over the rim of her teacup and saw the latter's eyes begin to mist. 'Of course,' she said hurriedly, 'that's conjecture. He was probably a confirmed bachelor.'

Miss Hancock's brow contracted. 'I don't think so. He said he was 'not unfamiliar with the married state'. That would mean that he was married . . . or had been married, wouldn't it?'

'You're right. He wouldn't say that unless he had some first-hand experience of matrimony. Did he often talk to you about personal things?'

'Oh goodness, no! Dear me, no! Mr Radcliffe was . . . very private.' The colour rose to her face as she realised this remark was contradictory. 'I mean . . . I . . .'

Amy smiled. 'There's no need to be embarrassed. It's impossible to work in such a small space without hearing snippets of conversations.'

Miss Hancock relaxed. 'He had such a clear voice . . . a strong voice. Unless he shut the study door, I could hear quite well. I wasn't eavesdropping. It was . . . Well, as you say, it was difficult *not* to hear.'

'Precisely. And fortunate, too, because without you the police wouldn't know where to start.'

'Start?' Miss Hancock looked alarmed.

'Of course. You worked more closely with him than anyone else, and you were privy to his conversations and his moods. There must be lots of things you can remember that will help the police discover who did that to him.'

Miss Hancock stared at Amy with dismay. 'But I don't know anything,' she whimpered. 'How could I possibly know who . . .?' She looked at Amy for confirmation, though she couldn't bring herself to utter the word 'killed'.

Amy shrugged. 'They can't be sure until the autopsy.'

Miss Hancock began to moan and rock backwards and forwards, her eyes closed, her hands gripping the china cup like a chalice. Amy was too intrigued by the uncharacteristic behaviour of the normally reserved, fussy little woman to express concern. Indeed, she felt little more than clinical fascination as she watched the bursar's public façade peel back to reveal a fear so primal that it outweighed any consideration of decorum.

She waited until the rocking ceased and Miss Hancock lowered her cup onto its saucer. 'Is there someone I can call, to stay with you? I can't leave you this way.'

'It will pass,' Miss Hancock replied dully, exhibiting no embarrassment and offering no apology. 'You've been very kind. I'll be all right, really.' She glanced up at Amy, who had risen and was standing next to her, touching her shoulder. Such a warm hand; the heat seemed to radiate from the point of contact, penetrating her neck. But Amy Graham's eyes were cold, and they seemed to look into her soul. Miss Hancock withdrew her gaze hurriedly. 'I'll just clear away these tea things and have a lie down. I'll be fine as soon as I've had a lie down. It's been a shock. I'll be all right tomorrow if the police want to talk to me, but there's nothing I can tell them . . . nothing at all.'

She began stacking the cups, saucers and uneaten biscuits onto the tray, which Amy took from her and carried into the kitchen. The two women walked to the front door, where they parted, with professions of concern from one and hasty assurances of well-being and gratitude from the other.

Amy Graham knew, as she pulled away from Miss Hancock's flat, that there was something troubling the bursar – something more than the shock of discovering the headmaster's body. She parked in the town centre and spent half an hour shopping for the items she'd intended purchasing that morning. Then she walked to the public library, where an impeccably dressed young man with a luxuriant moustache was exchanging pleasantries with a borrower. Selecting a book on gardening that she'd no intention of reading, she took it to the desk. As she suspected, her entry hadn't gone unnoticed.

'We're very speedy this morning, aren't we?' Martin McEchnie raised an eyebrow and glanced cynically at the book in his aunt's hand. 'Needed something to while away the wee hours?' He took the book from her and flipped open the cover. 'Last taken out in February 1970 . . . popular little piece!'

Amy smiled. 'Your powers of observation are wasted in a country library.'

'I have to eat, dear Aunt, and you know very well I wouldn't survive in the constabulary. Now what can I *really* do for you?'

'I need to know the sort of books taken out by someone who works at the school. It's confidential.'

'Of course.' He beckoned to an assistant who was replacing books on shelves, and retreated with Amy to a small office at the rear of the building. He brought his chair from behind the desk and gestured Amy to a seat. 'Can I get you coffee?'

'No, thanks. I've just had tea with Miss Hancock.'

'Ah . . . the spinster with the penchant for Spencer Tracey. He was a terrible man, if you believe Katherine's friends. I never cease to be amazed at women who profess to love bullying, alcoholic men. Is she the subject of your enquiry?'

'Yes. What sort of books did she take out?'

'Why do you need to know? Does it have anything to do with the rumour that our revered headmaster was visited by the police this morning? *Do* tell, dear. Is our headmaster under arrest?'

'No. He's dead, Martin. The news will undoubtedly be all over town by this evening, but I'd appreciate your discretion as to my queries about Miss Hancock. Poor woman found the body.'

Martin McEchnie digested his aunt's news. 'How did he die?'

'Can't tell you. The police are investigating.'

'Does that mean you don't know or you won't say?'

'A bit of both,' said Amy honestly. 'Until there's a post-mortem and the police are satisfied, I really can't speculate.'

'But you suspect someone bumped him off?'

'Martin!'

'Okay. But where does the spinster fit in? Not the woman scorned, surely?'

'You mustn't jump to conclusions. I just want to know a bit about her. I haven't really *any* right to pry.'

Martin sighed. 'Well, she's into herbs, charms, ancient remedies, aromatherapy and anything relating to mind control – including, I believe, witchcraft.'

'Witchcraft!'

'Don't look so shocked, my dear. Plenty of people read about things they'd never dream of doing. Can you picture your Miss Hancock dancing naked around a gum tree in the dead of night? There are too many things that crawl and bite for starters, and where in this godforsaken backwater would you find enough like-minded women to form a coven? I'd say her life's probably never gone the way she planned, and she's gullible enough to believe that she can exercise a degree of control by playing at pongs and potions. Little more than a hobby, really – like astrology.'

'Yes, I see. And I *am* aware that she's interested in such things, because there was the most dreadful odour in her flat when I took her home this afternoon. I can't imagine any spirit, good or evil, tolerating it. Where, I wonder, does she get her ingredients?'

'Well, if she's looking for eye of newt and toe of frog she might have difficulty, but otherwise there's a shop in Mittagong that sells everything from snake oil to mystical treatises. Failing that, she'd have to go somewhere like the Fisher Library to research recipes. They have books dating back to the seventeenth century that she could examine, but she couldn't remove them from the library, of course.'

Amy smiled and rose to her feet. 'Thank you, Martin. As usual, you've been most helpful. I won't keep you, but I do insist you come to dinner soon. Bring a friend.'

'You don't approve of my friends.'

'That's not true. I find them a little odd, but I know you wouldn't tolerate behaviour that didn't meet certain standards. You're quite conservative, you know.'

'Thank you for that vote of confidence, dear Aunt. What you're really saying is that I'm a stodgy, boring librarian who pretends to be avant-garde by surrounding himself with bohemians.'

Amy patted his arm. 'I'm saying you're my favourite nephew.' She rose and walked to the door.

'I'm your *only* nephew,' Martin reminded her in mock disgruntlement, re-enacting a scene they'd played out many times since his childhood.

'So you are, dear. So you are,' Amy replied, as if reminded of the fact for the first time.

Miss Hancock, as Amy's car pulled away, leaned against the inside of her front door, her right hand pressed to her forehead in the manner of heroines of the silver screen. Then she returned to the lounge room and flipped on the TV. It was a romantic comedy with Rod Taylor and Doris Day. She poured herself a generous glass of sherry and curled up on the lounge, awaiting transportation into a world a million times more satisfying than the everyday. For an hour and a half, reality would be held at bay as the plot moved inexorably through a romance tender and fiery, bumpy and smooth, towards its logical, reasonable, inevitable conclusion . . . marriage. For Miss Hancock, that was what life was all about – or if it wasn't, it certainly should be.

Horace Radcliffe, awaiting transportation to his stainless-steel container at Goulburn morgue, would probably have disagreed.

SIX

Edward Haines was tired. A recent visit to his doctor had revealed that his blood pressure was up. It wasn't a question of wanting to leave the force, because policing was his life. This was what worried him. What else did he have, apart from his job? His wife had left him, and drugs had deprived him of his only son. Peggy blamed him for not spending more time with the boy and for not being aware of what he was doing or what sort of people he was with.

He watched as Amy Graham led the bursar down the driveway towards her car, and thought of how he'd once fancied his chances in that direction. It was long before he met Peggy. Amy had numerous suitors, but he always fancied that she liked him. Then he'd been transferred out of the district, and when he returned she was engaged to someone else. He'd met Peggy at a dance, and any disappointment he'd felt when Amy became Mrs Graham was lost in the general excitement of falling in love and starting a family.

He'd sold the home he shared with Peggy and given her most of the proceeds. She needed something to start a new life. He moved into a furnished flat closer to the station and buried himself in his work. According to Peggy he'd been doing that for years. It was a soulless place with one bedroom, a bathroom and a tiny kitchenette. The latter he hardly ever used, preferring to buy take-away that, more often than not, he ate on the run. There were no photographs, no mementos, nothing to proclaim kinship with the past. It was a place to sleep and watch TV.

He looked at his watch. No sign of the coroner. It was nearly midday and he was hungry. He had two uniformed men searching the bins for the inhaler. He'd sent Lockyer back to the station to write a scene report and search for Radcliffe's next of kin. The report was to be on his desk by mid-afternoon. Fraser, who also had reports to write, he'd asked to return to the school after the coroner had been, so they could take a statement from Matron and possibly see the bursar. The ambulance was waiting at the top of the driveway.

Haines wasn't a career man. Any chance of rapid promotion had been lost during that first transfer to the city, when his intolerance of corruption led to his becoming an embarrassment to his superiors and an anathema to his peers. There'd been incidents – ugly incidents – with threats of physical violence and attempts to compromise him. But if being a loose cannon was not enough to get him transferred into the country, stopping a bullet at a siege during which he was denied effective back-up certainly was. It initiated a process of counselling, relocation and compensation that ultimately put him back where he belonged.

Nevertheless, it wasn't often a crime of this magnitude came Haines's way. Cracking it would look good on his record. He'd had several favourable reports and one commendation for bravery. Admittedly they were mostly to do with community policing, but that's what being a country copper was all about.

At twelve-thirty, to his great relief, the coroner's car turned into the driveway. He went to meet it and extended his hand as Leonard Pilkington, a gaunt tower of a man with grey hair, stepped out. 'G'day, Len. Not much I can tell you about this one. No obvious cause of death, but it's murder all right.'

The coroner shook the proffered hand. 'What makes you think it's murder?'

'A couple of tiny clues that only someone with my powers of observation and years of experience would pick up. Come and have a look.'

They moved into the cottage. 'I see what you mean,' said the coroner, peering at the paintwork and floral display. 'He could hardly have done that to himself.'

'Nah. It doesn't even match his suit.'

'Who found the body?'

'The bursar . . . middle-aged spinster. She decided to take him a cup of tea and found him like this. Haven't been able to get a statement from her yet, because she was too distraught. I'm going to see her this afternoon.'

'Jamieson's been?'

'Yep. He was here to do an infant death. You should have the brief soon. This one will take a bit longer.'

'Did he offer any opinion as to the cause of death?'

'Didn't have a clue.'

'Time of death?'

'Some time between late Friday night and Sunday. Autopsy's tomorrow morning, so I should know by lunchtime. Want me to give you a call?'

'Just to satisfy my curiosity. Never seen anything like it – looks as if he died of fright.'

'It's possible it was a natural death and someone decided to have a farewell party.'

'I doubt it. He lived on the premises?'

'Yes.'

'Alone?'

'Yes.'

'Perhaps he let his murderer in. No signs of forced entry?'

'Nothing. Back door was locked when we arrived. I'll have to ask the bursar about the front because she lets herself in with a key.'

'Well, I've seen enough for my purposes. I'll look forward to getting your brief. Happy hunting.' Haines escorted Leonard Pilkington to his car, relieved that the preliminaries were over. As the car moved down the driveway, he signalled to the ambulance officers to remove the body and walked slowly across the yard towards Edwards House.

By the time Fraser returned, Haines had scrounged a sandwich and a cup of tea from the kitchen and was feeling better. He'd asked Matron whether it was convenient for them to take a statement. 'We'll be here again tomorrow to interview staff, if that's easier. Or perhaps you'd prefer to come to the station?' Matron indicated that she'd prefer to do it immediately and suggested they use the common room.

When they were seated, and with very little prompting, she relayed to Haines what she'd told Amy about the threatening letters. She didn't know if they were posted, because she didn't see any envelopes. In fact, she only caught a glimpse of one letter, a cut-and-paste affair that the headmaster had on his desk. He wasn't keen for her to read it, although he evidently wanted her to see what it looked like. She hadn't discovered anything to indicate that it was a boarder, but then he only mentioned it to her a few days before he died. Had he asked earlier . . .

'Did you get on well with the headmaster, Matron?'

She threw him a complacent look. 'He was happy with the way the boarding house was being run. There were never any complaints.'

'But did you like him personally? Did you get on well with him?'

'My contact with him was purely professional, Sergeant. We spoke of nothing but the school and the boarders, when we did speak. Most of the time he kept to himself. I didn't like him or dislike him.'

'When did you last see him?'

'As I explained to Mrs Graham, he came into the kitchen on Friday evening to get some carrots. Later I saw him leaving in his car . . . at about six-thirty that would have been, or perhaps a little earlier. I didn't see him again . . . well, not clearly.'

'But you thought you saw him later?'

'Not on Friday night. On Saturday . . . well, Sunday morning. I couldn't sleep. It was about two a.m. I saw a light in the cottage and there were two people moving about.'

'Did you see anyone leave?'

'No. When the light went out I went back to bed.'

'Did the headmaster often have house guests?'

'Not to my knowledge, Sergeant.'

'And you definitely weren't aware of him returning to the school on Friday night?'

'No. Normally I'd hear his car, but I must have been sleeping too soundly.'

'To your knowledge, Matron, and apart from the threatening letters, was there anyone who had reason to dislike the headmaster enough to harm him?' Matron hesitated. A myriad of conversational snippets were tumbling around in her head, like pieces of glass in a kaleidoscope. How could she be sure the patterns they formed were real? People often said things they didn't mean.

She responded cautiously. 'There was always talk from the staff, Sergeant. The staffroom is next to the sitting room, so when voices are raised it's easy to overhear from the bottom of the stairs.

I've mentioned on several occasions that if they wish to raise their voices, they should close the sitting-room door. It doesn't seem to do any good.'

'Were they often indiscreet when discussing the headmaster?'

'Initially,' said Matron, 'they laughed at him, but as time went on they took him more seriously. Some of them sounded off quite a bit, but I can't be sure from the little I overheard if any of them felt strongly enough to harm him.'

'And what sort of things did you overhear, Matron?'

Again she hesitated. 'I heard Dennis Hinds call him a fascist. Georgina Stoddart called him a charlatan, but then, she believed she'd be the next headmistress so I suppose there was bitterness there from the start. I even heard Dr Deitz say that had he realised what they were in for he would have given Georgina more support, which is saying a lot because he can't stand her.'

'Anything else?'

'Some of them called him 'Horace the Horrendous'. Childish. Not the sort of behaviour one expects.'

'Did any of the staff ever express a desire to see him leave?'

It was the only time Haines had ever seen Matron smile. 'I doubt there was one of them, Sergeant, who would not have been happy to see the headmaster leave. The only one to express any preference about the manner of it, to my knowledge, was Miss Delhunty. She told me she hoped he and those amongst them who had 'fed his evil little mind' would slither out of the school and find . . . I can't remember her exact words, but it was something about finding a pit to share where they could live on each other's venom. That was shortly before she left.'

'Colourful language. She's on leave?'

'Yes. She's threatening to take the school to court. I don't have any details. Mr Fairweather would be the one to ask.'

'Anything else, Matron?'

'No, Sergeant. I believe I've told you everything.'

'In that case, I'll have your statement typed up and brought to you to read and sign. I think you should be aware that you may have to appear in the coroner's court, but that won't be for some time. Please call me at the station if you think of anything you wish to add.' Matron nodded and accompanied them to the door.

'Not a woman I'd care to cross swords with,' said Haines when they were back on the road.

'She's okay,' said Fraser. 'Just a bit isolated.'

'How do you make that out?' Haines was always nonplussed by Fraser's theories.

'She doesn't fit in with the academic staff, and teenage girls wouldn't be company for a woman her age.'

Haines grunted and changed the subject. 'How are you getting on with those statements about the baby? I'd like to get the coroner's brief together so we can concentrate on this one. I told Pilkington to expect them.'

'I've taken one from the nurse who found him, and the doctor who tried to revive him. The GMO is sending me the P-M report tomorrow.'

'Good. What about the drugs?'

'I haven't had a chance to get to the Thompsons yet. Do you want me to go first thing in the morning?'

'No. When we've finished with the bursar, I might drop in on them myself. Last time I saw Thompson, he swore blind he only had a couple of plants.'

Haines knew all of the hippies who'd settled in the district. Like Michael Thompson, they grew their own vegetables, gave their children strange names, kept chooks and goats, and built houses out of mud bricks. They also smoked pot, which was where he and they suffered a difference of opinion. If they had the occasional plant they were growing for their own use, he didn't see the point of turning it into an issue, but if he thought they were peddling it to the local teenagers, he'd have been down on them like a tonne of mud bricks.

Now, however, it was out of his hands. Goulburn had informed him that commercial quantities of marijuana were leaving the area for markets in Sydney, and he was determined to find out where it was coming from, even if it meant putting pressure on people like the Thompsons. He couldn't imagine Thompson or any of the others doing it alone, because their properties weren't big enough. For this reason he'd done little more than make cursory inspections of their greenhouses, but now he'd get tough. A small amount of evidence on one of them could yield information.

'It has to be someone who comes here regularly,' he told Fraser. 'A commuter with a legitimate reason for making the trip – a truckie or a sales rep, maybe. Keep your ear to the ground. I think you have to turn left here.' Fraser drove into the street where Miss Hancock lived. They parked, checked the numbers and knocked at the bursar's front door. At first there was no response, so Fraser, who could hear a TV, knocked louder. The door opened a crack, and a sliver of Miss Hancock became visible.

'It's Sergeant Haines and DS Fraser, Miss Hancock. I was wondering if it would be convenient for us to take a statement. If now isn't a good time, we can organise something for tomorrow?' The door opened a little wider, and the bursar peered at Haines as if she were having difficulty focusing. Haines held up his ID and nudged Fraser to do likewise. The bursar wasn't wearing her glasses. In fact, when the sliver of her that was visible suddenly became a whole person, it was evident that she was wearing little more than a frown. Fraser politely averted his eyes, and Haines tried to restrict his gaze to her face. 'Why don't we wait here until you're . . . ah . . . until you've had a chance to finish dressing. We can come back in twenty minutes, if that suits you?' Miss Hancock looked down, screamed, and slammed the door.

'Do you think that was a yes or a no?'

'I think she's a bit Adrian Quist,' said Fraser. 'Not worth waiting.'

'We'll give her a chance to climb into something and see what happens,' said Haines, loathe to miss the opportunity for a statement. 'If she's had a few, it might make her more likely to talk.' Fraser shook his head. 'All right,' Haines added. 'If she hasn't resurfaced in five minutes, we'll leave.'

Miss Hancock did reappear. She'd tidied her hair, powdered her nose, applied a little lipstick and donned a heavy towelling robe that on her could be described as full length. Her cheeks were pink, either from embarrassment or because she'd also applied rouge as part of her frantic toilette. Haines asked her whether they could sit at the table adjacent to the kitchen because it would be easier for Fraser to take notes. When they were seated, he explained that as she had discovered the body, her statement was important and she may be questioned on it in court.

'I want you to run through this morning's events slowly while DS Fraser here writes it all down. Later we'll bring you the typed-up statement, and if you're happy that it's accurate, you can sign it. Are you feeling up to this?' Miss Hancock eyes had glazed, and Haines was beginning to agree that they'd have to come back. But his direct question revived her. She assured him, primly, that she was quite capable of recounting the morning's events. She proceeded to do so at a leisurely pace, commencing with the time she arrived at the school and finishing with her appearance in the sitting room, where Matron had given her brandy and shut the door so they wouldn't be disturbed.

'Do you have your own key to the cottage, Miss Hancock?'

'Yes. Mr Radcliffe gave me a key to the front door so that I wouldn't have to interrupt him if he was working. Most mornings he was already in his study when I arrived.'

'Do you recollect any conversations he had last week, either with staff in his office or with anyone on the telephone, that could have a bearing on his death? Did he argue with anyone? Did he seem angry or worried?'

Miss Hancock closed her eyes. The alcohol she'd consumed had reduced her stress levels and only slightly impaired her powers of speech, but it had clouded her mind. This was probably an advantage, given her fearful and evasive reaction to Amy's questions earlier in the day. 'He had a call on Friday morning. I think it was from Mr Fairweather, because I heard him say "Gilbert". He was raising his voice at the end, and he seemed very put out.'

'Did you hear enough of the headmaster's side of the conversation to know what it was about?'

'Oh, no. He shut his door, you see, so although I could hear his raised voice, I couldn't hear what he was saying. I thought I heard the word "commitment" a couple of times, but that was all.'

'And what about his relationships with the staff? Was that all smooth sailing?'

Miss Hancock shook her head for much longer than was necessary. 'Dear me, no. He didn't seem to get on with the teaching staff.' She pursed her lips disapprovingly. 'You would think, wouldn't you, that they'd be grateful to work with someone as successful and . . . with someone like Mr Radcliffe. One of the newspapers said he was putting Eldersley on the map.'

'Did he argue with any of the staff?'

'Well . . . he had a terrible row with Miss Delhunty a few weeks ago. She was crying and calling him names. I couldn't hear what he was saying, but women's voices do carry so easily. She said it suited him to listen to lies, and that he had no right to judge her or pry into her affairs. She told him he'd hear from her solicitor and said she'd be lodging a complaint with the executive director and the union. She called him a pompous, righteous prig. At least, I think she said prig – it might have been pig.'

'What about the other staff?'

'I don't think they ever came to his office unless Mr Radcliffe asked them to, and they never looked happy when they left. Even when there wasn't any shouting, you could tell they weren't happy. He was rather strict.'

'Who came to his office most often?'

'Dr Deitz and Mr Vandegaard were both with him a couple of times in the last few weeks. Oh, and Miss Pendlebury saw him, too . . . I heard a bit of that. It was about the books the children were reading. He wanted her to remove some of them and she wouldn't. I think he meant he wanted her to take them off the course because he thought they were unsuitable. She was very red in the face when she left.'

'Anyone else?'

'Well, he had to see quite a bit of Mrs Stoddart, of course, because she's the senior mistress, but she had to report to him because she does the timetable and the duty rosters and he had to approve them. I never actually heard them arguing.'

'What about the girls, Miss Hancock? Did any of the girls argue with him, or leave letters for him?'

'Why would they leave letters for him? If their parents wanted to see him, they'd ring for an appointment, and if the girls wanted something themselves – special permission or exemption from sport – they'd go to their form mistress . . . or to Matron, if they were boarders. Matron looks after the boarders, and her decisions are final. Mr Radcliffe respected her.' This last comment was delivered somewhat wistfully.

'And I'm sure he respected you, Miss Hancock. You got on well with him?'

'Oh, yes,' she said vaguely, staring at Haines as if he had asked about her relationship with the man in the moon. 'He never shouted at me or anything – he was a perfect gentleman.' Her eyes misted over, and Haines signalled Fraser that they should take their leave.

'I think that's all we need for now, Miss Hancock. If you think of anything else, anything at all, please let me know. Your statement isn't valid until you've signed it, so you can change it if you feel it isn't right.'

'Will I have to go to work tomorrow?'

'That's not for me to decide, Miss Hancock,' said Haines. 'I can tell you that you won't be able to use the office until our scientific squad has been over it. Perhaps you should talk to the senior mistress . . . Mrs Stoddart, I think you said?'

'Oh dear, yes, I suppose there's nowhere for me to go. I don't have a desk in the staffroom. I'll ring Matron tomorrow and ask her what I should do.' She escorted Haines and Fraser to the front door.

'Do you think she'll be all right?' asked Fraser when they were back in the car.

'That's not our concern,' replied Haines.

SEVEN

After dropping Fraser at the station, Haines took the Moss Vale Road for a couple of kilometres and turned left into Kangaloon Road. At the intersection of Kangaloon and Old South Road, he turned north towards Mittagong. Thompson's property was off the Old South Road by about two kilometres. It consisted of a large mud-brick-and-timber dwelling set well back from the road and surrounded by a couple of acres of vegetable gardens, a single greenhouse, a chicken run, and a fenced paddock for goats and whatever other livestock Thompson took it into his head to keep. The shed at the back of the house was Thompson's workshop.

As it hadn't rained, the driveway to the house was passable, though Haines was beginning to suspect that Thompson used it as a quarry for his mud bricks. The car lurched and rolled over several potholes before coming to rest outside the yard where Thompson's wife had made an effort to establish a flower garden – something, she confessed, that was beautiful without being practical.

Haines felt sorry for Thompson's wife. The hard yakka of self-sufficiency probably wasn't what she'd envisaged when she and Thompson had paired up at a folk festival and exchanged their vows dressed in kaftans and surrounded by love, incense and peace. To give her credit, the house, with its cathedral roof and open plan, was always clean, although keeping it tidy with three small children running around was impossible. When she responded to Haines's knock, the fourth, a baby a few weeks old, was asleep on her back, like a papoose.

'Afternoon, Lily. I see the little one has arrived. Boy or girl?'

'Another girl,' she said, stepping back for him to enter. 'We're calling her Lucy. Michael's in the shed if you want to go through, or I can let him know you're here and make some coffee?'

'I want to talk to both of you, so perhaps you could let him know I'm here. There's no need for coffee. This visit is more official than social.'

When Michael Thompson followed his wife into the kitchen, he shook Haines's hand and gestured him to a seat. His leather apron was covered in golden dust, and there were wood shavings in his hair, which was long and unkempt. He was thin to the point of being emaciated.

'I won't beat about the bush,' said Haines when they were seated. 'You know I've never worried about the odd bit of pot you might produce for your own purposes, and you know, too, that I promised this leniency would change if you went commercial. Regardless of what I feel personally, it's still illegal. Now I've learned there are large quantities of it coming from somewhere in this area. I know you don't have the capacity, even if you had the inclination, but you're closer to the scene than I am and I think you might know where it's coming from. For starters, I want you to take me out to that greenhouse and show me how many plants you've got, just to convince me that you're not commercial. No blind eyes. Okay?'

Michael Thompson said nothing; nor did his wife. He rose from the table and gestured with his head for Haines to follow. They walked in silence to the back of the property, where the low afternoon sun was glinting off the roof of the greenhouse. It was probably about seventeen degrees outside, but inside the greenhouse it was warm.

'Okay,' said Haines, 'what's a tomato plant and what's not? And there's no point in lying, because I can have a car here within twenty minutes – full of officers who know what to look for. I'm giving you the chance to be straight with me.'

'All the ones along the outside are tomatoes,' said Thompson. 'Two rows of them. The inside row is hash.'

'That's a lot more than one or two plants,' said Haines. 'Are you telling me you smoke all of it yourself?'

'People keep more alcohol than they can consume themselves. What's the difference? Sometimes we have visitors and we share it around, but we're not growing it commercially. Anything we can't use we burn.'

'Can you honestly stand there and tell me that you've never sold any of this to anyone?' Thompson's eyes shifted to a point over Haines's right shoulder.

'He can, Ed, but I can't.' Haines swivelled. Lily had entered so quietly he didn't realise she was there. Her face was white, but outwardly she appeared calm. The child was still fast asleep on her back.

'For God's sake, Lily . . .'

'Someone came here one day wanting some . . . for himself, he said. I don't know how he knew it was here. He offered me more money than I get from the goat's milk or the vegetables or the eggs. He asked me to make him up half a dozen deals, and he came back for them. He's been getting them regularly ever since. I know you're going to ask, but I honestly don't know who he is. He's not young – about forty, maybe – and I think he works locally.'

'Did he ask you whether you could supply larger quantities?'

'No. But he has been buying more. He used to be happy with half a dozen, but now he asks for twenty.' Thompson groaned.

'Has he offered to purchase any plants?'

'No. Just the deals. What are you going to do?'

'That depends. For starters, I want to know who this bloke is, so the next time he pays you a visit I want you to write down the registration number of his car. Then I want you to tell him you won't be selling to him any more because you're frightened the police will find out. Tell him you're getting rid of all of your plants and ask him if he knows anyone who wants to buy them. Tell him you realise there are bigger operations around. See if you can draw him out on any other sources of supply.'

It was then that Thompson's anger focused on Haines. 'Do you realise what these people are like? You can't expect us to put ourselves at risk by nosing out information and then narking to you. I've got a family to think of.'

'You should have thought about that when you started selling the stuff, Michael. I'm sorry, but it's either cooperate with us or I do you for supply. Your customer's only a tiddler, but he might lead us to bigger fish. When do you think he'll be around?'

'He came about two weeks ago, so he could come any time,' said Lily.

'Phone me when he does – and don't forget the registration number. Get as much out of him as you can. If I'm not at the station, ask them to contact me.' He turned to Thompson. 'Burn the bloody stuff, Michael. I don't want to see it here next time I come, because next time I won't be alone. My report is going to say that you were found in possession of a few plants that have since been destroyed. Provided I hear from you or Lily, it won't say anything about intent to supply. In fact, if I get one good lead, I'll even think about torching the report. No promises. If I can't suppress it, I'll speak on your behalf when it comes before the magistrate. That's the best I can do.'

As he walked back to his car, Haines could imagine what Thompson was calling him. Coppers didn't have friends. It would have been nice to sit down and have coffee and some of Lily's home-made cake and take a closer look at the new baby. He felt like a bastard.

He drove back into town and picked up a hamburger and chips, which he ate in the car. Not much point in going home; there was nothing on the telly, and the book he'd been reading he'd finished last night. Having something to read or watch made being at home bearable. He decided to call past the station. It would keep the shift on its toes. As he drove into the station, the constable on duty strode out in a purposeful manner. That looked promising . . . a fight at the local?

He wound down his window. 'Trouble, Flynn?'

'Doherty is beating his wife again, Sarge. Pretty bad this time, they reckon. Neighbours have called an ambulance, and Spinner and I are gonna get him. I'll put him in the cells. Do you want . . .?'

Shaun Doherty had been beating his wife for years. It used to involve pushing and shoving, a few bruises and the odd black eye, but over the last six months the attacks had become more serious. At the last, he'd broken her arm. Molly had refused to make a formal complaint. Haines saw her at the hospital and tried to make her see that the attacks were worsening, but she'd laughed. She'd been Shaun's punching bag for so long that she couldn't imagine the violence escalating. Their conversation ended as all previous conversations had done: with Molly saying, ''E'll be ever so sorry in the mornin', Sergeant 'Aines.'

'I don't want to attend, Flynn, but I will. I'm in a mood to do something I might be sorry for. Spinner can go in the ambulance to the hospital, but I doubt Molly will be making a statement. I'll talk to the poor cow tomorrow, for all the good it'll do. Make sure you cuff the bastard this time. I'll see you there.'

He arrived at the Dohertys as Molly was being conveyed to the ambulance. She was semi-conscious. There was swelling on her right cheek, and her lower lip was turning black. Ignoring the inevitable cluster of neighbours, Haines entered the house. He found Doherty in the kitchen, trying to make himself a cup of tea. 'You fucking bastard, Doherty. I warned you last time that I'd shoot you if you did it again. Get up against the wall and put your hands behind you head.'

Doherty raised his head from the level of the gas jet, which he'd been attempting to light, and stared at Haines as if the latter had dropped out of a clear blue sky. He was already in the process of retreating from what he'd done. That was what made it so frustrating. Doherty was only ever violent with his wife and gave the police no trouble at all. This was one of many occasions on which Haines would have liked half an excuse, but Doherty was smiling, fawning and making incoherent apologies in a way that made him sick. Soon he would start to weep.

'Sheesh . . . sheesh . . . okay. Had a liddle acciden', but sheesh . . . okay. Makin' 'er a cuppa. Likes 'er cuppa . . . You want . . .?'

'She's on her way to hospital, arsehole. She needs medical attention, not tea and sympathy. As for you, I'd like to beat you senseless, and I would if you weren't brain dead already. She was unconscious this time. Do you hear me, Doherty? Am I getting through? Your wife is half dead and she's on her way to hospital.'

'Need any help, Sarge?' said Flynn.

'Yes.' Haines lowered his voice, aware he'd been shouting. 'Put the cuffs on this pathetic bastard and get him out of my sight. If he vomits on you, charge him with assault. Where's Spinner?'

'You said she was to go with Molly in the ambulance. She wasn't too happy about that. She wanted to arrest Doherty.'

'Tough. If she wants to be useful, tell her to persuade Molly to press charges. I'm off.'

Haines was left with his original dilemma of what to do. He couldn't face an evening of his own company, so he decided to mix business with pleasure and talk to a women whose attitude to domestic violence was in keeping with his own.

EIGHT

Amy Graham picked up her shopping from the passenger seat and locked her car. She was relieved to be away from the bustle of the town. She'd purchased Thyme Cottage ten years earlier with the money that came into her possession after her husband's death. Before that, she and John had lived in a much grander home on the outskirts of Bowral. Amy thought it pretentious.

Death had never been a part of John Graham's plans. It caught him unawares at the peak of his career in the form of a tumour that, like his business, grew until it became impregnable; 'inoperable', the doctors said. He bore the news with unphilosophical anger and became increasingly distant from his wife, whom he regarded in much the same light as his house and his car. He'd carried her off from under the noses of the country club set, with their old school ties and impeccable pedigrees, at a time when he was still unknown in the advertising world. Amy had been his entry into society.

The local papers reported John Graham's suicide in one of the upstairs rooms of his mansion where, had it not been for the housekeeper, he might have lain for days. Amy thought he'd caught a taxi to the airport and gone to Sydney on business. She bore her loss with dignity. The circumstances of his death distressed her only insofar as he'd denied her the right to mourn with him, and had left her feeling guilty that he died alone. When this guilt subsided, awareness that she was happier without him prompted her determination never to remarry. There were offers, many from men who'd courted her in her youth, but financial independence made the single state more attractive.

She walked up the path to the verandah, acknowledged the noisy greeting of her ginger cat, who'd been asleep on one of the wicker chairs, and entered the cottage. Marmaduke ran to the refrigerator, staring at the door. When she'd put away her hat and coat, Amy stood looking at the back of her furry freeloader with a fondness she rarely displayed for two-legged beings. 'So how was your day, my pet? Did the currawongs keep you awake?'

Marmaduke's limited facility for language never prevented him from knowing when he was being addressed. He tossed a peremptory 'miaow' at his mistress, which meant, 'Just do your thing, would you? I'm hungry and you're late.'

'If you insist. There's a nice bit of fish I've been thawing for you since this morning.'

Marmaduke's needs satisfied, she put on a record and set about preparing an omelette with the herbs that grew in her garden and the leftovers of the previous night's roast. The soothing strains of Mozart filled the little cottage, restoring Amy's belief that there was order in the universe. She's just finished her meal when the phone rang. 'Thyme Cottage.'

'Amy, it's Ed Haines. Thought I might pop around for a quick chat, if that's okay. I could come tomorrow if this evening's not convenient.'

'It's perfectly convenient, Edward. I'll make coffee.'

By the time Haines arrived, every trace of the evening meal had disappeared. It was replaced by the smell of freshly brewed coffee and warmed muffins that Amy had purchased that afternoon. 'Come in, Edward. Go into the lounge. I'll be with you in a minute.'

When they were seated, in mismatched chairs, Haines gave the reason for his visit: 'I wanted to go through with you, Amy, the backgrounds of some of these bods I'll be interviewing tomorrow. You've known them professionally and personally for many years. Anything you can tell me about them might help.'

'I'll do my best, Edward. I know the staff at Eldersley well, but I wouldn't have thought any of them capable of murder. I have absolutely no idea who could have done this, especially in view of the . . . er . . . decorative aspects.'

'Is that how you see it? As decoration?'

'Good heavens, no. I was at a loss for an appropriate word. If I had to find one, I'd say 'iconoclastic' or 'vandalistic'. The person that did that to him hated him very much. The murderer must have despised the image he presented to the world. Perhaps he or she was making a statement, but I can't think what, because I honestly believe that the headmaster was what he appeared to be – upright in his views and his behaviour.'

'He died in the right position, then.'

'Really, Edward!'

'Tell me about the staff. You'll have to remind me what they look like. I met most of them this morning, but there were a few at the hall I didn't meet. Just give me a quick rundown.'

'Well,' said Amy slowly, 'I'll start with the female staff. Apart from Matron, there's the cook, Mrs Watkins. She comes in daily and leaves after the evening meal. She's in her sixties, and very capable – rather short with a florid complexion.'

'Where was she this morning?'

'In the hall kitchen. The boarders had their breakfast there to keep them out of the way. I suppose she stayed to clean up. She does the ordering and shopping, so she may have driven into town. Life goes on when there are mouths to feed, and she and

Matron keep the show on the road as far as the boarding house is concerned.'

'Rather a peculiar woman, your Matron, wouldn't you say?'

'It depends on what you mean by peculiar, Edward. She's secretive – likes to mull over information. Which reminds me – how did you get on about the letters? Was Mildred able to show you any of them?'

'No. Radcliffe kept them, and he wasn't keen for her to see the contents. She caught a glimpse of one on his desk. It was made up entirely of letters cut from magazines, because the letters were coloured.'

'She has no idea what they said?'

'No.'

'How can she say they were threatening, then?'

'The one she glimpsed on Radcliffe's desk had the word "die" in it. Even upside down it stood out, because it was in larger print. When Radcliffe saw her looking at it, he put it away. He said the letters were always the same, and asked her to look for scraps of paper, magazines with holes, girls with scissors and such like. She said he assumed it was a vicious prank.'

'An assumption that may have cost him his life.'

'Possibly. Tell me about the other girl in the office – Brenda, you said her name is.'

'I don't know much about her, Edward, other than that she's been with the school for three to four years and seems efficient. She's young – about twenty-five – single, good looking in a brassy sort of way. She didn't hit it off with the new administration, and I suspect she was planning to leave. The headmaster wouldn't have been sorry to see her go.'

'No romance there, then?'

'Most definitely not. I doubt Horace Radcliffe needed female companionship, Edward. He was a self-sufficient man in every respect – a man devoted to his career.'

'A man who didn't need a woman, eh? I find that hard to believe, Amy.'

Amy coloured slightly. 'It's just my opinion, Edward. He was a cold man.'

'You didn't find him attractive, then?'

'Absolutely not, though I can't say the same for Miss Hancock. From her reaction and the photographs of him in her flat, I suspect she may have harboured romantic aspirations.'

'The bursar and Radcliffe? Good God! Still, she's not elderly, is she? Just not the sort you'd think of as . . . Well, it never would have crossed my mind.' He rubbed his chin.

'She was too distraught, Edward, for someone who'd just received a nasty shock. Plain women have feelings too.'

'And what about our Matron? Did she have the . . .? Did she fancy him as well?'

'I doubt it, though she had more in common with him that poor Laetitia. Mildred's world revolves around the school. I'm tempted to say that passion is something completely foreign to her – passion of that sort, in any case.'

'What other sort did you have in mind?'

'Well . . . if Mildred has a passion, it would be for power. She might have seen herself as a potential helpmeet – a sort of kindred spirit.'

'Together we'll rule the world?'

Amy laughed. 'Something like that. She has a nursing back-ground, but no academic qualifications. Marriage to Radcliffe would have enlarged her sphere of influence, and as his wife she would have presided over parent gatherings, women's groups. It would have been attractive . . . prestigious . . . for someone like Mildred.'

'You should have been a psychologist, Amy. What about the rest of the crew?'

'Well, on the academic side they're a mixed bag. To be honest, I find some of them quite strange. Bernard Deitz, for example. He's the science master. He came to the school two years ago after Mrs Appleby had her unfortunate accident. Hard to imagine that a woman familiar with the laws of physics could be so accident prone . . . Anyway, we had trouble finding a suitable replacement, and Deitz was the best of a bad lot. I was against his appointment.'

'On what grounds?'

'The worst possible grounds – dislike. You'd call it "gut feeling", Edward. And yet his qualifications and references are impeccable. He has a PhD, which is unusual for secondary-level teachers.'

'How's he turned out?'

'He doesn't socialise, so it's difficult to say. There have been no complaints, and he's too unattractive to be of interest to the girls. He seems to be covering the curriculum, but he's certainly not an inspired educator. Perhaps I'm being unfair.'

'Not necessarily. What is it about him you don't like?'

'I think he hates teaching . . . possibly hates children. There's something . . . a clinical detachment? Oh dear, I'm maligning the man without any evidence – other than what the girls call him.'

'And what's that?'

'Doctor Death.' Amy hesitated. 'Children can be cruel, Edward. They tend to search for weaknesses and personality disorders, sometimes with success. To be fair, I think the nickname had something to do with a biology lesson involving the dissection of a guinea pig. Some of the girls were upset.'

'Does he know?'

'All teachers know that children have names for them, but they don't necessarily know what they are.'

'How . . .?'

'Matron has good ears, Edward. I talk with her whenever I'm at the school. There's nothing she doesn't know.'

'Except who hated Radcliffe enough to kill him?'

'Yes . . . except for that.'

'You said that some of the staff had ambitions that were disappointed when Radcliffe arrived. Tell me about them.'

Amy hesitated. 'I feel as if I'm telling tales out of school, Edward. I have no proof of any of this, you realise. It's simply hearsay and personal opinion.'

'That's all I'm asking for, Amy. Nothing you tell me will appear in any statement.'

'Well then, I'd say your strongest contender as far as thwarted ambition is concerned would be Georgina Stoddart. She's the senior mistress and she teaches maths. Mrs Bridges retired when the Church relinquished control – or possibly because of it – and Georgina assumed, quite naturally, that she'd get the job. Had the school remained under the auspices of the Church, she probably would have, but the new regime was looking for someone different. She was bitter. Radcliffe was a mathematician too, you see, but he taught junior maths. He was appointed more as a figurehead.'

'Would you call her a dangerous woman?'

Amy laughed. 'I'd call her a *very* dangerous woman, Edward, but not in the way you're suggesting. I can't think her capable of murder, but she's capable of many lesser things. She's manipulative, unscrupulous and, according to some on the staff, two-faced. There were many who wouldn't have wanted to continue with her as headmistress.'

'So she became Radcliffe's right hand instead?'

'He certainly couldn't have run the school without her. No one would dispute that. She's always organised the timetable –

a thankless task – and collated all of the examination marks. She's very good at organising things and maintaining discipline. She's one of those people you need on a team but whom no one much likes.'

'Why is that, do you think?'

'She's . . . political, Edward. She likes to control everything and everyone. As senior mistress, she has the power to make everyone dance to her tune and she enjoys it. Anyone who falls out with her is issued extra playground duty or given a "bad" timetable. And she plays favourites amongst the girls, but she can always justify her decisions – she's far too clever to be caught out.'

'How did Radcliffe get on with her?'

'He was no fool. He knew that if she got half the chance she'd undermine him, but I don't think it worried him. Provided everything ran smoothly, he let her have her way. He was more interested in the big picture and in spreading the gospel according to Saint Horace. She wanted to control the school and he wanted to control the world.'

'You said she wasn't the only one who was ambitious. Who were the others?'

'There may have been a few, Edward, but the only one I'm aware of, apart from Georgina, is Veronica Ainesworth. She teaches geography and economics. She was appointed to the position after I left, so perhaps my opinion is unfair. I tend to form judgements based on what I've seen.'

'She's not a good teacher?'

'On the contrary – she's an excellent teacher and extremely well qualified, but her teaching skills go hand in hand with a somewhat vicious temper. I saw her tear strips off one of the girls in front of other students and staff, and Matron informs me that it happens from time to time. The girls are very wary of her. Her classes are usually productive, but they don't exhibit what Miss Weston would define as "constructive noise". A quiet classroom is not necessarily a good classroom.'

'What makes you think that she wanted Radcliffe's job?'

'She told me,' said Amy simply. 'I asked her a few weeks after her appointment how she was getting along, and she said that there were things about the school she wouldn't tolerate if she became headmistress, which was, she said, her ultimate ambition. She was quite open about it.'

'How did she get on with the Stoddart woman?'

'They didn't hit it off . . . two strong personalities, both with the same ambition. There was never any open bickering, though. I think Veronica realises that Georgina would make a formidable enemy, so she tows the line and keeps the peace.'

'And who's the tall, fast-looking piece with the buttons missing? She teaches art, she said, not to be confused with craft.'

Amy laughed. 'That's Madelaine Everhardt. She wouldn't mind what the girls called her. She's a great favourite because she isn't judgemental, and she allows them to talk as much as they like, about whatever they like, while they're painting and sculpting. She's a free spirit. She hears a lot, too, but she keeps her mouth shut. The girls know they can chatter without being reported. And the buttons aren't missing, Edward – she leaves them undone.'

'So what *do* they call her?'

'Well, Madelaine has her own theory. She had a dispute with one of our seniors some years ago, and the girl told her she was "nothing but an artistic fart". It so delighted her that she recounts it to anyone who cares to listen. I think she imagines alliteration still plays a large part in whatever the girls call her behind her back.'

'Which is?'

'Eveready . . . or "The Battery". Quite appropriate for someone as energetic and switched on as Madelaine.' Haines was about to expound his own theory, but thought the better of it and turned his attention elsewhere.

'There's the woman who teaches French. Looks like she has a bagel on top of her head.'

'It is unusual, I grant you. Perhaps Chauntel thinks it makes her look taller? She teaches Latin as well. It was quite a coup, obtaining a native French speaker. She's divorced but still uses her married name – Worsley.'

'Not a French name.'

'No. She married an Englishman, so possibly the marriage was doomed. She certainly dislikes everything English, which makes it difficult for our librarian, Mrs Westham. When I see them together I can begin to understand the Thirty Years' War.'

'Radcliffe was English, wasn't he?'

'No, Edward, but he was certainly an anglophile. That's how he got the job.'

'Come again?'

'The entrepreneur who runs the school uses anglophilia as a marketing tool. There are so many wealthy parents out there who grew up on English boarding school stories and adventures. Horace Radcliffe was the epitome of the English headmaster. If you could have seen him sweeping across the playground in his mortar board with his academic gown flying . . . He was almost fictional, Edward, in his expressions and mannerisms, not to mention his reverence for the royal family. I'm sure he grew up on a diet of *Biggles* and *Boys' Own*.'

'Why didn't he get a job in a boys' school?'

'Perhaps he would have preferred that, but Eldersley is a very prestigious post. It would have been too good an offer to refuse.'

'And you can always teach girls to play cricket.'

'Indeed,' replied Amy, ignoring his tone. 'In fact he introduced the GSTU – sorry, the Girls' Service Training Unit – which some would see as an exclusively male province. It fitted in nicely with his platform of discipline, order, and loyalty to the Crown. Parents seem to enjoy seeing their offspring march around in khaki trousers and slouch hats, saluting the flag.'

'And this appealed to you, Amy?'

'Don't be silly, Edward. I believe schools should cultivate responsible individuals, not militarised automatons, but I had to concede that there were benefits. The children seemed to enjoy it, and there were weekend camps and after-school activities that developed their team skills. It attracted media attention, which was very good for business, and it had the support of the board.'

'I didn't see anything in the newspapers.'

'Just a minute.' Amy disappeared briefly and returned with a manila folder from which she selected a clipping.

'Who's the bod with the swagger stick?'

'That's Horace Radcliffe doing his Alec Guinness impersonation. It's rather good, don't you think? I love the way the photographer has captured him like a giant in the foreground. You can't see his features of course, but they're not really what's important. What *is* important is the rigidity of that enormous hand stretching to the cap, and the little sea of echoing hands and upturned faces below him, moving and acting in unison.'

'Where did the uniforms come from?'

'The army supplied everything but the headmaster's uniform. Rumour has it that he got it from a disposal store, but I think not. It fitted him too well. I suspect he had it made, decorations and all.'

'You mean the decorations weren't his?'

'No, Edward. He wasn't old enough for the Second World War, and he didn't enlist for Korea. In any case, he had to stop wearing it because someone who *had* seen active service complained, and the army told him he wasn't entitled.'

'And that was the end of the . . .'

'The GSTU? Good heavens, no. For special occasions he simply organised one of the army officers to visit and take the salute. On other occasions the children saluted the flag.'

'Why would he want to wear a uniform if he'd never been in the army?'

'That's what's so interesting, Edward. I'm still not sure whether he was a marketer or someone who created fictions and liked dressing up. The mortarboard and gown were a bit of a blind as well. He didn't have a university degree.'

'But how . . .?'

'He had several teaching diplomas and a string of letters after his name. One of his qualifications was in photography, I believe. They went out on every circular to parents.'

'A poser?'

'One was never quite sure.'

'Whether he was taking you for a ride, or himself?'

'Well, yes . . .'

'So how did the other staff feel about him?'

'If they valued their jobs they got along with him. Attitudes towards him were varied, and I think I can say they ranged from the adoring – Miss Hancock – to the derisive. No one could dispute that he was good for business.'

'And you honestly can't think of anyone who would hate him sufficiently to . . .'

'I suspect,' said Amy carefully, 'that there were some who had cause to hate him. I have no evidence other than those hints I told you about – the ones he dropped at the last board meeting – but if he was prying into the backgrounds of certain members of staff,

I daresay someone may have wanted him silenced. The odd comment was passed, you know, that "so-and-so was holed up with him for an hour", or "carpeted" by him – nothing too specific, because the staff directly concerned didn't talk. He adopted a divide-and-conquer approach.'

'Who do you suspect?'

'Whom. Sorry, Edward. Once a school teacher . . . He seemed to target Deitz quite a bit, and Madelaine had crossed swords with him about her free-life classes. He apparently questioned the junior maths master, Vandegaard, but no one knows why. Rumour has it that it was something to do with his early years in South Africa. The English mistress, Jacquelyn Pendlebury, argued with him incessantly about texts and censorship – and Dennis Hinds, the history master, was caught giving him the Nazi salute. And, of course, he practically accused Miss Delhunty, our sports mistress, of being a lesbian – as a result of which she's currently on stress leave and undergoing counselling at the school's expense.'

'Jesus Christ!'

'Not really, but perhaps the headmaster felt they had something in common.'

'And *is* she? A lesbian?'

'Probably not. The point is that it's none of his or anybody else's business. She's responsible, hard working and genuinely concerned about the girls' welfare. She's a professional, not a pædophile.'

'What about the one who thought Radcliffe was a Nazi . . . the history teacher?'

'Dennis Hinds is a passionate supporter of Whitlam, and he belongs to some local activist group. He loves talking to the girls about "the lessons of history", so they dubbed him "Hindsight". He was always mumbling about rallies and propaganda and torch-light processions whenever the girls were in their khaki. I heard him say, "Dressed to kill, eh girls," to a group of them after a Parent–Teacher Day march.'

'A pacifist, then. Not a likely murderer?'

'Being passionate about peace can be as dangerous as being passionate about war, Edward.'

'You're right there,' said Haines, recalling the joke that fighting for peace was like fucking for virginity. 'So what about Vandegaard . . . the Afrikaaner. Why do you think Radcliffe had him in his sights?'

'I have no idea. I don't know how the rumour started, but people seem to believe that he had to leave South Africa in a hurry. There's a lot of pettiness and in-fighting amongst the staff, so possibly one of them mentioned the rumour to Radcliffe in an attempt to curry favour.'

'All in all . . .'

'You've got a lot of material to work with.'

Haines sighed, looking at his watch and then at the last muffin on the plate, which, in deference to his expanding waistline, he decided to resist. Everything about Amy's existence appealed to him, from the comfortable chairs in her cottage to the music she listened to. Even her huge ginger cat, though it shed all over his trousers, he tolerated because it was part of her world. He liked the way her mind worked. She seemed able to rise above things and remain detached. He'd never known a woman whose conversation he enjoyed more.'

'Time to be getting home, Amy. Thanks for the information – it's been a great help. It's always good to know a little about the people you're interviewing. If any other stray bits of information come your way, you will let me know?'

'Of course.' Amy accompanied him to the door. She watched him heave himself into the driver's seat of the Falcon, and waited until he was out of sight before locking up. Sometimes she thought favourably about male companionship, and she knew, too, that Edward Haines would be delighted to learn that she did not find him unattractive. He wasn't a sophisticated man, but she'd been associated, professionally and personally, with a number of sophisticated men who lacked his goodness and were obsessed with their careers. In the end they always wanted to dictate to her how she should live.

NINE

Haines brooded over the steering wheel, his window down to eradicate the lingering odour of hamburger and chips. Perhaps this was one post-mortem he should attend? Jamieson started early, but if they left the station by seven-thirty they'd be at Goulburn by nine.

In the vicinity of the school he slowed. The spire of the chapel and the chimneys of the residential block were silhouetted against the sky. There were hardly any lights in the residential block, and all the other buildings were in darkness. No harm in having a poke around? He parked and walked to the upper entrance, next to the chapel. From his vantage point above the quadrangle he could see the rear of the residential block and the kitchen. It was eleven-thirty, so they should all be in bed. Suddenly a sliver of light appeared in the kitchen doorway, obscured briefly by some-one leaving ... no, someone entering the kitchen. Could it be connected with the headmaster's death? Probably not – no saying what these cooped-up teenagers would do, and the doors of those old buildings were locked only from one side (deadlocks weren't popular, in case of fire).

He returned to his car, and quietness descended. Pigeons shifted and huddled in the eaves, and an owl swooped low over the playing fields in search of rats and mice. In the laboratory a caged rat, safe from such predators, ran in its exercise wheel. Clocks ticked in empty classrooms. In the kitchen a cockroach scuttled across Mrs Watkins' scrubbed and polished surfaces. In the bedrooms, which smelled of floor wax and cheap scent, the breath of the innocent and the not-so-innocent was drawn and expelled evenly from dreaming bodies as smooth and rounded as alabaster.

Peace, however, does not necessarily come with quietness, and darkness doesn't always bring release from the cares of the day. Had Haines stayed a little longer, he would have seen the lights in Edwards House go on and heard the echoing screams as one of the boarders, a pale girl with a secret, shattered her fellow pupils' rest.

At six-thirty he floundered with the alarm. It had interrupted one of those semi-waking dreams in which bloody Jamieson had been surrounded by pupils of Eldersley College, who'd been asked by Matron to watch him conduct a post-mortem on Amy's ginger cat. Hauling himself out of bed, Haines showered, dressed and made a half-hearted attempt to straighten the duvet. Then he locked the door and got into his car. Ideas were buzzing in his head.

Constable Spinner was at the desk, but there was no sign of Fraser. 'He's in, Sarge, but I just can't . . . I'm having trouble locating him.'

'Well, when you find him, tell him to move himself – and if he's getting breakfast, tell him not to bother because he's got a post-mortem. Going on past performances, he'll only waste it.'

'Okay, Sarge.'

'How's Molly Doherty?'

'Fractured ribs and concussion. Doctor says her injuries are consistent with being kicked. She can't talk yet.'

'Has Doherty been charged?'

'Yeah. Flynn did that last night. This morning I told the mongrel his wife might die, and if she does we'll be charging him with murder. He's down there, weeping. Do you want to see him?'

'No. I'll go and see Molly myself, tonight. Just find Fraser. Oh, and get me a telephone number for Pastoral Enterprises. Better still, get onto the bod called Fairweather that runs the show and tell him we need to talk to him urgently, and see what Lockyer's doing about tracking Radcliffe's next of kin, would you? Fairweather can ring me this afternoon. If I'm not at the station, I'll be interviewing at the school.'

'What Enterprises was that, Sarge?'

'Pastoral, Spinner. Pastor with an "al" on the end. Head office is in Sydney.'

Two hours later, Haines and Fraser were in the grounds of the hospital where Horace Radcliffe was to undergo his final medical examination. The trees flanking the hospital driveway made a tunnel of dappled light, and the adjacent lawns and gardens sparkled in the sun. It was the sort of day you wouldn't be dead for quids. They sauntered into the cool, white interior of the mortuary. Jamieson, capped, gloved and gowned, was bending over Horace Radcliffe's mortal remains, scalpel in hand. He looked up as they entered but didn't remove his mask.

'Had to start early. Good day for golf. Aiming to tee off at eleven. You ought to think about it, Haines – exercise and relaxation are the keys to longevity, and you look as if you could use both.' His eye travelled to the sergeant's waistline.

'I get my exercise walking to the funerals of my friends who get exercise,' Haines replied. 'Why waste time chasing a little white ball around a park?'

More dispiriting than the sterile atmosphere of the mortuary, and the smell of formalin and flesh, was Jamieson's indefatigable cheerfulness. Nothing gave the man greater pleasure, whilst he was working on a cadaver, than to conduct a one-way conversation with his audience in technicolour detail. He recounted gruesome case histories to anyone who cared to listen. Raw recruits weren't much more responsive than the cadavers, except when one of them fainted or threw up. In Haines's view, Jamieson had a personality disorder from working too long with people who couldn't answer back.

Transferring his scalpel to his left hand, Jamieson recovered a plastic bag that had been lying on an adjacent table. 'Liver for weighing and testing. No obvious signs of toxins, but proof of the pudding and all that.'

'No indications of how he died?'

'Too early to say. Nothing that jumps up and waves its hand about. If someone did him in, they made a neat job of it, because there's no apparent bruising or contusions. In fact, our man was in extremely good condition, for his age. His arteries are clean as a whistle. Haven't got to his lungs and heart, but if they're all right and there's no sign of embolism, we might be looking at cause of death unknown.'

'Give us a break, Jamieson. There's got to be something. What was that business yesterday about his hand?'

'Oh, that? Well, as your charming friend observed, rigor was interrupted in his right hand. Once rigor is interrupted it never returns. Smart woman, that. Is she in the trade?'

'Just observant.'

'Married?'

'Widowed.'

'Graham! Of course! Husband topped himself – whisky and barbiturates – and I did the autopsy. Brain tumour. Well, well,

well. She would have inherited a tidy sum. He was loaded, by all accounts.'

'Her finances aren't my concern, and they're certainly not yours,' replied Haines. '*How* was rigor interrupted?'

Jamieson sniggered. 'Someone interrupted it by moving his fingers. Maybe they wanted to shake his hand? How would *I* know? That's your job, not mine. Good-looking woman, that. Have you staked a claim or is she up for grabs?' There were times Haines wanted to smash Jamieson's face.

'What if he'd been holding something . . . clutching something that was subsequently removed?'

'That would do the trick,' said Jamieson, 'but . . .' (he paused, tracing with the point of his scalpel the line of the incision that had laid bare the headmaster's thoracic cavity) '. . . as we don't know what it was or whether it contributed to his death, it doesn't really help, does it?' Haines disliked rhetorical questions as much as he disliked the people who asked them. What Jamieson was enjoying, apart from the kick he got out of doing something that made other people want to throw up, was the fact that everything hinged on his findings.

Jamieson concentrated on his cadaver, over whose heart and lungs, which at a glance he could see were healthy, he hovered longer than necessary. He whistled and made clicking noises with his tongue. He mumbled under his breath in a way he knew would drive Haines crazy. The latter paced the floor, attempting to relieve the symptoms of aggravated suspense and mild nausea, and determined not to ask until Jamieson was ready. He wasn't the one who wanted to tee off at eleven.

'Nothing obvious there,' Jamieson was forced to say finally, 'but I'll send a sample for analysis.' He dropped a small section of the headmaster's left lung into a plastic bag and placed it alongside the others. Haines stopped pacing.

'So where does that leave us?'

'Well, it wasn't a heart attack. Didn't think it would be – arteries are too clean. Could have been a stroke, but I'll need to get to his brain for that. I'll get my little saw.'

Haines didn't fancy listening to the whining and screaming of Jamieson's little saw grinding away at the top of the headmaster's skull. His first impulse was to flee, but he wasn't about to give Jamieson the satisfaction. Instead, he held up his hand, indicating that he wanted Jamieson to wait. Then he beckoned to Fraser. 'Have a close look at that body. There's not a mark on it. What does that suggest to you?'

Reluctantly (he was looking pale), Fraser moved closer. After a brief glimpse at the corpse, he glanced at Jamieson. 'Well . . . if you're sure it wasn't a heart attack . . .'

'I'm damned sure he couldn't have had a heart attack and then painted his own face with lipstick and stuck a flower behind his ear.' Jameson grinned at Haines. 'I believe a flower behind the ear signifies availability in Polynesian circles. Damned good idea, that. Saves time and effort. Take the lovely widow Graham, for example. A man could make a fool of himself there, eh, Haines?'

'Shut up, Jamieson. Assume, Fraser, that Radcliffe's death was not from natural causes. How was it done?'

'Poison?'

'No immediate evidence of toxins,' Haines reminded him, waving his hand in the direction of the plastic bags. 'Try again.' Fraser stared at the body, taking in the handiwork of Jamieson's scalpel, a combination of distaste and concentration contorting his features.

'He wasn't a large man . . . I mean, he wasn't muscular. It wouldn't have been difficult to overcome him, particularly if he were taken by surprise. There are ways to kill someone without leaving a mark.'

'For example?'

'A blow to the carotid artery would do it, or a blow to the sternum about here . . .' (Fraser indicated the precise position on his own chest) '. . . would shear off a fragment of bone that might ultimately kill him.'

'Wouldn't blows like that leave bruises?' asked Haines.

Fraser, who wasn't sure whether the question was directed at him or Jamieson, looked from one to the other before replying. 'I . . . don't know, Sarge. I mean, I've never seen what happens afterwards . . . I've never seen the body of anyone killed like that.'

'Could be bruising, but not necessarily,' said Jamieson. 'No sign of bruising on his chest or lungs, but I'll examine his carotid cartilage. If he were dealt a blow to the carotid artery, there should be damage to his windpipe.'

'Anything else, Fraser?'

'Well . . . I was thinking, Sarge, of how he looked when we found him. If he'd been struck, you'd think his head would have been on one side, but he was bolt upright.'

'Then someone helped him stay that way,' snorted Jamieson. 'The head is bloody heavy, and it lolls about when we're unconscious. Ever gone to sleep in front of the TV? He must have been propped up.'

'Well, he was leaning against one of those curved, high-backed wooden chairs,' said Haines. 'Ugly bloody thing, like a throne. He was most likely struck and then rearranged.'

'Hang on! You're jumping the gun, old man,' said Jamieson. 'We don't know that he was struck. He may have died of natural causes and someone played around with the body. It wouldn't be the first time.'

Edward Haines ignored him and turned to Fraser. 'Anything else?'

'Pressure points, Sarge. You can black someone out in seconds by applying pressure to the carotid artery and stopping blood flow to the brain. If you keep up the pressure, death would take . . . maybe three minutes?' Fraser looked at Jamieson for confirmation.

The latter nodded. 'Could be quicker. There was a case in Leeds in the UK where a perfectly healthy young lass dropped dead on the dance floor. It was only from eyewitness accounts that they were able to determine what killed her. Boyfriend was grasping her neck a little too fondly and rendered her more relaxed than he anticipated.'

'Are you saying there was no other way the pathologist would have known?'

'That's exactly what I'm saying. Didn't show up in the post-mortem. Young, healthy girl dies, though – it arouses suspicion, eh, Fraser? Lots of questions asked. If an older person dies the same way, your average pathologist wouldn't pick it up. Might be anything. Our man was asthmatic, wasn't he?'

'Yes.'

'Could he have inhaled something?'

'It's a possibility,' said Haines, feeling no inclination to share with Jamieson the question of the missing inhaler.

'Well . . . I was about to look at his brain, but let's try Fraser's theory first. If you'd like to stand a little closer, Constable, we'll just open up his neck.' Fraser, who did not care to stand closer, glanced desperately at Haines and made his escape only after the latter inclined his head in the direction of the door.

'You're mollycoddling that boy.'

'Maybe, but I'm not a sadist,' said Haines mildly. He waited and stared at the ceiling while Jamieson, whistling and humming snatches from *The Merry Widow*, laid bare the carotid cartilage and exposed the windpipe of the deceased.

'Well, well, well.'

'Well what?'

'Well I never . . . Come and have a look at this.' Reluctantly, Haines joined Jamieson and studied his handiwork. Even he could see that there was some sort of trauma. 'Definitely bruising and some crushing of the windpipe. Blood flow to the brain stops, heart stops, everything stops. Life extinct. Who's a clever dick, then?'

'So will that be the basis of your report? Death by a blow to the neck?'

'Haven't finished yet. Paperwork can't be done till the job's finished. Still have to examine his brain and analyse the other bits.'

'But you're convinced that was how he died?'

'Unofficially?'

'Unofficially.'

'I'd say it looks promising. You won't get any more out of me until I've finished. You know the rules.'

'It's good enough for me,' said Haines. 'We know the how. Now it's a question of why and who.'

'That's two questions,' said Jamieson, 'but who's counting?'

Haines walked towards the door, turning at the last minute. 'Let me know if you decide on a more precise time of death, and if you discover anything else. I don't want to wait for your report. If I don't hear from you by midday, I'll assume that your report confirms what we've already discussed.'

'What have we discussed?'

'Have it your way.'

'Give my regards to the widow Graham.'

Outside, Haines breathed in the sunlight. Fraser was examining some distant shrubbery. Jamieson was right – Fraser *was* a clever dick. He had twice as much grey matter as Lockyer, but none of the latter's cockiness.

As Fraser approached, Haines held up his hand. 'Do me a favour, would you?'

'What's that, Sarge?'

'If I die of unnatural causes, make sure that bastard Jamieson isn't given the job of finding out why.'

Fraser managed a weak smile and slid into the driver's seat. 'Back to the station?'

'Aren't you even going to *ask*?'

'Ask what?'

Haines sighed. 'What the bastard found.'

'I didn't think he'd finished. Has he found something already?'

'A contused windpipe, Fraser! A contused windpipe! Good call. Got it in ahead of the expert. I'll offer your services as a consultant the next time he gets a suspicious death.'

Fraser looked pleased. He repeated his earlier question.

'No. I want you to help me with the interviews. But we might as well make a detour via the hamburger shop. I didn't have time for breakfast.'

TEN

Bernard Deitz was indulging in the rare pleasure of a joint on school premises. He stared out of the window at the empty quadrangle and wished every day could be a pupil-free day. In his peripheral vision he could see the rodent galloping around inside its exercise wheel, driven by something humans would pay a fortune for if it could be bottled. He exhaled, closed his eyes and waited for the weed to take effect. Round and round from the beginning of the curriculum to the end of the curriculum, and back again until you fall off or get replaced.

Although the assignments in front of him were inaccurate and badly written, they had to be marked, and he was wasting the legacy of time bequeathed to him by the headmaster's death. His attention strayed again as two of the boarders appeared in the quadrangle, dragged wooden benches off the verandah and into the sunlight, and then hitched up their skirts and stretched their legs between the benches in pursuit of the all-important tan. Why, he wondered, did he bother talking to them about holes in the ozone layer?

There was something else worrying Bernard Deitz, something he'd tried unsuccessfully to push to the back of his mind. From his wallet he retrieved a neatly folded piece of paper and read again the unsigned words that he'd almost committed to memory. Then he touched the corner of the note with his joint and watched, mesmerised, as it burst into flame. At the very last moment he dropped it into the waste basket, where it lay, blackened and curled.

Haines and Fraser parked outside Edwards House. There were only a few remaining boarders, most having been granted permission to catch the bus into Bowral. The interest of the girls was aroused by Fraser's height and good looks. He was pronounced 'dishy', 'spunky' and 'cute'. Haines, who might well have been invisible, wondered to what extent Fraser was aware of his power over women – not just the gaol bait, but women in general. He'd often witnessed Fraser's ability to reduce the female of the species to simpering stupidity. They either wanted to mother him or . . .

'Good morning, Sergeant,' said Matron from the verandah.

Then again, thought Haines, one day young Fraser was bound to meet his match. 'Good morning, Matron. Constable Fraser has a draft statement for you to look at.' Fraser handed Matron an envelope.

'Thank you. I'll let you have it back before you leave this afternoon. I take it you'll be here all day?'

'Yes,' Haines responded. 'I was wondering if we could use one of your offices with a telephone . . . perhaps the one next to your staffroom? We'd like to interview staff, and there are a few other things we need to organise.'

'You could use the bursar's office,' said Matron.

'I'm afraid not. Our scientific squad will be going over the cottage for prints. The area has to remain sealed.'

'Then you can use the sitting room by all means.' Matron turned and the two policemen followed her starched exterior into the room through which Haines had passed the previous morning.

It was large and comfortable, with a bay window overlooking the front gates. The wallpaper was yellowing and the furniture had seen better days, but the room had an atmosphere Haines liked. He could imagine candles on the mantelpiece above the fireplace, and servants lifting lids off steaming dishes of lamb, beef and boiled potatoes. The room's centerpiece was a round wooden table with high-backed chairs. In the corner, nearest the staffroom, was a small table with a telephone.

'Thank you, Matron. This will do very nicely. You have no objection, I take it, to us availing ourselves of the odd cup of tea?'

'Not at all. The kitchen is at the end of the corridor. Mrs Watkins will be happy to provide you with cups and saucers and a pot. The toilet is at the other end of the courtyard. You have to go through the kitchen door.'

'Thank you. There's only one other thing I'd like to ask.' Matron, who had been about to leave, turned to face him, hands clasped. 'Do you have any idea where the headmaster kept his personnel records – job applications, résumés, records of interview, contacts in an emergency?'

'If they exist they'll be in the cottage somewhere, Sergeant, unless Mr Fairweather has taken them to Sydney. I imagine one of the filing cabinets in the bursar's office would be a likely place. Brenda Stokes would know.'

'Would you, or she, have any idea of the headmaster's next of kin?'

'None whatsoever. I can't answer for Brenda Stokes.'

'He was a bit of a dark horse, your Mr Radcliffe.'

'The headmaster was a private person. I can't say that I would describe him as "dark".'

'Possibly not the right word. Don't let me keep you any longer, Matron.' When she left, Haines gestured in the direction of the telephone. 'See if that will stretch across here, and when you get a chance, relay the number to Lockyer.' With the telephone in place, Haines leaned back and pressed the tips of his fingers together. 'Notebook.' Fraser obliged, seating himself opposite Haines with his pen poised. 'There are things we need to do immediately, not the least of which is to get the scientific squad. I'll do that. What I want you to do is get hold of Radcliffe's personnel files. As Attila says, they're most likely to be in the cottage. Wear gloves and avoid the obvious parts of the drawers – we don't want to wipe any prints.'

'Attila?'

'The Hen,' said Haines. 'I've asked Lockyer to phone the bloke who runs this place . . . Fairweather of Pastoral Enterprises, would you believe? Ask him how far he's got. Maybe the records are in Sydney.'

'Anything else, Sarge?'

'Do me an interview schedule – twenty minutes each with ten minutes between. Say a midday start. I want you to take notes. Anyone in there?' He jerked his thumb in the direction of the staffroom.

Fraser opened the door. 'No.'

'Good.'

'But there's another entrance from the verandah.'

'Stick a note on their side saying 'Interviews in progress. Please keep door shut.' By the way, Fraser, how did you hit upon a blow to the carotid artery?'

'You said there were no marks on the body but to assume that death wasn't natural. That narrowed it down. If it wasn't poison or asphyxia, and it was quick – when I saw him, he looked sort of surprised – it could only have been something like that. I don't know of any other way to kill someone without leaving a mark.'

'Who would know how to do this?'

'Anyone who practises karate. I go to self-defence classes twice a week, but I'm still a novice. Army recruits are trained in unarmed combat, and I suppose there's special training for the select few.'

'Could a woman have done it?'

'Yes, I think so. It's a question of accuracy, not brute force. If he were unconscious, it would have been no trouble to deliver the lethal blow, and . . .' He hesitated, loath to commit himself, but keenly interested nevertheless.

'And?'

'Well, I was thinking about what Jamieson said about the boy and girl on the dance floor. Getting close to a man's neck without arousing suspicion would be difficult, but a woman who pretended she was . . . you know . . .'

'My knowledge doesn't arise from recent experience, Fraser, but yes, I get your drift. See if you can find other places in the area that teach that sort of thing, and have a look at their membership records.'

'Will do.' Fraser added the latest instruction to his notebook and wondered how quickly Haines expected him to get all of these things done.

After ringing Goulburn to inform them of events and request the scientific squad, Haines wandered to the window. It was eleven-fifteen. Three cars entered the driveway – staff arriving late, he assumed. Still, it was a pupil-free day, and with Radcliffe dead, who cared what time they got to work? In their wake came a stocky, gnomish man with a broom, and a dog whose body was too big for its legs. Haines had seen both at the bottom of the drive on the morning Radcliffe's body was discovered. Haines liked dogs. He left the room and stood on the verandah. 'Who's the chap with the broom?'

The boarder he'd addressed was engrossed in a paperback.

She looked at him in a startled way and almost dropped her book. 'Mr O'Flaherty, the handyman.'

'Thank you.' Haines nodded to the staff alighting from their cars, only two of whom he recognised. The third fitted Amy's description of Brenda Stokes. As the girl began walking towards the cottage, he intercepted her. 'I'm afraid, Miss Stokes, that the cottage has to remain closed. Perhaps you haven't been told what's happened? I'm Detective Sergeant Haines.'

Brenda was chewing gum. 'I know he's dead,' she said simply, 'if that's what you mean, because Lettie rang me last night. Who's answering the phones, then? The phones won't stop ringing just because he's dead. In fact I can hear one of them now.'

'Does the school have an answering machine?'

'Yeah. Lettie switches it off when she comes in.'

'And do you have the telephone number of Mr Fairweather's office in Sydney?'

'Yeah.'

'Then I'll ask my constable to accompany you inside so you can put a message on the machine.'

'You want me to put a message on the machine?'

'Yes.'

'But I don't know what to say. What will I say?'

'Something to the effect that you regret there's no one who can attend to their call, and that Eldersley College is temporarily closed due to the unexpected death of the headmaster. You could add that the office will re-open soon and that, in the meantime, urgent enquiries should be directed to . . .'

'All right, then – if I have to. You couldn't write that down, could you?'

'With pleasure. Why don't you just sit over there on the verandah. Apart from the phone, don't touch anything, and I'd like you to leave as soon as the message is in place. Please excuse me for a moment.' Haines could see Fraser talking to two girls who were sunning themselves in a way Matron would not, he felt sure, approve.

He approached the trio. 'I'm sorry to deprive you of Constable Fraser's company, girls,' he said with mock gallantry. 'I'm sure he'd be delighted to chat with you all morning, but we have work to do.' Fraser looked sheepish as he followed Haines back towards Edwards House. 'Can't leave you alone for five minutes and you're at the mercy of predatory females, and these haven't even finished high school. How are you going on the interviews?'

'I've asked Dr Deitz to see you at twelve and Vandegaard at twelve-thirty. I thought you might want some lunch then, so I've left the others until after two. Oh, and Lockyer has left a message for Fairweather to ring you here.'

'Good. Speaking of phones, jot this down and give it to the brazen piece on the verandah.' He ran quickly through the message for Brenda Stokes. 'I want you to take her into the cottage so she can leave a message on the answering machine. Get her out of there quickly, but while you're there, ask her where the personnel records are. And see what's in those filing cabinets, will you? Bring me anything that looks interesting.' He was about to leave when he heard a dog bark. 'Oh, and before we start with Dr Deitz, have a look round for that handyman, O'Flaherty. Ask him to keep an eye out for the inhaler. He seems to spend most of his time wandering about the grounds. And tell him not to touch it if he does find it. We don't want his grubby prints all over it.'

'Will you want to interview the brazen piece?'

'Yes. Her name's Brenda Stokes. Some others have arrived too. They're probably in the staffroom, so add them to your list.' Then another thought struck him. 'If you're going to chat to the lassies,

Fraser, and I certainly have no objection, find out what you can about this paramilitary organisation . . . the GSTU. Every now and then they climb into khaki trousers and slouch hats and march around saluting the flag.'

'Do they do self-defence?'

'Now you're cooking, Fraser. Use that God-given talent of yours. I'd suggest you try your charms on Attila, but I think she's a lost cause.' He introduced Fraser briefly to Brenda Stokes and made his way back to the sitting room to await the arrival of Bernard Deitz.

When the science master entered the sitting room, Haines's first impression was that he was stoned. 'It must be relaxing to have a day away from the pupils, Dr Deitz.'

'I can't imagine why you say that, Sergeant. Perhaps you're just naturally perspicacious. In any case, there's no escaping them. If they aren't there in person, they're there in the form of abysmally written essays that have to be marked in those periods we jocularly term free.'

'You sound cynical, Dr Deitz. Are you sure you're in the right profession?'

'How observant, Sergeant! But then, that's what policemen do, isn't it – they observe?'

'Tell me about your relationship with the headmaster. I haven't had a chance to observe that, although I've heard that he wasn't flavour of the month with many of the teaching staff. Did the two of you get on?'

'Oh, we got on famously – on each other's nerves, that is. I couldn't stand the bastard, but then you already knew that, didn't you? Now, I suppose, you're going to ask me where I was between Friday evening and Monday morning. Let me see. I drove home about four on Friday afternoon, and I saw no one between then and arriving at the school at seven-thirty on Monday. In fact the only person who can vouch for my existence over that period is Mr O'Flaherty, who waved me into the driveway from his usual position by the front gate.'

'You get to work early, Dr Deitz, but not quite as early as Mr O'Flaherty.'

'I get to work early, Sergeant, so I can prepare for classes and get some marking done. I try to get out of this place as early as I can in the afternoon. Mr O'Flaherty probably sleeps here, judging by his body odour. This place is his *raison d'être*.'

'But he's paid . . . to caretake, or whatever it is he does?'

'The Church paid him a nominal salary. I have no idea what his financial arrangements are with the new administration. He's a dinosaur – a survivor from the era of *noblesse oblige*. The Dean probably insisted that he be kept on.'

'Do you live far from here?'

'I commute from Goulburn, Sergeant.'

'So it would be unlikely for you to come here at weekends to prepare lessons?'

'I've never been that desperate, Sergeant. Six weeks' annual leave and two days away from this place at the end of every week is the very least I ask.'

'Have you always taught science?'

'Do you mean, have I experimented with other disciplines or have I dabbled in other professions?'

'Both.'

'No, Sergeant. I had dreams of one day discovering a formula that would make my name a household word and simultaneously make me obscenely wealthy, and then I grew up. Since then I've been teaching basic physics and chemistry to cretins.'

'Can you think of anyone who would want to harm the head-master, Dr Deitz? Do you know if anyone threatened him?' Bernard Deitz raised his left hand to his brow, his thumb and index finger pressed to his temples, his palm obscuring the upper half of his face. When he removed his hand, his eyes were creased with laughter and his shoulders shook.

'Just about every member of staff, Sergeant. They detested him. If one of them in a fit of pique exceeded my wildest expectations and did away with him, I think that person deserves a medal.'

'What was it, in particular, Dr Deitz, that you disliked about him? I didn't know him, so it's difficult for me to form a picture.'

'There were always little things, but overall I think the fact that he was a raving lunatic had something to do with it. The man was as mad as a meat axe – a little to the right of Genghis Khan. He even wanted to get into politics, God help us! He saw himself as a leader of men, and he was fond of poncing around in fancy dress, raving about teachers being pastors and not allowing technology to replace chalk and talk.'

'Was he critical of your teaching methods?'

'He was critical of everything the staff did, Sergeant. Whether he singled me out for special treatment I'll never know, because I don't know what he said to anyone else. Let's just say I wasn't his golden-haired boy. But if you're considering that as a motive for doing him in, you'd be mistaken.'

'He didn't suggest that you leave?'

Deitz snorted. 'He could suggest all he liked, but he couldn't do anything about it.'

'So he did suggest that you leave?'

'He said he thought I wasn't committed to the ideals of the school and that I might be happier elsewhere.'

'And what did you say?'

'I agreed. I told him that if I could find a school where the pupils were less concerned with their looks and their love lives, and more concerned with science, I'd be a much happier man. I asked him if he knew of a vacancy at a school where there were pupils like that.'

'And?'

'He told me to get out – out of his office, that is – but perhaps the comment was open to interpretation.'

'Thank you for your frankness, Dr Deitz.' Haines stood and moved towards the door. Deitz rose, almost reluctantly. He thrust his hands into his trouser pockets and, with a brusque nod in Haines's direction, left without another word.

Hans Vandegaard, delivered to the door by Fraser, was a well-built, suntanned man in his early forties. He had piercing blue eyes and a smile that seemed to extend across his whole face. Haines shook his outstretched hand and then looked enquiringly at Fraser. Fraser shook his head and gave him the thumbs down. Haines turned his attention to the interview.

'Thank you for coming, Mr Vandegaard. If you don't mind, Detective Constable Fraser will join us and may take notes. You have no objection?'

'None at all, Sergeant.' Vandegaard seated himself in the chair vacated by Bernard Deitz. He looked relaxed and confident.

'You might like to begin by telling me why you left South Africa and came to this quiet little backwater,' said Haines. 'Have you been in Australia long?'

'About two years, Sergeant, and although this backwater, as you call it, is quiet, it is also very beautiful. I travelled extensively in the first six weeks after my arrival and I had not intended to stay anywhere for long, but my funds were running out. When I saw this position advertised, I decided to apply. The holidays are generous and I can travel extensively during the breaks. I am on what you might call a working holiday.'

'Your family is in South Africa?'

'I am divorced, Sergeant, but there were no children from my marriage. As my parents are no longer living, there is nothing to keep me in South Africa. I was born here, in any case, but I grew up in South Africa. My father, who was what you call a jackeroo, told me much about Australia and I have not been disappointed.' He flashed Haines and Fraser a brilliant smile.

'Will you return to South Africa?'

'Perhaps, one day. It is my first home, but I may make Australia my second.'

'What did you do in South Africa, Mr Vandegaard? I assume this is on your résumé, but we haven't been able to locate the head-master's personnel records. The executive director has agreed to provide us with copies.'

'When I left university, I worked for a company in Johannes-burg that conducted medical research. I am a doctor by degree, although I have never practised medicine.'

'Have you visited other countries as well as Australia?'

There was a slight hesitation in Vandegaard's response. 'No, Sergeant. Australia has been my only port of call.'

'And what was your opinion of the headmaster? Did you get on well with him?'

'I understand that it is usual to say something nice. You have a saying, do you not, not to speak ill of the dead? Unfortunately, this is not possible. It would be foolish of me to disguise my dislike of Mr Radcliffe because it is common knowledge that we argued on a number of occasions. He was a petty, narrow-minded autocrat, but more than that, he was an actor. I could not abide his performances and his speeches and his dressing up. He was a salesman, not a scholar . . . a charlatan, as Mrs Stoddart says.'

'That's a very comprehensive description, Mr Vandegaard. Is that what you and he argued about – his role at the school?'

There was a perceptible hesitation. 'We argued about a variety of things, Sergeant, some of which I scarcely remember. At a school, differences of opinion arise all the time.' Haines was silent. His policy was to wait, if an answer were evasive. 'We differed on a number of issues,' Vandegaard said finally. 'He believed in capital punishment, whereas I do not. He believed that technology is undermining society, whereas I believe it is beneficial. He believed that totalitarian ideologies are infiltrating our western way of life – reds under the bed, as you say – and I think he was paranoid. I think . . .' (he hesitated) '. . . I think he yearned for an old British order and a position of rank for himself. He liked a society where birth brought privileges, but where someone like himself could rise to wealth and rank and take his place amongst the elite. He was a dreamer, perhaps?' Vandegaard shrugged.

'Did he criticise your teaching or threaten you, or ask questions about your background?'

'He certainly did not criticise my teaching, Sergeant, and why should he threaten me or ask questions about my background? I have nothing to hide. Has anyone suggested otherwise?'

'Not at all, Mr Vandegaard. I understood that the headmaster crossed swords with many of the staff on a number of issues, both personal and professional. I'm simply trying to determine what those issues were in your case. I was informed that he had lengthy discussions with you, and I'm assuming you didn't discuss capital punishment or the socio-economic aspects of British democracy.'

'You are misinformed, Sergeant, if you believe Mr Radcliffe

spent any more time with me than he did with other members of staff. My fellow teachers are great gossipers, mindful of everyone else's business but their own. In any small group there are petty jealousies, would you not agree? Here there is much hissing in corners and it is wise to believe only a small proportion of what you hear.'

'I'll bear that in mind, Mr Vandegaard. Tell me, when was the last time you saw the headmaster?'

'I was working late on Friday evening and I saw him getting into his car at about six o'clock. I was using one of the classrooms to mark some homework because I didn't want to do it in the staff-room. From the quadrangle you can see the cottage quite clearly.'

'How was he dressed?'

'He was . . . I was about to say "dressed to kill", but that is a very bad joke. He was dressed in a suit and a tie.'

'And that's the last time you saw him?'

'The very last time. Although I live quite close, I do not come to the school on weekends unless there is something I have forgotten.'

'So you didn't return to the school over the weekend?'

'I did not.'

'Can you think of anyone who would want to harm the headmaster, or anyone who had a grudge against him?' Hans Vandegaard's response, sans the manic laughter, was similar to that of Bernard Deitz. He spread his hands broadly.

'It would be difficult, I think, to find a member of staff who did not have some reason to dislike him. He was an intolerant man.'

'Thank you, Mr Vandegaard, for your time. When the personnel records are at our disposal, I may wish to speak with you again.'

'Any time, Sergeant. I am always happy to assist the police.' With a smile and a nod in Fraser's direction, he left.

'Why do I get this feeling he's not what he seems, Fraser?'

'Too practised . . . too smooth. He's got an answer for everything. I wonder where he stands on apartheid?'

'Amy Graham mentioned a rumour that Radcliffe was grilling him about his early years in South Africa. It could be hearsay, but it wouldn't do any harm to run checks. If there's anything suspicious, we'll try Interpol. No one checks résumés nowadays. Who's next?'

'The bloke who teaches history. Hinds. Bit of a hippie.'

'We'll have a break after we've done him. Who's after that?'

'The two English teachers, and then the French teacher and the art teacher. Haven't managed to line up anyone else. Anyone in particular you want?'

'There's a senior mistress – the one Vandegaard mentioned. Stoddart. See if you can find her. In the meantime, wheel in the history bod. I'm just about ready for a cup of tea.'

Dennis Hinds was already striding across the verandah when Fraser opened the door. He was tall and angular, like an overgrown adolescent, with a shock of untidy, reddish-brown hair. He had spectacles with heavy, unbecoming black frames. He kept his hands in his pockets, even when slouching in his chair.

'Good afternoon, Mr Hinds. It is "Mr", isn't it? I don't wish to overlook anyone's qualifications, and I've just been talking to Dr Deitz.'

Dennis Hinds snorted and was about to say something derogatory, but thought better of it. 'I don't have a PhD, Sergeant. It is "Sergeant", isn't it?'

'That will do nicely, Mr Hinds. Perhaps you'd like to tell me how you got on with the headmaster. Some of your colleagues didn't see eye to eye with him. Was that your experience as well?'

'You might say that. He saw himself at the forefront of education, but I put him somewhere on the lunatic fringe.'

'You thought his ideas harmful?'

'If that's your way of asking me whether I assassinated him to save generations of children from becoming militant drones, the answer is no. Pity someone didn't do it to Benjamin Spock, though. He was loony tunes, too. No, Sergeant, I wasn't worried that the headmaster was directly harming the students – it was more a disagreement in principle over the messages students were getting from the militancy and flag waving. So much a celebration of uniformity! I would have liked a little more emphasis on understanding differences and tolerating diversity. These children are living in a different world. The British Empire is dead.'

'Did you convey your feelings to the headmaster?'

'I did, and they went over like a lead balloon. He made it quite clear that he was running the show, and that if I felt I couldn't celebrate unity and nationalism and uphold his cherished ideals I could go elsewhere.'

'Did he threaten you?'

'Not in so many words. The implication that I could either conform or get out was there, though.'

'You must have resented that. You were here before he came.'

'I resented the fact that the company running this place selected a narrow-minded anglophile rather than an enlightened educator,' said Dennis Hinds. 'It would have been nice to work with someone I could respect.'

'When did you last see the headmaster?'

'It would have been . . . ah . . . Friday afternoon. I left early because I planned to come in over the weekend to do some marking. I passed him on my way to the car and he gave me a nod.'

'And did you come in over the weekend?'

'Yes, but I didn't see him. I put in a couple of hours at my desk on Saturday and then went home.'

'Do you often come in on weekends?'

'Yes. I live close and the atmosphere in here on weekends is conducive to working, whereas at home . . .'

'You have children?'

'Two, but they make enough noise for six.'

'Do you have any idea, Mr Hinds, who may have wanted to harm the headmaster?'

'None whatsoever. He argued with most of the staff, and he had a flaming row with Jacquelyn Pendlebury a few days ago. I saw her leave his office and try to slam the door. There must've been something heavy on the back of it, because it remained ajar and spoiled the effect. She just looked at me and raised her eyebrows.'

'Do you know what they were arguing about?'

'Probably the literature in the junior courses. It's been a bone of contention since he arrived. I think Radcliffe had theories about decadent art, like the Nazis. He couldn't do much about the senior texts, but he liked to check what they were studying in the other years.'

'Well, thank you for your help, Mr Hinds. We may need to talk to you again a bit further down the track. In the meantime, please call me if you think of anything else.'

Dennis Hinds removed his hands from his pockets, dragged himself to his feet and loped to the door. When he reached it, he hesitated and turned.

'How did he die? I mean, what was it that killed him?'

'I can't answer that, Mr Hinds, until the results of the autopsy are known.'

Haines and Fraser shared a brief lunch of sandwiches and tea brought to them on a tray by Mrs Watkins, after which they resumed the interviews. The English mistress, Jacquelyn Pendlebury, was a woman in her mid-thirties with a severe case of what Haines later described as 'terminal vagueness'. She recalled her argument with Horace Radcliffe, but wasn't sure whether she had seen him since; nor could she recall what time she left the school that Friday afternoon. She did not return to the school on the weekend. It was her practice to take marking home.

On the subject of Horace Radcliffe she was mercifully clear, proclaiming him to be a philistine and censor. 'If he'd had his way, Sergeant, the senior girls would not be studying any of D.H. Lawrence. He seemed to think that poetry has to rhyme and that anyone who couldn't spell wasn't any good at English. I tried on at least two occasions to explain to him that three pages of beautifully spelled English that didn't answer the question were worthless, but he thought of English as a soft option rather than a test of a student's ability to think.'

'Did he ever threaten you, Ms Pendlebury?'

'No . . . well, not exactly, but it may have been implied in his tone and attitude. I usually just refused to do whatever it was he wanted. I had no intention of changing any of my texts to suit him.'

'Do you have any idea who may have killed him?'

'I'm tempted to say someone with literary taste, but in truth I haven't a clue. It seems incredible that anyone here could have done it. My theory is that there was something in his private life that led to his murder, if it was murder . . . something not related to the school. That's the best I can do.'

'Thank you, Ms Pendlebury. If you think of anything later that you feel may be relevant, please contact me.'

Next was the French mistress, Chauntel Worsley — a short, plump woman who was an ardent fan of Jacques Tati's classic character, Mr Hulot. She was delighted that Haines had seen most of Jacques Tati's films. Unfortunately, Mr Hulot's mannerisms and staccato movements, which she attempted to emulate, lent themselves to someone taller, thinner and of the opposite sex. Chauntel's attempts made her appear like a badly wired mechanical hen. Fraser, who'd never heard of Jacques Tati or Mr Hulot, was at a loss to record anything in his notebook.

The only bone of contention between the French teacher and the deceased was her smoking and drinking. Chauntel ('Ms Worsley sounds so *gauche*') was in the habit of organising social soirées for her students, during which they would speak only French. Sometimes they would leave the school and go for a picnic to discuss 'ze birds and ze bees'. On other occasions she would provide savouries and wine and music, and they would listen and eat and discuss and compare. At these little soirées she would smoke Gauloises, but this the headmaster had strictly forbidden. He had also forbidden her to provide wine for the girls, regardless of the small proportions. He had dismissed her argument that to learn social French, one must speak it in social situations, and warned her that any further lapses would mean the end of her job, native French speaker or not.

By the time Chauntel left the sitting room, Georgina Stoddart had appeared on the verandah, chatting to the geography teacher, Veronica Ainesworth. Both had been informed by Matron that Sergeant Haines wanted to see them.

Mrs Stoddart chose to be interviewed first. After Amy's comments the previous evening, she wasn't at all what Haines expected. She was relatively young – late thirties, maybe – and she smiled a lot. In fact, there was something decidedly girlish and flirtatious about her that didn't reconcile with the image of an ambitious, manipulative woman. She impressed him as helpful, cooperative, and knowledgeable about the workings of the school. She was coy about the headmaster's direct dealings with staff, preferring to drop hints. For example, in her comments about the colleague to whom she had been chatting on the verandah, she alluded to a potential scandal in such a lighthearted, jocular fashion that Haines could be forgiven for thinking there was no venom there at all. They'd been discussing the headmaster's tendency to criticise, when she suggested that he didn't restrict his criticism to his staff's professional behaviour.

'Do you mean he got involved in their private lives?'

'It's possible he might have been extremely shocked if he had,' she replied, 'but then I've never attended one of Veronica's parties, so I wouldn't really know.'

'Veronica being . . .?'

'Oh, Veronica Ainesworth. That was just an example, Sergeant. I don't really listen to hearsay.'

'And what sort of hearsay would it be, Mrs Stoddart, that you didn't really listen to? I'm curious, because the headmaster appeared to take the calibre of his staff very seriously. Indulge me, please.'

'Well, it was something one of the older women on the staff said who was invited to Veronica's house. She got the impression the invitation included an arrangement involving other people's spouses, and as she wasn't inclined to share anything, let alone her husband, she declined. Perhaps she was mistaken. Who knows?'

'The headmaster, perhaps, Mrs Stoddart? Someone, in the best interests of the school, may have told the headmaster?'

'It's possible,' said Georgina Stoddart with a smile, 'but if he knew, he didn't say anything to me.'

'That surprises me. You must have seen him regularly, in your capacity as senior mistress. Did he never complain to you about other members of staff?'

She raised her eyebrows innocently. 'No, Sergeant, I can't say he did. He may have made the odd comment, but nothing of any significance.'

'And how did you get on with him, Mrs Stoddart? I believe the day-to-day running of the school has always depended largely on you. Was he happy for this to continue, or did he envisage relieving you of some of your responsibility as he became more familiar with the school?'

'He was more than happy for me to continue, Sergeant, either because he liked the way I handled things or because he didn't feel capable of handling them himself.'

'He taught maths, I believe, before he took this post. It gave you something in common, I suppose?'

'He taught *junior* maths, Sergeant, for approximately seven years. I have been teaching senior maths for fifteen, and I am degree qualified. He was not. We had very little in common.'

'I do recall,' said Haines, 'someone saying that they expected you to become headmistress when Mrs Bridges retired. I can see why. You're better qualified, more experienced, and more familiar with the running of the school. It seems to me you would have been the logical choice.'

'The thought crossed my mind, Sergeant, but the powers that be thought otherwise. I have continued to serve the school to the best of my ability. I always gave Mr Radcliffe my full support.'

'I'm sure you did. I wonder what the powers that be will do now that Mr Radcliffe is dead.'

'That's not for me to say,' said Georgina Stoddart. The flicker of interest in her grey eyes was unmistakeable. 'Of course, if I were called upon . . .'

'You would step into the breach and do the job admirably,' said Haines.

Veronica Ainesworth, who replaced Georgina Stoddart in the

seat opposite Haines, was an older woman. He put her at between forty-five and fifty. She was softly spoken and sophisticated, if slightly overweight. She wore bright-red lipstick and there were lines around her mouth, which were explained when she asked whether she could smoke. She was conservatively dressed.

'You teach geography, Mrs Ainesworth?'

'Geography and economics, Sergeant.' She removed a silver cigarette case and lighter from her purse.

'Times have changed. They didn't study economics when I was at school.'

'Times have changed for the better, Sergeant, I believe.' She selected a cigarette, lit it, and put the case and lighter back into her bag.

'I agree,' said Haines. 'Tell me,' he asked, leaning forward confidentially, 'did you find Mr Radcliffe very open to new ideas? Some of the staff have suggested he was rather old-fashioned and conservative.'

'In the extreme,' Veronica Ainesworth replied, holding her cigarette beneath the level of the table so the smoke did not drift in front of Haines. 'He was offensively narrow-minded, and he had ideas about women that bordered on biblical. How on earth he obtained a position in a girls' school is beyond me.'

'I take it you didn't like him?'

'You take it correctly, Sergeant.'

'Was he ever critical of you personally, Mrs Ainesworth? I'm asking that question of everyone because it appears he spent a great deal of time arguing with staff.'

'He didn't know anything about the subjects I teach, Sergeant, so he couldn't interfere. In any case, my public examination results have been good, so there was no cause for scrutiny.'

'I believe he could be critical of things other than public

examination results,' said Haines. 'In fact, I believe one of your staff is currently threatening legal action over his scrutiny of her personal life. Was that your experience too, Mrs Ainesworth?' She drew on her cigarette, blowing the smoke sideways but at no point losing eye contact with Haines. Her expression was challenging.

'Are you calling my private life into question, Sergeant?'

'Not at all, Mrs Ainesworth. I'm merely trying to establish whether Mr Radcliffe did.'

'Then the answer is no. Mr Radcliffe knew nothing of my private life, and if even he had, there's nothing there that would have interested him.'

'Can you think of any reason why anyone would want to harm him?'

'Not off hand. I can think of plenty of reasons why people would dislike him, but none of them warranted killing him. *Was* it murder?'

'We don't know yet, Mrs Ainesworth. So as far as you're concerned, he had no enemies?'

'I didn't say that, Sergeant. He was surrounded by enemies. What I said was that I couldn't imagine the reasons his enemies had for disliking him becoming legitimate reasons for killing him. There's a difference.'

'Yes, I appreciate that. I've also known murderers to kill for reasons other people see as insignificant. The relative importance to the murderer could be great.'

'In that case, Sergeant,' said Mrs Ainesworth softly, 'I think you may find yourself with a great many more suspects than you anticipated.'

ELEVEN

By the time Haines and Fraser had completed eight interviews, the art teacher being the last, the sun had lost much of its warmth. The few staff who'd not yet been interviewed were anxious to leave. Haines stretched and yawned. 'Tell them they can go, Fraser. I'll be back over the next couple of days, and I can catch them in what they call their free periods. I'm interviewed out. Anyway, I want to get to the hospital to see Molly Doherty.'

'Not much point, because she won't press charges. Spindles has already spoken to her. All she says is "'E'll be ever so sorry in the mornin', Constibule Spinner."'

'He's always sorry,' said Haines. 'He'll be sorry after he kills her. Probably weep over her grave. I thought I'd try a different tack.'

'What's that?'

'I'll let you know if it works,' said Haines. 'We haven't heard from Fairweather yet, have we? That's strange. I'll have to make a statement to the press without him. You'd think he'd be mildly concerned, wouldn't you?'

'Maybe that's him just coming up the drive,' said Fraser, who was at the window. He whistled. 'Old roller . . . classy!'

It was indeed the executive director who had just driven, or been driven, from Sydney. He'd stopped only long enough to book into a motel. He was ushered into the room by Matron, whose animation and brilliant smile astounded Haines. Amy was right – it was power that turned that woman on.

Gilbert Fairweather reminded Haines of a used car salesman. He was wearing an immaculately tailored, grey pinstriped suit, from the breast pocket of which a peacock-blue handkerchief protruded to complement its owner's tie. As Matron introduced him, he smiled broadly and stretched out his hand. There was a glint of gold bracelet, cuff links and wristwatch, the combined value of which probably exceeded several months of Haines's salary. His hand was soft and white, like a woman's, and Haines noted with distaste that the manicured nails were varnished – clear varnish, but varnish nonetheless. He shook the proffered hand briefly without returning the director's smile, and involuntarily glanced at Fairweather's shoes. What had he expected – spats?

Fairweather oozed charm. He was basking in the attention of a transformed Matron, who'd just included Haines and Fraser in her offer of tea and cake. 'No thank you, Matron,' said Haines, taking the opportunity to establish control of the interview and the conditions under which it would occur. 'We won't be needing anything for the next half hour, and then DC Fraser and I will be on our way. I'm sure Mr Fairweather would like a little refreshment once we've finished.' Matron looked put out. She withdrew and Fraser groaned inwardly, tormented by the hunger pains that were gnawing at his guts.

'I'd like you to tell me about your headmaster, Mr Fairweather,' said Haines, leaning back in his chair. 'I never met him, but I understand he was hand-picked for the job. You were happy with his performance?' As he said this, he leafed through and glanced at the contents of a manila folder, which he subsequently closed and placed in front of him, tapping it lightly with two fingers.

Fairweather's response was effusive: 'I was extremely happy with him. I'm a very good judge of character, Inspector – I mean

Sergeant – and I'm happy to say that Horace met all of my expectations. He was dedicated, hard working, and he projected the kind of image we needed.'

'What image was that?'

'Horace,' said Fairweather with an expansive gesture, 'was precisely what the parents wanted. He was a drawcard – salute the flag, uphold traditions, preserve moral values, and all that. Straight out of a movie, I sometimes thought.'

'And as an educator?'

Fairweather shrugged. 'He didn't have to teach them. The academic staff did that. Horace was a frontman, and I paid him to look good and promote the school. It's what he did best.'

'He received a generous salary,' said Haines, who knew nothing of the dead man's finances. Fairweather hesitated, unsure of what Haines had been able to glean from Horace Radcliffe's bank statements.

'I'm a businessman, Sergeant. I pay for results, and Horace got results. I fail to see what that has to do with anything. It hardly makes me responsible for his death. Quite the contrary.'

'He was more valuable to you alive?'

'I would have thought that was obvious. I don't know what you're getting at, but whoever killed Horace, it had nothing to do with me.'

'I haven't accused you of anything, Mr Fairweather. I'm just trying to establish what kind of relationship you had with the deceased. By the way, what makes you think that someone killed him? The cause of death isn't known, and I'm sure I couldn't have given you that impression . . . or any of my staff, for that matter.'

'I know nothing about how he died, but you wouldn't be bloody interrogating me like this if he'd died in his sleep. In any case, Matron indicated that he'd been . . . mucked about a bit. I take it *that* wasn't natural?'

'Well, it depends . . . naturally,' said Haines. 'We'll know more when they complete the autopsy. When did you last see him?'

Fairweather hesitated, considering whether to withhold a piece of information that might, if he were lucky, remain unrevealed. What if they'd been seen? It was a small restaurant, and Radcliffe wasn't exactly low key. There were the waiters, for starters, and there was no way of knowing what this fat bastard had already found out, so he decided on the truth. 'We had dinner at a place called Mandibles in Mittagong on Friday night, and when I left him he was walking towards his car.' Fraser realised, with a jolt, that they'd not yet discovered the whereabouts of the headmaster's car. He glanced at Haines, but the latter kept his attention fixed firmly on the director's face.

'Just a friendly meal, was it?' It was a casual question, but there was a barely perceptible emphasis on the word 'friendly' that pushed Fairweather's patience beyond its limit.

'I've had enough of your insinuations, Sergeant – on top of which I've had a long drive and I'd like to return to my motel.' He stood up, producing as he did so a slim, expensive looking wallet from which he selected a card. 'You can contact me here for the next couple of days, after which I'll be returning to Sydney. If I'm not available, leave a message with my secretary.' He hesitated briefly, as if expecting Haines to detain him. Instead, Haines arose and preceded him to the door. He did not, however, open it.

'There are just a few things, Mr Fairweather, that I'd like you to assist me with before you go. First, could you draft a statement for the newspapers? If we don't give them something soon, they'll be printing hearsay, and a formal statement from you would, I think, project the right kind of image. Anything speculative or gory might do untold damage to your marketing strategy.'

'It will be with you first thing in the morning. And?'

'A temporary replacement for Mr Radcliffe is in order. I've someone in mind, and I'm sure you could have no objection.'

The director flushed, lost for words. When he recovered, his response was terse. 'I certainly do object, Sergeant. You may have jurisdiction to investigate Horace's death, but you have no jurisdiction to appoint his replacement. The running of this school is not your concern.'

'The people who are running the school are my concern for the moment,' Haines replied mildly, 'particularly if they're involved in a police enquiry. Finding someone local who's qualified and familiar with the school . . .'

'. . . and not a suspect?'

'. . . won't be easy. Mrs Graham is, I believe, a member of your school board who taught English here for many years. She's retired, but I'm sure she could be persuaded to accept a short-term contract. I know she has no desire to return to full-time teaching.'

Fairweather was torn between maintaining his rage and conceding that it was an excellent suggestion. Finding someone to take charge at the school was one of the problems he could see keeping him in this godforsaken hole, and from what he knew of Mrs Graham, she'd do very nicely. She'd resisted every attempt he'd made to establish her as an ally on the board, and she'd also declined his one invitation to dinner. In spite of this, or perhaps because of it, he had every confidence that she'd be adept at maintaining order. She was respected, and no one would get the better of her. She wasn't marketable, like Horace, but she could do the job. 'I'll let you know, Sergeant, when I've decided on Horace's replacement, but in the meantime I'll consider your suggestion.' With a curt nod in Fraser's direction, the director turned and was about to open the door.

'Just one more thing, Mr Fairweather. It's very important that we find the personnel records. There appear to be none in the headmaster's office or in the bursar's office. Can I assume that they're with you?'

'I have duplicates, but Horace had the originals. I can't say whether the two sets are identical, and I have no idea where Horace kept them. He insisted on sending me copies of everything in case of . . . well, fire I suppose.'

'I'll need those records as soon as possible, so could you ask your secretary to courier them tomorrow? Even more urgently, I need to locate Horace Radcliffe's next of kin, and there should be a name in your records. Please ask your secretary to phone it through to Detective Constable Lockyer at Bowral Police Station.'

'She won't be there now, but I'll call her first thing in the morning.'

'Thank you.' Haines opened the door and stood back as the director made his escape. 'We'll be in touch.' He shut the door and turned to Fraser. 'Rattled his cage, eh? More than a few interesting things in there – a bit more footwork for you, Fraser. It's marvellous what waiters and waitresses overhear.' He began to pace. Fraser watched, all too aware of what was worrying him. At last Haines looked up. 'We'd better find his bloody car.'

'It wasn't in the yard when we were called, Sarge. Maybe he garages it somewhere else. I don't even know what he drives . . . drove.'

'Ask Matron. She'd know what he drove and where he parked it. I'll be in the car. Try not to be too long. I want my dinner.'

Fraser began his search by investigating sounds from a room to the left of the stairs. He knocked, entered, and immediately regretted his decision. Twenty pairs of eyes stared at him. It was the evening meal, and the boarders were seated at long tables. The smell of food aroused his slumbering hunger, making him feel faint. He turned to a large girl at the nearest table and, in his most authoritative voice, asked where he could find Matron. Within seconds, the titters that had heralded his entry became a torrent of explosive laughter. The girl he'd addressed pointed, just as he heard Matron's voice behind him.

'What can I do for you, Constable?'

'Can I see you for a moment, please?'

'Well?' said Haines.

'It's a vintage job – one of those late-1930s Jaguars. He usually parked it near the steps underneath his office window, but there's a garage next to the art room, according to Matron, that he used from time to time. She assumed it was there.'

'Is it unlocked?'

'No. She's given me the key to the art room, and there's a door leading into the garage. Apparently the art teacher used the space for storage and wasn't happy about making room for the Jag. They didn't see eye to eye, but then . . .'

'But then murdering someone to obtain his car space seems a bit drastic.'

They drove around the block and parked in front of the old house that served as the art room for the school. There was a light inside. Fraser was about to knock, but Haines shook his head and pointed at the key. 'Just get on with it.'

A smell of linseed oil and turpentine greeted them as they stepped into the hallway. From an adjacent room came a barely audible rustling and what might have been a stifled exclamation. Fraser, with great intrepidity, was about to enter the room but Haines held him back.

'Police here. Who's that?'

'Oh, my God! You nearly gave me a heart attack.' A heavy walking stick appeared in the upper space of the doorway, followed rapidly by a pair of legs descending from a stool. Madelaine Everhardt returned the walking stick to its place in the hat stand, brushed down her skirt and held a beringed hand against her throat. 'I heard the gate and then the key. Matron might have let me know you were coming. I assume it was Matron who gave you the key?'

'Perhaps she didn't think that you'd be working so late. I'm very sorry we startled you, Ms Everhardt.'

'It's Madelaine, Sergeant.' She ran her hand down her throat and let it rest, fingers spread, where her cleavage began.

Madelaine Everhardt wasn't young, a fact Haines had noted at her interview, but she exuded youth and vitality. She was physically attractive and sexy; in fact, she was one of the sexiest women he'd ever met. Men obviously delighted her.

'So, what can I do for you, Sergeant?'

'We'd like to look at the headmaster's car. I believe there's a connecting door through to the garage. Do you have a key?'

'It isn't locked. Mr Radcliffe had the keys to the outer garage doors, and he used them to get in and out when there were classes. He preferred not to come through the art room. We didn't see eye to eye, as you know. Undoubtedly he would have found something to criticise, either in the way I was teaching or the nature of the work.'

'Particularly if it were a work of nature?'

'Ah . . . I told you about that, did I? I'm sure that other members of staff have embellished the story, because nothing's sacred around here. It wasn't as if the young man was naked. He was simply beautiful, and he inspired my senior girls to do some of their finest work. Look – I'll show you.' Before Haines could object, she darted into a corner and returned with exhibit one, propping it against the vase on her desk. 'Is that or is that not beautiful? Natasha's my best student. She's doing honours, of course.'

It was good, Haines had to admit. The flesh looked real and there was something about the sitter's face that drew your attention, though he couldn't have pinned it down . . .'

'It's innocence, Sergeant,' said Madelaine, reading his mind. 'How anyone could construe my life classes as dirty is beyond me. Philistines. Thank goodness the students are more sensitive than the staff. I don't suppose,' she said, casting an appreciative eye over Fraser's broad shoulders and narrow hips, 'that you've ever thought of sitting?' Fraser looked startled and the blood rose to his cheeks.

Haines knew he shouldn't have laughed, but Fraser's expression made restraint impossible. 'Sorry,' he said, wiping his eyes. 'It's been a long, amusement-free day. Some of your girls have already taken note of Constable Fraser's potential, but whether or not they want to immortalise him on canvas I couldn't say.'

'I'm sorry, Constable Fraser, if I've embarrassed you. It's so difficult to find suitable subjects, and the sergeant's response is typical. I wasn't suggesting, in any case, that you should wear as little as the young man in this picture. Jeans and an open-neck shirt or a T-shirt would be fine. My senior girls are not giggling voyeurs, although I can't speak for the bulk of the students in this establishment. Let me know if you change your mind.'

Fraser recovered his powers of speech and nodded in the direction of the painting. 'It's not something I've ever thought of doing, but if it would help and if something that good came out of it, I might be able to find time. I used to do some painting myself, but I didn't have Natasha's talent.' Madelaine Everhardt beamed, clapping her hands with delight.

It was Haines's turn to feel embarrassed. 'Now that we've got that settled, Madelaine, could we look at the garage?'

'Oh, I'm sorry. I forgot that's why you'd come. You're welcome to look in the garage, but you won't find Radcliffe's car. It hasn't been there since . . . Well, I think the last time I saw it was Friday morning. I'm sure I would have heard him take it out during the day, so it must have been taken out on Friday evening, or some time over the weekend. Do you think it's been stolen? Do you think the person who . . .? Well, assuming he was murdered, do you think the murderer could have taken the car? It was valuable, you know – a vintage Jaguar.'

'Rather conspicuous,' Haines answered shortly, 'and not easy to get rid of. I'll check out the garage anyway, if you don't mind.'

'Not at all. Follow me.' She led them back into the hallway and into an adjoining room filled with more canvases, cupboards, and what looked like props and painted backdrops. In the far wall was a door bolted from the inside. She slid back the bolt and waited for Haines and Fraser to enter.

'Where's the light?' said Haines.

'No light. He used a torch if he went out in the evening – one of those huge, powerful things with a handle on the top. He used to wander the grounds with it, according to Matron, checking that all the boarders were safely tucked up in their beds.'

Fraser rattled the outer doors. 'Locked, sir – from the outside.'

'Okay, Fraser. We'll leave it at that.' As Fraser re-emerged, Haines turned to Madelaine Everhardt. 'We'll leave you to it, Madelaine. Don't work too late.'

'I won't, Sergeant – and please feel free to drop in if there's anything I can do.' She walked them to the front door and waved cheerily as they left.

'Well, Fraser, what are our options?'

Fraser, who was prepared for this, had already formulated his response: 'According to Fairweather, he was walking back to his car, and since he got here and the car is missing, someone – perhaps the murderer – must have driven it away. I'll put out a description.'

'And alternatively?' Fraser was momentarily stumped. 'If he got here but the car didn't . . .?'

'Then the car's still there?'

'Which means?'

'He either got a taxi or someone gave him a lift?'

'Let's establish, Fraser, whether the car's still there before we issue a description. After I drop you off, I'll try the restaurant – and if I find the bloody thing, I'll have it towed back to the station and the fingerprint boys can go over it. If I don't, we'll revert to plan A. There were car keys in the drawer of his desk. Unless they were spares, the murderer couldn't have driven it away. My bet is, it's still in the car park.'

'Why would he leave it? Perhaps it wouldn't start?'

'That would be my guess. If I find it, check the taxis to see if anyone picked him up. Failing that, it's back to the restaurant staff. He may have returned to make a phone call.'

'Okay. By the way, did you see the bloke outside the school? I think he might have been waiting for us to leave. I spotted him when we came out of the front door, and he turned away when he saw us. Reckon he might have been visiting Madelaine.'

'Recognise him?'

'No. I couldn't see his face. He was under a tree and there wasn't enough light. Might have been any of those bods on the staff, because they're all about the same height and build.'

'You think he was an admirer?'

'I got the feeling she was expecting someone,' said Fraser.

'I can think of better places for an assignation. Not exactly comfortable, unless you fancy the floor.'

'There was a bed in the room leading into the garage.'

'You could have fooled me.'

'One of those things that fold vertically from the middle . . . wheels, so you can move it about. My mother had one for visitors.'

'Your powers of observation are remarkable, Fraser. That's a triple score, starting with our friend Jamieson. He said you were a clever dick, and I'm beginning to agree with him.' Fraser grinned.

When he'd dropped Fraser off, Haines drove to the hospital to have another chat with Molly Doherty.

TWELVE

Fraser glanced at his watch. It was six-thirty. He'd taken Haines's advice and chatted to 'the lassies', one of whom told him there was a new gym in Goulburn managed by the brother of one of the day girls. He decided to check it out.

A gym on the scale of Fit for Life was foreign to Fraser – a far cry from the community hall in which he attended his own self-defence classes. Were there enough people in Goulburn to support such a venture? The girl at the desk, assuming he was a prospective customer, offered to find the manager. He declined, saying he preferred to look around, but he chatted to her briefly. The club was doing well, she boasted. The Sydney backers visited the site frequently and even stayed on the premises, so comfortable and well equipped were they. He was tempted to point out that anyone with the money to put into such an enterprise shouldn't need to sleep on an exercise mat and use a communal shower.

The rooms for classes in judo and karate were empty, so he wandered into the area containing the exercise equipment. It had full-length mirrors, giving the impression of more space and multiplying the equipment into a forest of gleaming metal. Half a dozen male patrons grunted and sweated their way through routines by which they aspired to resemble the photographs of champion body builders adorning the walls. They were totally self-absorbed, and

Fraser disliked the way they strutted when they went from one piece of equipment to another. Their bulging thighs and biceps prevented them from walking normally, and their heads were too small for their bodies.

From a doorway that led to the toilet block and showers, there emerged two men deep in conversation: one was an instructor, judging by the 'Fit for Life' emblazoned across his yellow T-shirt; and the other, when he spotted Fraser, plunged forward with practised ease, hand outstretched and a welcoming smile. 'I do apologise. I had no idea we had a visitor. I'm George Papandopolous. Are you looking for somewhere to work out? If you are, look no further. We've got everything here you could possibly want, except maybe a pool, and we're hoping to get council permission to start one next year.'

Fraser shook the proffered hand, and then his head, to indicate that he wasn't seeking gym facilities. 'I'm not into body building, Mr Papandopoulos, although I do study self-defence. I suppose you have classes in that sort of thing?'

'We certainly do. Karate, self-defence, judo ... I have two instructors that come here from Sydney once a week, and both are black belts. Why don't you come through to reception. I'll get Ginny to give you an application form.'

'Actually, Mr Papandopoulos, I'm not looking to join. I'm here in a professional capacity, although I'm off duty at the moment. I need some information about your membership, and I didn't think you'd appreciate a formal visit.' He displayed his ID.

Papandopoulos's smile faded. 'What information do you need, exactly ...' (he looked closely at Fraser's ID) '... Detective Senior Constable Fraser?'

'I need to look at a list of your members – and your employees,' Fraser added as an afterthought. 'Is it possible I could do that now, or would it be necessary for me to return with a warrant?'

'You don't have any authority, then?'

'No. I was hoping that wouldn't be necessary. However, if you wish to reassure yourself, I can give you a telephone number for Detective Sergeant Haines. I'm requesting this information on his behalf.'

'What are you investigating?'

'I'm not at liberty to reveal that, Mr Papandopoulos. I can only assure you that our investigations are not related to the administration of this establishment. I've been instructed to make enquiries in an entirely unrelated matter.'

They reached the reception area, where Ginny smiled. 'You found him, then.'

'Ginny, would you please find a list of members and bring it into the office – and a current staff list if you have one? If you don't, write one out.'

'It's okay. I've got them. Do you just want names, or contact details as well?'

'Both,' said Papandopoulos, looking towards Fraser, who nodded his assent.

'Just one more thing,' said Fraser. 'Is it possible to indicate which of your members attend classes? You said you have instructors from Sydney who take classes in judo and karate. If possible, I'd like the list to indicate whether your members are just attending the gym or attending a particular class, or both. Would this be difficult?'

'Ginny?'

'It won't be on the list,' said Ginny, 'because they pay Gary and Nick separately, but I keep a record . . .' (she waved an exercise book) '. . . so I can tick off on the list the guys that are doing classes, if you like.'

'That would be great. Do any women do classes?'

'There was one,' said Ginny, 'but she had to compete against the guys and I think she went somewhere else. Anyway, she doesn't come any more.'

'Can you remember her name?'

'Yeah. Well, I only used her first name and that was Victoria, but I should have her surname in here somewhere.' She flicked back through the pages of her exercise book. 'Here it is. Delhunty. Her name was Victoria Delhunty.'

THIRTEEN

Day two following the discovery of Horace Radcliffe's body dawned bright and cold. A mist hung in the trees, and the only sounds to break the stillness were the cries of the currawongs. Haines still had a couple of interviews to complete, including one with Brenda Stokes. In the afternoon, fingerprints would be taken.

In the bedrooms of Edwards House, girls were excited at the prospect of going home. The school was to close for the rest of the week, but the boarders, with the exception of those whose parents had agreed to take them away until the weekend, would remain.

Mrs Watkins arrived at seven to do breakfasts. At seven-thirty, Ira and Mr O'Flaherty alighted from the latter's panel van and headed for the shed at the back of the kitchen, where the brooms and gardening implements were kept. They bid Mrs Watkins good morning, Ira with a short bark and Mr O'Flaherty with 'Top o' the mornin' to yer, Mrs W,' the same greeting he'd delivered for the past fifteen years. At the head of the driveway he removed a few persistent weeds; then he swept the gravel as far as the gates and took up his position on the footpath, where he remained, leaning on his broom, to greet the academic staff.

In a kitchen one hundred kilometers away, a middle-aged man was reading the *Sydney Morning Herald*. The hand that held the newspaper was weathered, its knotted veins and broken nails testifying to a life of manual labour. The table hosted the remains of two breakfasts, and there was a lingering odour of burned toast. Cornflake remnants in the empty bowls had hardened to the consistency of cement and were being explored, along with spillages of sugar and milk, by a lone fly. Suddenly the man lowered the newspaper and exclaimed, 'Bloody hell!' Then he bellowed, 'Shirley . . . come 'ere!'

'What?'

'Come 'n' listen to this.' The woman lowered her cigarette and eyed him wearily. With a glance to ensure that she was listening, the man read aloud:

DEATH AT PRIVATE SCHOOL

The death of the headmaster of Eldersley College in the southern highlands of New South Wales has shocked local residents and college staff. Police are treating the death as suspicious.

The body of 52-year-old Horace Radcliffe was discovered in his office on Monday, 23rd May. Although Mr Radcliffe had been headmaster for only eighteen months, he was respected for his administrative ability and his commitment to education. 'He'll be a great loss and very difficult to replace,' Mr Gilbert Fairweather, Executive Director of Eldersley, said yesterday.

Police urge anyone with information relating to the headmaster's death or to his whereabouts between Friday, 20th May and Sunday, 22nd May to come forward.

'Wha' d'yer reckon?'

'Reckon we shoulda sold 'em to 'im when 'e asked. Now we're stuck with the bloody things. You should'na told Gill. God know what 'e's gone an' done.'

'Don't be stupid, woman! We *had* to tell Gill. Can't you get it through your thick skull that he's got first option? We could'na sold 'em behind 'is back. It weren't legal. We signed a contract, remember?'

'Well, either way 'e's dead an' we're stuck with 'em.'

'Yeah. Well, Gill would'na had anything to do with that . . . would 'e?'

'E's your bloody brother, so why ask me? 'E went berserk when 'e found out that poncey little twerp'd made us an offer.'

'Said 'e'd kill the bastard,' her husband returned. His wife shrugged and left the room. The man continued to sit, reliving the conversations he'd had with his brother and with Horace Radcliffe, deceased.

In another kitchen, closer to where Mr O'Flaherty was leaning on his broom, storm clouds were brewing. The kitchen was light-years away from the first, and separated by a social stratum or two. Shirley's counterpart, a wife similar to those paragons of virtue seen in television commercials, was cutting the crusts off sandwiches. She was wearing a white blouse, a linen skirt, and black-leather court shoes with sensible heels. Her jewellery was subtle and tasteful.

The kitchen, straight out of the pages of a magazine, would have appeared sterile but for the fresh flowers, expensive glassware and colourful furnishings. The fruit in the cut-glass bowl was real, and there was the smell of percolating coffee. A transistor radio was playing 'Bridge Over Troubled Waters', but the woman was too preoccupied to notice.

Daddy did not breeze into this tableau of domestic felicity and put his arms around mommy; nor did mommy turn to give him the obligatory tippy-toe kiss. They did not stand together at the door and wave their delightfully behaved offspring off to school. Instead, the woman worked alone, quickly and efficiently – all the more efficiently because she was angry. She wrapped the sandwiches in greaseproof paper and placed them in separate lunch boxes, together with two pieces of fruit. Then she sat down to await the departure of her children and the arrival of her husband.

She intended having things out with him. Why had she waited so long? For months she'd pretended that it wasn't happening, which he'd construed as acceptance, or perhaps consent. His absences had become more blatant, and he less furtive and apologetic.

When the children, scrubbed and uniformed, swept out like twin tornadoes, she listened at the kitchen door. Upstairs she could hear the sound of his electric razor. She poured two coffees, sugaring her own, and for the umpteenth time ran over what she was going to say. Outwardly she appeared calm.

Her husband rushed in with his briefcase, his tie in his other hand. He glanced at the coffee. 'I'm a bit late. I wasn't going to have any.'

'I want to talk. Please sit down.'

'Can't it wait?'

'No. It's waited long enough. Either we discuss it now or . . .'

'What's the matter? What are you on about?'

She knew he'd start blustering. He was good at that. No matter how calm and controlled she was, he always managed to imply that if anything was wrong, it was her fault; she was making some-thing out of nothing; she was working herself up; she was getting things out of proportion. He was the injured party, all innocence and bluff. He sat down, doing up his tie and avoiding her gaze.

She went through her speech. She knew about the affair. She related times and dates, and explained that she had documented evidence of his infidelity sufficient to divorce him and apply for custody of their children. If he didn't end the affair and make something of their marriage, she would return to the UK. Her parents would welcome their grandchildren with open arms, and she could get a job that, together with the alimony he'd undoubtedly have to pay her, would allow her to live comfortably.

For some time, he sat stirring his coffee. He didn't deny anything; nor did he attempt an apology. He sat like stone. She wanted to scream at him and beat him – hurt him as he'd hurt her.

When he did speak, it wasn't what she'd expected. It was, he said, more than an affair. He was in love with another woman. He hadn't wanted it to happen, but it had. He'd not set out to hurt her or the girls; nor did he want to lose contact with them. If she divorced him, he'd see to it that she was well provided for. He'd make a settlement to her liking . . . whatever . . . provided she agreed not to take the children away or turn them against him. He'd do anything to avoid that, but he couldn't give up the woman he loved.

How she regretted, now, her decision to have it out with him. Why had she insisted on knowing the truth? Wouldn't it have been better to go on pretending? He'd stuck a knife in her chest and she had nothing, except her girls. Bitterness engulfed her. She would have considered doing away with herself, but that would have suited him perfectly – no scandal, no messy divorce, a home for his fancy piece to move into. Oh no . . . she was not going to leave her house until she was ready. She would not make it easy for him.

The first of the staff to be greeted by Mr O'Flaherty were Georgina Stoddart and Bernard Deitz. They walked to the staffroom, where

Bernard Deitz dropped his briefcase and went to open the lab. It wasn't necessary, given that it was a pupil-free day, but it released him from the necessity of making small talk.

As he was leaving the staffroom, Hans Vandegaard arrived, followed shortly by Chauntel Worsley, Jacquelyn Pendlebury and the librarian, Mrs Westham. There was an air of excitement, because they were all suspects in a murder enquiry. One of their number had done Radcliffe in, and the intense pleasure of speculating who and why would occupy the better part of the day.

'We could establish odds and lay bets,' said Hans Vandegaard, who'd been drawing up a list of front-runners. 'You know . . . like your Melbourne Cup?'

'If you mean a sweep,' said Jacquelyn Pendlebury, 'that's not the same as betting. The names of the horses are pulled out of a hat and everyone puts in the same amount of money. The person who pulls out the name of the winning horse gets most of the money. It's like a lucky dip.'

'I have never heard this expression . . . lucky dip. Is it common?'

'It probably wasn't the right term,' Jacquelyn Pendlebury sighed. 'A lucky dip is where people pay to pull out a gift or a prize. Perhaps I should have said "raffle". A sweep is more like a raffle. There's no skill involved.'

'So, you would rather select a member of staff who might have killed him, and bet on that?'

'I didn't say I wanted to bet at all,' Jacquelyn Pendlebury replied. 'I think the whole idea is tacky.'

'I agree,' said Georgina Stoddart. It would be in appalling bad taste. I don't know what you're thinking of, Hans, but if you try to do anything of the sort I'll nip it in the bud.'

'This is another of your expressions? To nip something in the bud? Very vicious.'

'A simple, horticultural metaphor,' said Jacquelyn. 'And you're stirring, Hans. I know you have a very sophisticated grasp of figurative language.'

'Stirring? Is this another of your metaphors?'

'Oh, for God's sake shut up, Hans,' groaned Bernard Deitz, who'd returned in time to pick up the thread of the conversation. 'Give me a look at that.' He snatched the paper from Hans Vandegaard's hand and exploded. 'You've got me top of the list, you bastard!'

'I consider you to be a very good bet, my friend,' said Hans calmly. 'You must admit that you have been less than complimentary about the headmaster, and it is common knowledge that he argued with you in his office on many occasions.'

'He argued with just about everyone in this room, including you. Where have you put yourself? You're not even on the bloody list!'

'I would hardly put myself on the list when I know I am not in the race. I didn't do it, but of course only I can be sure of that.' He smiled and spread his hands apologetically. 'But you can put me at the head of *your* bloody list, Bernard. I will not be offended.'

'Could we scrap the bad language?' said Georgina Stoddart.

'*And* the figurative language, if you don't mind,' said Veronica Ainsworth, mocking Georgina's schoolmarmish tone. She'd followed Bernard Deitz into the room and was immensely amused by the whole exchange.

At that moment Mrs Westham nudged Jacquelyn Pendlebury and pointed in the direction of Chauntel's desk. The little French woman was weeping quietly into her handkerchief – apparently, or so they thought, as a result of their banter. Georgina Stoddart put her hand on Chauntel's shoulder.

'Are you all right? You're not sick, are you?'

'He's dead,' came the response, and it was followed by a violent bout of weeping that left everyone feeling embarrassed – and more than a little guilty that one of their number felt the murder so keenly, while they'd been treating it as a joke.

'Well of course, Chauntel, we're all very conscious of that,' said Georgina Stoddart soothingly, 'and I think perhaps some of us express our concern in very different ways. It's not that we don't deplore what's happened as much as you do – it's just another way of dealing with things and coming to terms with them. I'm sorry you're upset. Is there anything I can do?'

'No. Zank you. It was just so unexpected. I have 'ad him for so many years, you see, and you get fond, so veree attached. Everyone will say to get anozer one, but I cannot.'

'You're talking about one of your pets, aren't you?' said Mrs Westham, who believed weeping in public was something only continentals would do.

'My terrapine,' said Chauntel, wiping more tears from her eyes.

Hans Vandegaard was genuinely in the dark. 'Your what?'

'It's a sort of turtle,' Bernard Deitz explained. 'She kept it in a tank without any rock to climb on, and it scrabbled incessantly around the edge, staring frantically at the outside world. It probably died of exhaustion.'

'When did you discover it had died, Chauntel?' asked Jacquelyn Pendlebury.

'Zis morning. I went to feed it and it was dead. I have buried it in ze garden.'

'Was it floating, or did it sink?' Bernard asked.

'*Really*, Bernard,' said Georgina as Chauntel burst into a fresh flood of tears.

'I was merely trying to establish, out of scientific interest, what happened when it died. Fish tend to float, but they don't have shells, do they?'

'It's a pity she buried it,' said Mrs Westham. 'She could have hollowed it out and used it as an ashtray for those dreadful black-and-gold things she smokes.' Hans Vandegaard guffawed and Bernard Deitz sniggered, but everyone else managed to control the impulse to laugh. Georgina Stoddart whispered to Chauntel, and together they left the room.

At that moment Dennis Hinds rushed in, his face flushed and his hair uncombed. It was obvious that something had happened, and he was pleased insofar as it diverted attention from his lateness. 'Have I missed anything?' he asked breathlessly.

FOURTEEN

Fraser leaned back in his chair with his hands clasped behind his head. There was a satisfied grin on his face. He was anticipating with pleasure the moment he could relay to Haines his success at the gym. Lockyer, who'd been on until midnight, rolled in at ten past eight looking seedy but excited. 'Come 'n' have a look at this beauty,' he chirruped, jerking his head in the direction of the garage. 'Got towed in last night. Bloody classy. Wouldn't mind taking it for a spin, but there aren't any keys.'

'Wouldn't be a vintage Jag, would it?'

'How'd you know?'

'It's Radcliffe's. It wasn't at the school, so Haines figured it was at that restaurant in Mittagong where Radcliffe had dinner Friday night . . . Mandibles. It's possible the murderer disconnected something and gave Radcliffe a lift back to the school. It's got to be dusted for prints.'

Lockyer's enthusiasm evaporated. 'Shit.'

'Oh no,' groaned Fraser. 'What have you done, you stupid bastard?'

'I just wanted to look at the donk. Never seen one like it before. I opened the bonnet. He'll kill me. Do you think if I wiped it . . .?'

'Don't be stupid. You'll wipe away the only chance we have of getting any others. You'll have to come clean. If he finds out he's wasted time trying to identify your pinkies, it'll be a lot worse. Anyway, I might as well have a look at it now that it's here. I didn't know he'd found it.'

'You buggers don't tell me anything.'

'If he brought it in himself, he should at least have warned you. It's not like him.'

'Why would he bring it in himself?' asked Lockyer, looking even more desperate.

'He went looking for it yesterday. Weren't you here when it came in?'

Lockyer looked evasive. 'Spindles was here. I had to nick out for half an hour. Hang on.' He picked up the phone and dialled the extension of the female constable who was bent over a typewriter keyboard in a far corner of the station.

'Constable Spinner.'

'It's me. Who brought the Jag in last night?'

'The Sarge. Got the guy in the local garage to tow it in.'

'Did he leave any message for me?'

'Yeah. I told him you were in the loo, and he said to tell you if you touched the Jag he'd have your guts for garters.'

'You didn't tell me that!'

'I left a message on the pad next to your phone. Are you blind?'

'Okay.' Lockyer picked up the notepad and turned back the pages. The message was printed inside a large heart with an arrow, from the tip of which fell drops of blood. It read: 'The Sarge sends his love, but says if you touch the Jag he'll be wearing your balls for a bow tie.' On the next page were the details of a telephone call Locker had taken. 'Must've flipped it over without reading it,' he mumbled, his misery acute.

'I'll tell him, if you like,' said Fraser. 'That way you'll miss the worst of it. There are some statements that need to go to the hospital to be signed. Why don't you take them over? No point in hanging around.' Lockyer agreed.

At eight-thirty, two members of the scientific squad arrived from Goulburn. Fraser ushered them into Haines's office and offered them coffee. He was scrounging for clean cups when Haines came in, demanding to know who was in his parking space. Fraser pointed. 'Bradley and Frenshaw are waiting to see you, Sarge. I was just about to make them coffee. Like some?'

'No, thanks. You make bloody awful coffee. Any sign of those personnel records?'

'Not yet, but . . . ah . . . I . . . there are a couple of things. One of them you're not going to like.'

'Spit it out.'

'Well, the good news is that there's a Delhunty on the staff list at the school, and a Victoria Delhunty was taking karate classes at that new gym in Goulburn until a few months ago. Could be a match.'

'Good. And?'

'You might find Lockyer's prints on the bonnet of the Jag. He didn't get the message you left about his gonads.'

'Christ! That bastard's a liability. Did he touch anything else?'

'Only the bonnet as far as I know. I'd like to have a look myself if I can borrow one of those fingerprint blokes for a few minutes. There's an easy way to immobilise an old car and it wouldn't be at all obvious to anyone looking at the engine, provided the distributor cap was replaced. If I'm right, and if the murderer didn't wear gloves, there might be prints on the cap and the clips.'

'This is assuming that whoever disabled the car also killed Radcliffe. So if they are one and the same, what do you think he did?'

'Removed the rotor button. A few seconds work. Radcliffe

wouldn't have noticed with the distributor cap in place. He probably wasn't mechanically inclined.'

'Okay. Get someone else to make the coffee and meet me in the garage.'

The car was beautifully preserved. Its seat leather showed little signs of wear, and on the body there wasn't so much as a scratch. Detective Frenshaw whistled appreciatively. 'Nice!'

'How long do you think it will take you to do the bonnet?'

'Five or ten minutes. You don't want us to go over the whole thing?'

'I want you to lift what you can from the bonnet, distributor cap and clips, and any other engine part that looks promising. Oh, and Fraser would like to know whether the rotor button has been removed. Isn't that right, Fraser?' Fraser nodded. 'And then,' said Haines, 'perhaps you could lift some prints from the steering wheel so we can compare them with what we find in Radcliffe's office. One of our PCs is bringing you coffee. When you've finished, give me a call and I'll take you to the school.'

Haines left, signalling for Fraser to follow. Fraser did so reluctantly. He would have preferred to watch the experts work. Back in his office, Haines gestured Fraser to a seat and began rummaging through one of his drawers. Eventually he found a brown bottle from which he shook a couple of tablets. He swallowed them without water.

'Blood pressure?'

'Yeah. Doc keeps telling me to get exercise and lay off the burgers. He doesn't know about Lockyer yet. Anyway, I want you to chase up three things for me. First, I want you to ring Fairweather's Sydney office and find out if those personnel records have been sent. Here's his card. If they haven't, threaten to come and get them. I want them here today. Second, I want you to go to the restaurant and see what you can dig up regarding Fairweather's dinner on Friday night. I've borrowed this photograph of Radcliffe from that fat little bursar. She wants it back, so you'll have to keep it in its frame. Last, ring Attila and tell her it would be nice if a cup of tea and a sandwich could be arranged for lunch. Okay?'

'Okay. Is Fairweather still in town?'

'He can't go back until he's seen Amy Graham. At least, I hope he plans to see her. Which reminds me, I'd better warn her that I've dropped her in it. I'll give her a call. Off you go.'

Fraser had come off lightly. Two of his tasks would take minutes. He called Fairweather's secretary, who said the files had been couriered the previous evening and would be with them before lunch. Then he telephoned Matron to explain that the scientific squad would be working in the headmaster's cottage, and that Detective Sergeant Haines had asked whether it was possible to provide them with sandwiches for four around midday. Finally, he rang the number for Mandibles, but there was no answer.

He returned to the garage, where the two officers had progressed from the bonnet to the engine. Both were wearing surgical gloves, reminding him of the post-mortem on the car's owner. They'd already dusted the distributor cap and were in the process of gingerly removing it. As it was lifted, Fraser's patience was rewarded. He couldn't help grinning when Haines rejoined them.

'Well?'

'No rotor button.'

'And prints?'

'Plenty,' replied Frenshaw, 'but there's no saying whose. Could belong to the last mechanic who worked on the car.'

'It's a start,' said Haines. 'When you've packed up your equipment, we'll take a look at the scene of the crime.'

FIFTEEN

While Haines and the officers of the scientific squad were on their way to Eldersley, an economic disaster was unfolding in a small upstairs office in the main street of Goulburn. The sign at street level said 'Brand & Associates, Financial Advice, Market Research, Private Investigations'. Harold Brand, reclining in his vinyl swivel chair, was a jack of many trades and master of none. He stared gloomily at the page from the local rag that his secretary had left on his desk. It was accompanied by a short note: 'Harry – isn't this the guy you've been working for?' The newspaper clipping was headed 'Suspicious Death at Local School'.

He screwed up the clipping and hurled it across the room. Ten days of surveillance down the drain, and his chances of getting anything for the last month were Buckley's! Radcliffe had made it quite clear that he was footing the bill, so it was pointless contacting anyone else. Radcliffe had also insisted on monthly payments, the last of which was due at the end of the week.

He'd crossed to the wrong side of the law for this one – a bit of snooping involving a spot of break and enter . . . nothing really criminal. He drummed his fingers on the desk. The thing was, he may just have stumbled onto something that could pay *real* dividends. How could he capitalise on it with Radcliffe dead? He didn't know whether that other slimy bastard from the school was involved. From his filing cabinet he retrieved a folder containing photographs, which he spread out on his desk. Something was going on, and he might as well pursue it since there wasn't anything else on the horizon. He shuffled the photographs back into their envelope and returned them to the filing cabinet.

He could go to the police, of course, but that would leave him with nothing. No. He'd see if there were something in it for him, and then, if nothing came of it, he'd earn a few brownie points with the constabulary. He locked up and left. It was going to be a long night. Might as well go home and pack a thermos and something to eat.

SIXTEEN

Leaving Bradley and Frenshaw at the headmaster's cottage, Haines made his way to the sitting room to continue his interviews. First was the cook, Mrs Watkins, whose sole memory of the headmaster was that he refused to eat her food. 'My cookin' weren't good enough for 'im,' she said in an injured tone. 'Nothin' wrong with my cookin'. I don't get no complaints from the girls. Not good enough for 'im, though. 'E'd rather squeeze a carrot than 'ave a nice baked dinner. One of them vegetarians . . . skinny as lizards, the lot of 'em. 'Ow they can expect to put meat on their bones if they don't eat it, I'll never know. It ain't natural.'

The librarian, Mrs Westham, was even less helpful. She spent more time in the library than in the staffroom, and knew little of the dramas that occupied the rest of the staff. She preferred it that way. Apart from a couple of occasions when the headmaster had asked her advice about junior English texts, she saw little of him. He was, she admitted, over zealous in his desire to protect the minds and morals of the younger girls. Jacquelyn Pendlebury had complained to her on a number of occasions that he was trying to censor her reading lists. Of course, she couldn't be seen to take sides, but she did go so far as to assure the headmaster that she would personally vet any novel about which he had qualms. If she believed it to be unsuitable, she would remove it from the library. He had to be satisfied with that.

Brenda Stokes was, in Haines's opinion, a mindless bimbo. Although she'd worked in the office adjacent to Radcliffe's, she knew sweet f.a. Miss Hancock had observed and heard far more. Brenda was either totally self-absorbed or not inclined to cooperate, but as the latter presupposed some intelligence, Haines opted for the former. Not sharing Miss Hancock's romantic aspirations, Brenda had paid little attention to the traffic to and from the office and couldn't recall whether the headmaster had argued with any of the staff. Breaking one of her long, varnished nails on the type-writer keyboard would have had more impact.

She did, however, tell Haines that one of the girls had been ask-ing who paid her fees. 'I don't know why she was asking. She also wanted to know who paid some doctor's invoice, and I told her *she'd* have a better idea of that than I would. In any case, Lettie pays the invoices. She looks after the fees as well, and does the banking.'

'So Miss Hancock types up the accounts and sends them out?'

'Oh no, I do that. Lettie doesn't type.'

'Then perhaps the girl thought that as you did the typing, you might remember whose name went on the account for her fees.'

'Oh, yeah . . . I suppose so. But sometimes the parents just send a cheque. We don't always post anything. Anyway, I told her I didn't know.'

'What was the girl's name?'

Brenda Stokes looked vague. 'I don't remember. She was one of the boarders, I think, because it was late in the afternoon and she was still hanging around. All of the other girls would have gone home.'

Encouraged by this evidence of cerebral activity, Haines tried one last question: 'Can you remember what she looked like?'

'Oh, yeah. She was skinny and pale, and she had straight hair. Brown. She wasn't pretty or anything.'

'Thank you, Miss Stokes. You've been very helpful.'

He returned to the cottage to see how Bradley and Frenshaw were faring. They were still working upstairs. Bradshaw told Haines there were signs of recent entry on the sill of the bathroom window. 'The paintwork's pretty old, and it's flaking. You can see where it's been disturbed, and quite a few flakes have been knocked off. Reckon they'll be under the window, but I haven't been around there yet to have a look. The wood underneath looks fresh . . . I mean, it isn't weathered, so someone's climbed in and out recently. No prints.'

'Pity,' said Haines. He looked at his watch. 'I've asked the cook to make us some sandwiches for about twelve-thirty, and it's a bit after twelve now. Why don't you knock off in ten minutes and come over to the sitting room. It's in the building with the verandah on your left. Oh, and while I remember, tell the cook, Mrs Watkins, that her sandwiches are superb, because she's mortally offended that the headmaster wouldn't eat her food. A couple of compliments from you will keep her sweet for days.'

When Bradley and Frenshaw took their break, awaiting them was a hot meal comprising steak and kidney pie with mashed potatoes and vegetables. There was roly-poly pudding and custard to follow. Mrs Watkins was one of those women who believed men needed feeding. 'Tell me, Mrs Watkins,' said Bradley with a wink at Haines when she came back to clear the table, 'are you single by any chance? Only I've never in my life met a woman who could cook like that. Bloody fantastic, that was.'

'I'll second that,' said Frenshaw. 'My wife can't cook.'

'Get away wi' yer, yer cheeky divils,' Mrs Watkins responded with a throaty chuckle. There was a smile on her florid face as she bustled out of the room.

While Haines and the scientific squad were filling their faces,

Amy Graham was standing at the cosmetics counter of the Bowral chemist studying the array of lipsticks. Perhaps she'd been too optimistic? Even if she found one that matched, how was she to know that there weren't similar colours in six different brands? She avoided the expensive cosmetics and concentrated instead on those marketed to teenagers. She took the handkerchief from her handbag and studied it again. It could be a match for any of the names in the row in front of her: 'Spicy Pink', 'Pink Minx', 'Candied Rose' . . .

'Can I help you?'

'Well, yes, you may be able to help. I'm looking for a lipstick for my niece and I have a sample here of the colour she wears, but it isn't easy to match.'

'What brand?'

'Well, that's the other thing,' said Amy. 'I'm not sure. I know it's not an expensive brand . . . well, not like those.' She waved her hand in the direction of the Helena Rubenstein display. 'How much are they?'

'They're fourteen dollars, ninety-five.'

'It's more likely to be something like this. These are . . .?'

'They're normally ten dollars, but we have them on special at the moment for seven dollars, ninety-five. Couldn't you just ask her what she wants?'

'That would be sensible, dear, but I wanted to surprise her. She always seems to wear the same shade.'

'That's unusual. Most of the girls who come in experiment with different colours.'

'I suppose you get a lot of girls from the school?'

'Sometimes a few day girls come in during the week, but at the weekend lots of the boarders come in. They don't wear their uniforms, but I know several of them because my sister has pointed them out. It's hard to tell when they're out of uniform.'

'Your sister is a boarder?'

'No, she's a day student. We live locally.'

'It must be handy for her, living so close to her friends. She can meet them to go to the movies, and I suppose they sometimes come to your house?'

'Not really. She doesn't have close friends amongst the boarders. She thinks they're snooty.' A sudden thought struck her. 'You don't teach there, do you? I shouldn't be rambling on. Your niece isn't a boarder, is she?'

'No, dear. I used to have a connection with the school many years ago, but not any more. It was just idle curiosity. Every now and then I wonder about the latest gossip, but now, particularly with the headmaster . . . Dreadful, don't you think? And such a good man, I was told.'

'Rebecca – that's my sister – is worried that it'll mean post-poning the dance at Balmoral. Apart from that, I don't think she or any of the others really care. They're not exactly in mourning.'

Amy sighed. 'The indifference of youth. Still, one can't expect them to weep and wail. He was little more than an authority figure to them, I imagine.'

'Well, one of the boarders has been screaming in the middle of the night since it happened, according to Rebecca. Wakes up the whole place. The other boarders have been complaining, and I think the mother of one of them is threatening to take her to another school.'

'Really? I wonder what's troubling the poor girl . . . the one who has nightmares, I mean.'

'She was strange to begin with. She has counselling, but no one knows why . . . Well, I mean, the girls don't know. Excuse me for a minute. I'll just see to this customer. If you need some tissues, there's a box on the counter.'

'Thank you, dear. I'm fine.' Amy started along a row of pink 'testers', marking the back of her hand and wiping off the colour onto the end of her handkerchief. The sample had darkened, and none of the fresher samples seemed to match. She jotted down the names of a couple that were close and returned the handkerchief to her bag. It had seemed like a good idea, but it was too imprecise. A number of girls might use the same shade; and the original sample, which had darkened, might begin to look like any of the others if they darkened too. No. It wouldn't hold up in court. She left the shop, giving the assistant a cheery wave as she did so.

SEVENTEEN

Bradley and Frenshaw had only just returned to the cottage when a call came through. They were to drop what they were doing and attend a break-in at Goulburn. 'Since when,' grumbled Haines, 'does a break-in take priority over a murder enquiry?'

'Since the local MP's house got done over,' said Bradley. He can't touch anything until we've been over it. He's twitchy. Not much use coming back this arvo, so we'll see you tomorrow. We'll only need a couple of hours.'

Haines grunted. When they had left, he stuck his head into the staffroom. There was no sign of life. 'I think,' said Matron, 'you'll find them in the library. They're having a meeting.'

The library was a freestanding building with lots of glass to capture the light. Haines could see the staff seated in a semicircle with Georgina Stoddart presiding. He knocked and entered. 'I'm afraid,' he explained, 'there's been an emergency and our scientific squad's been called away, so they won't be able to do any fingerprinting until tomorrow. If tomorrow is inconvenient, please let Mrs Stoddart know and we'll make alternative arrangements.' He left, preferring not to wait for questions. Besides, he'd seen Mr O'Flaherty on the other side of the quadrangle and he wanted a quick word.

Mr O'Flaherty was raking over the soil in one of the gardens and mumbling to himself as he removed the occasional lolly wrapper and shook the soil from the roots of weeds. Haines bent down to pat Ira. 'Nice dog,' he said. 'Handy little fella?'

Mr O'Flaherty straightened, brushing the soil from his hands. ''E's good wi' rats. Shakes 'em, 'e does.' He clenched his teeth and shook his head from side to side in a demonstration of Ira's rat-despatching methodology.

'Constable Fraser spoke to you about an inhaler that's missing from the headmaster's office. We thought it might turn up in one of the bins or in the grounds. No sign of it, I suppose?'

'Not a sign of it anywhere at all now,' said Mr O'Flaherty, 'but I'll be keepin' me eye out for it, you can be sure o' dat.'

'And if you find it, you'll not pick it up with your hands, will you? We'll want to examine it for fingerprints.'

'To be sure,' said Mr O'Flaherty, raising his grubby hand to his forehead.

Haines was about to leave when he had second thoughts. It was possible Mr O'Flaherty knew something that might help, and he was the only member of staff they hadn't questioned. 'Tell me, Mr O'Flaherty, what do you make of all this? I mean, it's not the sort of place where you'd expect a murder to occur – a quiet little school. I suppose you were shocked, like everyone else?'

Mr O'Flaherty's eyes widened, and his pleasure at being so consulted was patently obvious. ''E was done away wi', den?'

'It appears that way. We'll know more later. Did you have much to do with him?'

Mr O'Flaherty, who was accustomed to verbal exchanges with staff lasting no more than a few seconds, was overjoyed at the opportunity to conduct a real conversation. He became loquacious, recounting for Haines several exchanges he'd had with Horace

Radcliffe, including the very last during which the headmaster had asked him not to use pesticides or herbicides in the garden. He was not, he said, privy to conversations between the headmaster and the academic staff, but he understood there was ill feeling. To Haines's surprise, he alluded to Mrs Stoddart's envy and Miss Hancock's unrequited love. He also suggested that the headmaster had some of the male members of staff 'on the run'.

'You're very perceptive, Mr O'Flaherty. Why is it, do you think, he had them on the run?'

Mr O'Flaherty couldn't say. He'd formed the impression from observing the body language of Bernard Deitz and Hans Vandegaard after their late-afternoon sessions with the headmaster.

'You work late, then? Do you work on weekends as well?'

Mr O'Flaherty shook his head. He did not work at weekends, his normal hours being Monday to Friday, seven-thirty a.m. to four p.m., but he did sometimes work back in the evenings, particularly summer evenings when there was more to do in the garden.

'So you'd often be in the grounds at a time when most other people are indoors, and you'd notice anyone unfamiliar, I suppose?'

'To be sure,' said Mr O'Flaherty. 'There's dat feller who was visitin' 'im regular like . . . maybe two, t'ree times dis month.'

'Do you mean Mr Fairweather, the executive director?'

'No, not 'im,' Mr O'Flaherty said patiently. 'Someone unfamiliar, like you said. Didn't know 'im at all.' He'd observed the headmaster receiving regular visits in the afternoon or early evening from a man who came with a briefcase and stayed for about twenty minutes. He could describe for Haines the man's height, age and build, the colour and make of his car, and even recalled the first three letters of the car's number plate.

'That is excellent, Mr O'Flaherty,' said Haines. 'I wish every witness were as observant as you. I'm going back to the station now with this information, so you have a good day.' Mr O'Flaherty, looking more than a little pleased with himself, trundled off with Ira in his wake, and Haines, after informing Mrs Watkins that her fan club would be returning in the morning, headed back to his car.

At about four, Mrs Watkins was busying herself with the evening meal. For dessert there would be bread-and-butter pudding, which she'd prepared earlier. She checked the temperature of the oven. In a few moments she would pop into it the two large stainless-steel trays of cottage pie, with their snowy blanket of mashed potato that she'd glazed with beaten egg.

She was prevented from doing so by a knock at the kitchen door. Through the screen, she could see Mr O'Flaherty. She retrieved from the refrigerator a plastic bag containing two well-hacked lamb bones and carried them to the door. Ira's stump of a tail was wagging, and he was quivering and whimpering excitedly at the thought of what the plastic bag contained.

'T'anks kindly, Mrs W. I suppose now that yer wouldna ha' any o' dem pincer t'ings, w'dyer?' said Mr O'Flaherty, taking the plastic bag and ignoring Ira's demands that he relieve it of its contents.

'Them what?' asked Mrs Watkins, with equal disregard for grammatical nicety.

'Pincer t'ings . . . ter pick up t'ings wi'out puttin' yer 'ands on 'em.'

'Tongs, you mean,' said Mrs Watkins. 'Yes, I have tongs, but I wouldn't want you picking up any dead rats or pigeons with them. What do you want them for?'

'Polis said if I found 'is puffer, not ter pick up wi' me 'ands,' he offered.

'What puffer? What are you talking about?'

''Im that's dead. Polis's been lookin' for 'is puffer.'

'But he didn't smoke,' said Mrs Watkins impatiently.

Mr O'Flaherty grunted. 'One of dem t'ings t' 'elp 'im breathe,' he explained.

'Didn't know he used one,' said the enlightened Mrs Watkins, 'let alone that the police were looking for it.' She went to a drawer and extracted a pair of tongs that she took to Mr O'Flaherty with an injunction that he should wash them and return them to her as soon as he'd finished with them.

Mr O'Flaherty saluted her with his free hand and trundled off in the direction of the garden where he'd spotted the inhaler, Ira salivating in his wake. When he got there, he realised he had nothing to put the inhaler in, so he gave one of the lamb bones to Ira, put the other one in his pocket and, with the help of the tongs, dropped the inhaler into the plastic bag, which he had the presence of mind to turn inside out.

When Haines got back at the station, Spinner greeted him with a message from Lily Thompson. 'She said you wanted this registration number, Sarge. I rang the motor registry, and it belongs to a Bernard Deitz of Goulburn. I've got his address, if you want it.'

'I don't need his address, Constable Spinner. Well, well. Dr Deitz smokes quite a lot of pot, it would appear. He and I will have to have another little chat. In the meantime, why don't you try Rosebery on a more difficult one. I've only got the first three letters of this number plate.' (He handed her a piece of paper.) 'That's D for Delta, V for Victor and F for Foxtrot. You can tell them it's a dark-blue Vauxhall registered to someone in this area. That should narrow it down.'

'Could take a couple of days, Sarge, without the complete number. I'll tell them it's urgent, will I?'

'You do that. Oh, and do you happen to know if Lockyer has heard from Fairweather's office on our headmaster's next of kin?'

'Yeah, he found the guy's father.'

'His father!'

'Yeah. He's pretty doddery, Lockyer said. Lives in a retirement village in Kiama. Someone's driving him to Goulburn tomorrow to identify the body.'

'Must be over ninety,' said Haines. 'I hope Lockyer didn't break the news to him over the phone or we might be responsible for another dead Radcliffe.' When Constable Spinner didn't answer, he groaned. 'Tell me he didn't, for God's sake.'

'No, Sarge, he didn't,' she reassured him. 'As far as I know, he asked one of the local police to go there and talk to the people at the home, so I assume one of the nursing staff told him.'

'Never doubted him for a minute,' said Haines as he walked back to his office.

EIGHTEEN

Mandibles was on the highway outside Mittagong. Fraser, dressed in the only good suit he owned, intended having a quiet meal and then explaining to the manager that he was looking for information relating to two of their patrons. He was met at the front desk by a smiling concierge, whose patronising manner annoyed him.

'Good evening, sir. You have a reservation?'

'Yes. Fraser. I booked this afternoon.' The concierge made a great play of searching the register.

'Ah, yes. Here it is. Fraser. A table for . . . one?' He looked at Fraser with slightly raised eyebrows, and eyes that seemed to hold a question other than the one he'd just asked.

'For one,' Fraser repeated.

The concierge pursed his lips and gestured towards a small table adjacent to a dusty potted palm whose fronds were waving in the draft from the air conditioner. 'Please follow me.' If the look and the gesture raised doubts in Fraser's mind, the concierge's body language as he minced ahead and pulled out the chair confirmed them. This little creep thought he was gay! He sat down in the chair that the concierge tucked neatly beneath his rear. Why hadn't he made it a formal police visit?

'Would sir like to see the wine list?'

'I'd like a beer, please – a VB – and I'd like you to check your register for last Friday night. I'm making enquiries about two men who dined here.' He held up his ID in the manner of someone holding up a crucifix to ward off a vampire. 'The booking would have been in the name of either Radcliffe or Fairweather. Would it be possible for you to find out where they were sitting, and the name of the waiter who served them?' He placed the photograph Haines had given him on the table. 'This is one of the men. I'm afraid I don't have a photograph of the other.'

The concierge recoiled, his manner reverting to one of superior indifference. 'I'll see what I can do, sir.'

Fraser suspected he'd committed a tactical blunder. The waiter, who'd been working the previous Friday night, didn't recall anything about the men or notice anything unusual in their behaviour. No, he did not overhear anything. He was not in the habit of listening to the conversations of patrons, and they'd been particularly busy that night. Fraser had the distinct impression that the waiter's lack of cooperation had something to do with the concierge. He was on the verge of cancelling his meal when a woman's voice drew his attention.

'Constable Fraser, isn't it? Amy Graham.' She smiled. 'I'm a friend of your sergeant. Do you mind if I sit down?' Fraser, remembering his manners, started to get up, but she pulled out her own chair and gestured for him to remain seated. 'I hope I'm not intruding. Are you waiting for someone?'

At first he was at a loss, but something in her manner prompted him to explain. 'No. I came for information, but I've drawn a blank.' He could see why the Sarge was smitten. She was classy in an ageless sort of way . . . like Radcliffe's car.

'Would you like to join us? My nephew is buying me dinner and we'd love some extra company. I hate eating alone . . . I don't know about you.'

She was so gracious that Fraser accepted. 'Are you sure your nephew won't mind?'

'He'll be delighted . . . someone closer to his own age to talk to. I'll get Francis to move you.' She gestured to the concierge, who was watching from a distance, and waited until he was simpering at her side. 'Francis, could you please move Detective Constable Fraser to our table? And bring another glass?'

'Of course, Mrs Graham. I'll attend to it immediately.' He pronounced 'immediately' with a heavy second syllable, and a 'j' instead of a 'd'. Another of his poofy little mannerisms, Fraser thought as he followed Amy. Their table was set into a small alcove. Amy introduced her nephew – a tweedy, nerdy type in his late twenties or early thirties. He had a thick, glossy moustache, and his eyes were sharp and intelligent. Fraser's first impression was that they would have nothing in common, but he soon discovered that Martin McEchnie, like his aunt, had the happy knack of making total strangers feel at ease. He could converse on any subject, and seemed particularly adept at choosing subjects to suit the company he was in. Fraser began to enjoy himself, particularly after a glass of Martin's excellent wine.

He was not at all surprised when the latter asked how the investigation was going. He knew that it was the one topic he and Amy Graham would be most curious about. Until now, they'd politely avoided any mention of the headmaster's death. 'You can't expect Constable Fraser to discuss it, Martin,' Amy expostulated.

'It's okay, Mrs Graham,' Fraser assured her. 'There are some things I can discuss. It's early days and we still have leads to follow. It's one of the reasons I'm here. We believe that Mr Radcliffe and . . . another gentleman ate here on the Friday night before he died. I wanted to find out if the staff noticed anything unusual about the dinner, and . . . well, I was hoping to get some information about the headmaster's last hours. There are other leads we're following up, and, of course, Sergeant Haines is interviewing all of the staff at the school. We're still very much at the foot-slogging stage . . . nothing exciting.'

'And was Francis able to tell you anything?'

'He confirmed that they ate here, but the waiter who served them didn't hear or see anything. They were very busy, apparently.'

'Was it the waiter over there?' Martin inclined his head in the direction of the waiter who'd brought Fraser's VB.

'Yes.'

'Not much gets past him, so I find it difficult to believe he couldn't tell you anything. I know him rather well. Would you mind if *I* asked him?'

'Not if you think it'll do any good,' said Fraser dubiously.

'I'll go powder my nose and leave you to it, Martin,' said his aunt. 'He may talk more freely if I'm not here, since he doesn't know me.' Amy began making her way between the tables. When she reached the waiter, she stopped to exchange pleasantries and nodded in the direction of Martin and Fraser. He smiled delightedly and, within minutes, was at Martin's side.

He replenished their wine and generally made a fuss about removing used entrée dishes and brushing away imaginary crumbs. 'Have to look busy, Mr M,' he explained, conspiratorially. 'Saint Francis's watchful eyes are upon me, you know. That delightful lady is a relative of yours, I believe? She said you wanted to see me. Is there something else I can bring you to drink? Another bottle of that superb wine, perhaps?'

'Not just yet, Ceddy. It's information we want. I can't believe that you can't tell us anything about those two you served last Friday night . . . Detective Constable Fraser here spoke to you about them, I think?' Fraser nodded and forced himself to smile. 'I told him,' Martin continued, 'that you had an uncanny knack of piecing together snippets of conversation. Isn't there anything you can recall that might help, or has Saint Francis made you take a vow of silence?'

'Well, he's not fond of the constabulary, as you know . . .' Ceddy responded with a knowing look, 'and, of course, we have to be discreet. If we chatter about our customers' private conversations, soon we will have no customers. I mean to say, you never know who's a private investigator, or a Mafia hit man . . . or . . . an auditor from the ATO for goodness sake!'

'Very droll, Ceddy, but this is different. You do remember some-thing, don't you?'

'Well, yes I do, if you *insist*.' He breathed a sigh of relief, happy to be able to unburden himself of the sought-after information. 'They were having a right royal row, if you must know. It didn't seem to me that they were at all enjoying each other's company. Why they had dinner together in the first place is beyond me, because it was an absolute *fiasco* from beginning to end. Half a bottle of lovely wine gone to waste . . . well, not exactly gone to waste . . .' He winked. 'But I had visions, I can tell you, of them coming to blows. I don't know what we would have done – call the police, I suppose.' He cast a furtive glance in Fraser's direction. Fraser, taking his cue from Martin, laughed, which was all the encouragement Ceddy needed.

'So you can tell us what they were arguing about?'

'Of course I can, darling. It was all about shares in some business. The big one . . . he's the one who booked the table, Fairweather . . .' He giggled. 'Bit of a misnomer, under the circum-stances. Well, he said, "It's my bloody company," and "You've got a gall, approaching my family," and "I'm running this show," and various other bits and pieces along the same lines. He called the other one – the one in the photograph who got himself bumped off . . . called him "a little tin-pot general" and told him to back off or he'd break him and make sure he never worked again.'

'Ceddy, you're wonderful. Tell Detective Constable Fraser how you do it,' said Martin. 'He probably thinks you've got bionic ears.'

'My sister is profoundly deaf, Constable Fraser, and when we were kids I not only learned to sign but to lip-read. I wanted to know what it was like to live in a silent world, so I'd sometimes put plugs in my ears and we'd watch people in the street, or we'd turn down the sound on the television and watch movies together. Everything she learned she passed on to me. We went to different schools, but we were always very close.'

'You're very fortunate, Ceddy, and I'm very grateful,' said Fraser sincerely. 'Thank you for the information. It's precisely what I was looking for. It tells us a bit more about what was going on in his life before he died, and it's given us some leads to follow. Investigating a death can be a bit like working on a jigsaw, and you've just provided some important pieces.' As he expected, Ceddy asked the inevitable question.

'Do you think the big guy did him in?'

'Not necessarily . . . Well, no I don't, actually, but that's a gut feeling. There are too many people who disliked the headmaster for us to draw that conclusion. Anyway, I do the footwork and leave the thinking to my superiors. I'll tell the sergeant how helpful you've been.'

'Well, I think this calls for another bottle,' said Martin, 'and perhaps you and Francis will both join us for a glass? Later, when you're not so busy?'

'Well I will, for one,' said Ceddy, 'and I've never seen Assisi turn down a glass of vintage plonk. Maybe when it gets a bit quieter? People don't usually start leaving until ten.'

By the time Amy rejoined them, Fraser was in a celebratory

mood and halfway through his third glass of wine. He'd concluded that Martin wasn't such a nerd after all – and even if he were, he was a bloody useful one. He'd also concluded that poofs were okay if you kept on the right side of them.

NINETEEN

Fraser's celebratory mood survived long enough for him to get home and fall into bed. Like Radcliffe, he left his car outside the restaurant, but, in spite of the amount of alcohol he'd consumed (Saint Francis had come up with a couple of complimentary bottles), he could remember saying to Mrs Graham when she drove him home that had his Cortina possessed a rotor button, he would have removed it to ensure that it wasn't stolen. It was these words that came into his head when he awoke the next morning, furry tongued and desiccated. If Radcliffe was having engine problems, perhaps he removed the rotor button himself. He'd have to mention the possibility to Haines.

When Fraser arrived at the station, Haines was reading the personnel files that had arrived the previous afternoon. Lockyer, looking pale and unhappy, was tapping away at a traffic report at the front desk. He looked up as Fraser walked in.

'How'd it go?' Fraser asked.

'Worse than I expected. I've got the bite marks to prove it.'

'You can go out and get some nosh, if you like. You're looking seedier than I feel.'

'Not until I've finished this,' said Lockyer. 'He wants you in there to work on those files, anyway, so I'll have to wait until Spindles gets in. Why should you be feeling seedy? Don't tell me you actually had a night on the piss? Which pub'd you go to?'

'Not a pub. That restaurant. Mandibles. I was only going to have a beer, but I ran into some people who were drinking wine, so I had a skin full. Had to go back and pick up the car this morning.'

'Anyone I know?'

'That woman who's friendly with Haines – Amy Graham. She was with her nephew. He's the librarian at Bowral. Skinny guy with facial hair and specs.'

'Sounds like a wild night.'

Fraser stuck his head around the door of Haines's office. Haines acknowledged his presence by pointing to a chair. 'The Delhunty woman is living in Sydney with her sister while she's receiving counselling,' he said. 'There's a memo here from Radcliffe to Fairweather. I'll say one thing for the bloke – he kept his files in order. There are photographs here, too, at least of the more recent additions to the staff. You can send this one to Interpol.' He slid a photograph of Vandegaard across the desk to Fraser. 'How'd you get on at the restaurant?'

'Bit of luck. I ran into your friend Mrs Graham, and her nephew. He knows the staff very well, and I think it's fair to say he got a lot more out of the waiter than I could have done. Apparently there was quite an argument about shares. Fairweather was laying down the law about who owned what, and he said some rather unflattering things about Radcliffe. Called him a "tin-pot general". Appeared to be incensed that Radcliffe had approached his family without his knowledge to try to buy them out. What do you think Radcliffe was trying to do? Take over the business?'

'Could be . . . could be. Do some digging. If you don't come up with anything, we'll talk to Fairweather again. At least we have evidence now that they didn't part amicably, and he's still the last person who saw Radcliffe alive. I'll make the bastard squirm.

So what did Amy and that poncey nephew of hers have to say for themselves? Anybody else there?'

'No. They were very helpful, as I said. Do you think he's queer?'

'I'm bloody sure of it, but Amy thinks the sun shines out of his arsehole – and he's got a degree from Oxford, so he's no fool.'

'Why's he working in a country library?'

Haines shrugged. 'Beats me. Why don't you get that picture off to Interpol. I don't trust anyone who smiles as much as Vandegaard. I'm going to spend a bit more time going through these files, then I'll pass them over to you. You might pick up something I've missed.'

Fraser took the photograph of Vandegaard. 'I've been thinking.'

'Always a good sign,' responded Haines. 'Do you think you could teach Lockyer?'

'If there was something else wrong with Radcliffe's car, he might have removed the rotor button himself to prevent it being stolen. And another thing – that gym in Goulburn that the Delhunty woman went to . . . a lot of money's been poured into that. In fact, I was wondering how a population the size of Goulburn's could support that kind of investment.'

'So, maybe they'll do their dough?'

'The receptionist said they had Sydney backers, but why would a Sydney investor take a punt on something that big down here when he's likely to get a better return on one in the big smoke? The guy who runs it says they hope to put in a pool if they can get the okay from the council. He's talking big bikkies.'

'What's his name?'

'Papandopolous.'

'Never heard of him, but go with your instincts. Check him out.'

Fraser made no attempt to leave. 'Remember when we were on the way to interview the bursar and you said it had to be someone with a legitimate reason for coming here regularly? Papandopolous has instructors in karate and judo coming down regularly from Sydney to take classes. The receptionist mentioned that sometimes people from Sydney stay in the building overnight.'

At last Fraser had Haines's full attention. 'Now that's interesting! I *like* it. Wouldn't it be just . . .? Can you imagine the sheer bloody joy of pulling a little stoned bunny out of the inspector's hat? Right underneath his nose? Take as much time as you need on this one, Fraser, but keep me up to date and don't go rushing in. Just imagine . . .' He was still imagining when Fraser returned to his own desk and reached for the *A to K*.

While Fraser, between cups of black coffee, was making trunk calls in the relative peace of the police station, an anything-but-peaceful confrontation was occurring on the second landing of Edwards House. Girls had gathered on either side of the combatants, like supporters at a mediæval joust. In one corner was one of the girls who'd almost witnessed the arrival of the police on the morning the headmaster's body was discovered: a pretty girl with masses of auburn hair. Her accuser, who could not be described as pretty, was a pale, thin, straight-haired girl of about fifteen.

'You . . . bloody bitch,' the thin girl screamed, creating shock-waves that raised the adrenalin levels of all within earshot. All, that is, except Matron, who found Annabelle Friedman and Josie St John facing each other outside the door to the former's bedroom. 'Just stay away from me or I'll do you in, you cat, I swear. Just stay away from me and stay out of my room.'

'I was just looking for my magazine, Matron,' Josie said sweetly over Annabelle's right shoulder. 'I thought Annabelle might have borrowed it. She often borrows things.' There *was*, thought Matron, something decidedly feline about Josie St John. Her eyes were narrowed, like a cat's, and she moved with the same insinuating grace – creeping into your presence almost before you knew she was there and curling up on the most comfortable piece of furniture. Matron could not, however, appear to favour one girl over the other. Annabelle was shaking, her breath coming in huge gasps.

'I think you'd better look for your magazine downstairs, Josie. *Now*, please,' she added, when Josie made no attempt to move. Scowling, Josie flounced off and danced lightly down the stairs, although anything other than walking on the stairs was forbidden. 'And the rest of you can return to your rooms or join Josie in the common room,' she said. The onlookers drifted away to whisper and speculate. Matron knew she'd have to do something before parents began taking their girls away, or before Annabelle did herself an injury. The nightmares were becoming more frequent, and counselling wasn't making a blind bit of difference. She had no faith in psychologists.

Beneath her starched exterior Matron was a kind woman, but she was a victim of her own undemonstrative upbringing. She patted Annabelle's hand and led the girl back into her room. 'I'll give you something to put behind your door. It's heavy enough to stop people barging in. Will that help?' Annabelle nodded, unable to speak. 'Do you have your inhaler handy, in case you have an attack?' Annabelle nodded again, her eyes brimming with tears. 'Well, then, you lie down and I'll shut the door. I'll come back with a cup of cocoa in a few minutes, but I'll knock.' She was about to leave when it crossed her mind that the girl might be a little more communicative. 'You can talk to me, if it helps, Annabelle. You know that, don't you?' A sniff and a nod were, as usual, the girl's only response.

At the instant Matron was shutting Annabelle's door, Amy Graham was alighting from her car in front of Edwards House.

She'd just had a most unsatisfactory conversation with Gilbert Fairweather about the possibility of her accepting the role as temporary headmistress. It was a position she wasn't inclined to accept, but the executive director wouldn't take no for an answer. He kept offering her more money. She resented the implication that she could be bought, and that it was simply a matter of finding a figure she was prepared to accept. In vain she'd tried, as politely as possible, to make it clear that in declining she wasn't holding out for money. The man was crass and insensitive.

Then he undermined her resolve completely by saying that it was Edward Haines's suggestion that she should take up the position. Why would Edward do such a thing without consulting her? And why would he suggest it at all? Was he thinking she would be able to help him discover who'd murdered Horace Radcliffe? The thought that she might be able to assist Edward prompted her to tell the executive director she would get back to him after she'd discussed his offer with Detective Sergeant Haines. His manner indicated that he interpreted this as capitulation.

It irked her into being blunt. 'Mr Fairweather,' she said, 'nothing, other than the thought that I might be useful to Detective Sergeant Haines, would tempt me to accept the position of temporary head. If it transpires that DS Haines simply mentioned my name in passing, my rejection of your offer will stand. If, on the other hand, I can be useful to the police, I will reconsider your offer. My decision will be based on that, and that only . . . *not* on money. Do I make myself clear?'

'Absolutely, dear lady. Absolutely,' he'd replied.

Amy entered the front door of Edwards House just as Matron descended the stairs. Both, though outwardly calm, were inwardly flustered. Matron acknowledged Amy with a nod of her head and indicated that she should follow her into the kitchen. There she set about making cocoa, to the annoyance of Mrs Watkins, who was preparing food for lunch.

'It's 'er again, ain't it? 'Erd 'er screaming a few minutes ago. Needs a good clip around the ear 'ole, if you ask me. Better'n cocoa.'

'I'll be the judge of that, Mrs Watkins, if you don't mind.' Mrs Watkins did mind, but she sniffed and went on with her preparations.

Amy, her conversation with Gilbert Fairweather forgotten, approached Matron while she waited for the milk to heat in the saucepan. 'Is one of your charges sick, Mildred? I did hear that one of them was having nightmares. Is it the same girl?'

Matron hesitated, but common sense got the better of her. With this girl she was out of her depth, and she knew it. She made what was, for her, an unusual admission: 'Yes. I don't know what to do.'

'You always do the right thing, Mildred, because you have the girls' best interests at heart. Sometimes, though, there are problems that cocoa can't fix. Is this one of them?' Matron sighed and nodded. A single glance in the direction of Mrs Watkins indicated that at the moment she didn't wish to talk. Amy took the hint.

'Are the police coming this morning, Mildred?'

'Yes. That overweight sergeant is bringing back the other two to finish going over the cottage for fingerprints, and they'll be taking fingerprints from the staff in the afternoon. He's asked whether we can do something for them for lunch. Is that possible, Mrs Watkins?' The latter grunted her assent, and then, as an afterthought, pointed in the direction of the kitchen door.

'Better tell 'em Mr O found somethin' they was lookin' for. 'E's 'ung it out there in a plastic bag . . . Says it belonged to the 'eadmaster. Used my tongs, 'e did, 'cos they told 'im not to touch it if 'e found it. Says it's 'is "puffer". Didn't even know 'e used one.'

'Mr O'Flaherty found the headmaster's inhaler? Why didn't you tell me this before? I would have rung the police immediately.'

'E only found it last night, and it weren't goin' nowhere,' said Mrs Watkins in an injured tone. 'I knew they was comin' back.'

Matron shook her head as she poured scalded milk into a mug. She put the saucepan into the sink, filled it with water, and then followed Amy into the hall.

At the bottom of the stairs, Amy placed her hand on Matron's arm. 'Mildred, I know this is going to sound strange, but I want you to do something for me. I want you to keep that mug when . . . Who is the girl?'

'Annabelle.'

'. . . when Annabelle is finished with it. Now that they're taking fingerprints, they may want to do the girls as well – and this would be a less stressful way of obtaining hers, given her condition. Of course, if you don't feel right about this, I'll understand. I don't want to compromise you. I'm just being practical.'

'I'll collect it myself and keep it in my room.'

'Thank you, Mildred. And when you've seen her, would you have time for a talk? There's something I'd like to discuss with you, and I'm sure there are things you'd like to discuss with me. I'll be on the verandah.'

By the time Haines, Fraser and the scientific squad arrived back at the school, Amy had consulted with Matron and decided to accept the position of temporary head of Eldersley. Under the circumstances, she felt it irrelevant now to discuss Edward's motives for putting her forward, so she simply told him that she had accepted the position. She also told him what she knew of Annabelle Friedman and the nightmares that had been disrupting her fellow boarders' sleep since the headmaster's death.

'She's been going to a professional counsellor since she arrived at the school. I have the name of her counsellor. She's got an office in Bowral.' She handed Haines a business card. 'And I thought the girl's prints might be useful, so Mildred is going to keep a mug she's been drinking from this afternoon.'

'That's great,' said Haines. 'The boys will be finishing the cottage today, so if anyone has been prowling about in there, we'll soon know about it. Good thinking, Amy.'

'There might be something else for your forensics people, too, Edward. It's hanging on the back door in a plastic bag. I believe you asked Mr O'Flaherty to keep an eye out for the headmaster's inhaler? Apparently he found it and picked it up with tongs, so if there are prints they should be intact.'

'Brilliant. Why didn't someone call me? I would have sent an officer to pick it up.'

'Mrs Watkins said she knew you'd be coming back.'

'And in the meantime, a vital piece of evidence has been hanging in a plastic bag on the back of the kitchen door.'

'The front of the kitchen door, Edward. Mrs Watkins refused to have it in the kitchen because the bag is greasy. She keeps bones in it for the dog.'

'Better and better! Now tell me, Amy, has Fairweather gone back to Sydney or is he still hanging about?'

'He's waiting for me to call him about the position. He doesn't know yet that I plan to accept. Perhaps you could tell him, Edward? I don't relish the thought of another conversation.'

'With pleasure. I have a few bones of my own to pick over with him. And just one more thing, Amy. The sports mistress – the Delhunty woman – anything else you can tell me about her? I'm going to Sydney to interview her. She must have hated Radcliffe's guts.'

'I can't tell you much more than I did before, Edward. She's an intelligent, dedicated young woman. She didn't take any non-sense from the girls, because of which I think some of them spread rumours about her. She's not what you'd call "girlish" . . . and please understand that I'm trying to see her as most men would. She's muscular and statuesque. She has close-cropped hair and she doesn't wear make-up, which to me is practical, because she's running around a sports field or doing gymnastics most days. If she is a lesbian, and frankly I don't care, why does it follow that she's corrupting the morals of young girls? Are the heterosexual male teachers to be suspected on the same grounds? If you do see her, please say I'd be happy to have her return to the school.'

'What if she murdered him?'

'Really, Edward. If everyone who hated Horace Radcliffe is a suspect, you'll still be interviewing this time next year.'

TWENTY

Gilbert Fairweather looked at his watch. They were determined to keep him waiting. There'd been something in Haines's manner when he rang – a greater smugness than usual? Did Haines have something up his sleeve? He looked at his watch again. Half past three. Even if he left now he wouldn't be back in Sydney before dark, but he didn't want to spend another night in this hole.

When Haines and Fraser entered the office, Haines looked grimly triumphant and Fraser was flushed. But if there were any reason for them to feel elated, they were certainly not going to communicate it to him. Haines sat at his desk, and Fraser on a straight-backed chair that he carried in for that purpose. Haines began: 'You mentioned, Mr Fairweather, that you went to dinner with Horace Radcliffe on the evening of Friday, twentieth of May. Can you tell me, please, the substance of your conversation with Mr Radcliffe during dinner?'

'Our conversation was predictable, Sergeant. We talked about the school.'

'Did you discuss members of staff?'

'I dare say. Horace frequently discussed members of staff, but we didn't necessarily see eye to eye on this issue. Qualified teaching staff aren't thick on the ground – at least, not the ones prepared to bury themselves in this godforsaken hole. One of Horace's shortcomings was his intolerance of . . . let us say, people's pecca-dillos? He tended to involve himself, unnecessarily, in their private lives. He couldn't leave well alone – always prying and inves-tigating. Yes, investigating,' he repeated, in response to Haines's quizzical look. 'I suspect he even paid to have someone look into the backgrounds of some of them, because there were things he knew that he couldn't have found out any other way.'

'Such as?'

Fairweather hesitated, aware that in his nervousness he had already said too much. 'He discovered that the Delhunty woman was in a relationship with another woman. It's costing us a fortune, and we might end up in court. Stupid bastard.'

'And?'

'He dredged up lots of things, some of them petty, others that I would say should be buried in the past. I don't recall all of them.'

'Do try, Mr Fairweather. I shouldn't have to remind you that this is a murder investigation and that any information Mr Radcliffe was holding over members of staff could have provided a motive. What else did he reveal to you? Vandegaard, for example. Did he talk about Vandegaard?'

'Said he thought he'd been involved in something dodgy overseas.'

'In South Africa?'

'Yes. That's all he said. I don't know any more.'

'What about Deitz? He disliked Deitz. Did he have anything on him?'

'He was contacting someone at another school. Said he thought there was something odd about him. He wasn't explicit, but I think he was thinking alone the lines of some kind of perversion. Horace had a nose for that sort of thing. I told him to lay off.'

'Who else was he digging dirt on? Hinds? Everhardt?'

'Don't know about Hinds, although I recall him saying that

he thought he was politically unsound. Everhardt was a favourite target. I think he suspected her of enjoying herself too much. She's a bit of a goer, that one.'

'And is this what you were arguing about, at the restaurant? The staff?'

'What makes you think we were arguing?'

'I don't think you were arguing, Mr Fairweather – I *know*. Was the headmaster trying to muscle in on your business? Did he want more control?'

'What makes you think that?'

'Who owns Pastoral Enterprises, Mr Fairweather? Is it a family company?'

'It is.'

'Do you prepare annual reports?'

'If you know so much already, Sergeant, you'll know that I'm not obliged to prepare annual reports because the company isn't publicly listed.'

'No. But under Section 293 of the Corporations Act, you *could* be obliged to prepare annual reports, Mr Fairweather, if five per cent of your shareholders asked you to do so. Did the headmaster have a five per cent holding in Pastoral Enterprises? Or was he attempting to obtain one by purchasing shares from your family?'

Gilbert Fairweather had gone pale. Fraser noticed a pulse beating in his temple. 'My brother owns shares in the company, but Horace had none – it wasn't part of the deal. He was a salaried employee. My brother is obliged, under the terms of our agreement, to give me first option to purchase any of his shares. He told me Horace had approached him, and I was livid. I'll admit I felt like beating him to a pulp, but I didn't. I never laid a finger on him, I swear. The last I saw of him, he was walking towards his car. I left before he did.'

'It follows, then,' said Haines, 'that the more information you give us about the headmaster's investigations into his staff, the more your own anger with him will appear as only one motive among many.'

'If I knew more, I'd tell you more. I wish I'd paid more attention to his infernal ramblings about morality, but I always tended to switch off and take the attitude that he was interfering in things that were none of his business. I'd asked him many times to lay off, so probably he stopped telling me what he was doing. One thing I do know is that he would have kept records . . . files. Horace recorded everything. It was an obsession. He probably recorded his own farts.'

'In date order?' said Fraser.

'There are no records in the cottage,' said Haines. 'Not even the original personnel records. That's why we got copies from you.'

'Then someone lifted them. Find them and you'll find the person who killed him. Can I leave now? I've told you everything I know. I have to get back to Sydney.'

'Just one more thing, Mr Fairweather. Annabelle Friedman. I need to know why she's receiving counselling and something of her family background. Who pays her fees?'

'Who *paid* her fees, said the executive director bitterly. Horace paid her fees. I don't know what's going to happen to her now. Why should I be expected to pick up the tab?'

'The headmaster paid her fees? Why?'

'I have no idea. He said it was a charitable matter. I assumed she was a relative of his . . . maybe an illegitimate child?' He laughed. '*If* that were possible, which I doubt. As to her mental condition, Horace never mentioned any details and I didn't ask. Can I go now?'

Haines, stunned by this latest piece of information, nodded. 'I think that's okay. Oh, by the way, Mr Fairweather, I have a message for you from Amy Graham. She'll be accepting the position of temporary head after all.'

In spite of everything, the executive director looked relieved. 'Tell her I'll be in touch. She can have anything she wants, provided she stops it all falling apart. You know where to contact me. Good afternoon.' He nodded curtly in Fraser's direction and left the office.

'Do you think Radcliffe was the girl's father?' Fraser asked when he'd gone.

'Stranger things have happened. Better start looking into their backgrounds. Find out what school she came from, and see what you can dig up on Radcliffe. You'll need these.' He handed Fraser a folder. 'Fairweather sent us Radcliffe's letter of application and résumé, along with all the others.' Fraser took the folder and was about to leave when Haines added: 'He thought he was dealing with ignorant country plods . . . arrogant bastard. No wonder Amy can't stand him. Did you see him change colour when I mentioned the Corporations Act? Do you reckon he's up to something?'

'It would be easy to fiddle the books if the other shareholders were apathetic and you weren't required to lodge annual reports,' said Fraser. 'Maybe he's salting away some of the profits and Radcliffe was onto him. He said himself that Radcliffe had a nose for that sort of thing.'

'He said Radcliffe had a nose for perversion, but I'm sure it was capable of sniffing out fraud as well. I wonder how Bradley and Frenshaw are getting on with those prints. Did you give them the inhaler?'

'Yes. And the mug that Mrs Graham got from Matron. Could the girl have done it, do you think?'

'We know he thought one of the girls was threatening him, and these nightmares only started after the murder, although she was already having counselling. We'll go and see her psychologist tomorrow . . . at least, we will after you've made an appointment.'

He handed Fraser a business card. 'And then, we're off to see Ms Delhunty, *who* is living in what appears to be a lesbian relationship in Glebe, but with *whom* she is living I do not know. Glebe's near Sydney University. I looked it up.'

'Been looking up your old grammar textbooks as well?'

'Too right. She's not going to catch me out on that one again.'

'I hear there're some good finishing schools in Sydney. Don't know whether they take middle-aged men, but I could find out.'

'Piss off.'

'Before I do,' said Fraser, 'I want to put something on the record that's been worrying me. Something happened this afternoon. It was when I got the mug from Matron. I was holding it and the headmaster's inhaler in plastic bags. The handyman, Mr O'Flaherty, joined us. He was quite proud that he'd only handled the "t'ing" with tongs. Anyway, that little dog of his started barking. I think he thought I had something for him in the bags. Matron came over all peculiar, and I thought she was going to faint. She looked at me and O'Flaherty as if she'd seen a ghost. And he was staring at her. Then she came to and laughed and said that cook always put scraps for Ira in plastic bags, and that's why he was barking. I started to think she'd gone barking mad.'

'And you expect me to make something of that?'

'No. It's just for the record.'

'You're not developing an obsession for recording things, are you?'

'Like your farts, do you mean?'

'If you do, make sure they're in date order.'

Bradley and Frenshaw made their verbal report to Haines before returning to Goulburn. Apart from verifying signs of entry through the upstairs bathroom window, their findings were disappointing.

The headmaster's prints were, of course, all over the cottage and the interior of the car. Apart from Lockyer's, there were no other prints on the bonnet or distributor of the car, or in the headmaster's study; nor were there any discernable prints on the filing cabinets, which was strange. There were, however, clear prints on the type-writers, the drawers, and the crockery in the kitchen, presumably those of the administrative staff. It was as if parts of the cottage had been wiped clean.

'What about the inhaler? And the mug?'

'Ah, that's the interesting bit,' said Bradley. 'I was saving that till last. The prints on the mug were the same as the ones we found on the inhaler. Does that help?'

Haines's heart beat faster. He looked at Fraser and then back to Bradley and Frenshaw. 'Were they the only prints? Were there any others?'

'We thought at first we'd picked up one of the headmaster's, but it's pretty fuzzy. Can't be certain. Probably wouldn't stand up in court.'

'Bugger. Still, it's somewhere to start. We'll need to have either her psychologist present or some other responsible adult. Maybe Amy would do it . . . or Matron?'

'We'll be seeing her psychologist tomorrow at nine-thirty,' said Fraser, 'and she's seeing the girl herself at eleven, but I don't think she'll agree to any kind of questioning by us and Matron. If the girl's unhinged, it's better to have a professional on hand.'

'And on side,' said Haines.

TWENTY-ONE

Ms Hestleton's offices were above a shop in Bowral's main street. A steep flight of stairs took them to a small landing, from where they could hear the clicketty-clack of a typewriter. It ceased when they knocked, and the door was opened by a young woman in a brown slacksuit with lace-up shoes and an open-necked shirt. She had short, unstyled hair and round, fine-rimmed spectacles. There were no concessions to femininity either in her attire or in the room that she occupied. That was the way things were now, Haines thought. He might just as well have left Fraser at the station.

'Ms Hestleton? We rang yesterday. This is Detective Constable Fraser and I'm DS Haines.'

'Come in. Take a seat. I don't know that I can help you, but I'm happy to spare you some time. I gather you wish to see me about Annabelle Friedman.' She gestured to some comfortable-looking chairs and perched herself on the edge of her desk, which gave her a height advantage. Haines declined. He moved towards the window and stood with his back to it. 'I'll try to be brief, Ms Hestleton. I believe you've been counselling Miss Friedman for several months. Her condition has worsened since the death at the school, and I'm afraid that we'll be obliged to question her, along with the other boarders. I need your advice if I'm to do this without putting the girl at risk. She was hysterical yesterday, because one of the girls entered her room while she was sleeping. What, exactly, is her problem?'

'I can't tell you that. Annabelle has a right to privacy, and as her counsellor I'm bound to preserve that privacy.'

Haines sighed. 'I expected that would be your response. I was hoping it wouldn't be necessary, but you do realise that we can and will subpoena you and your records – and in the meantime, we still have to interview the girl?'

'When I'm under a legal obligation to reveal information in a closed court, I will. Until that happens, there's nothing I can do except to say that Annabelle is psychologically disturbed. She has no next of kin since her mother died last year, so please treat her gently. I'd like you to promise me that when you interview her, there'll be a woman she trusts present – perhaps the Matron?'

'Would you be prepared to undertake that role, Ms Hestleton? I assume she trusts you?'

Ms Hestleton hesitated before shaking her head. 'I'd like to say yes, because I'm concerned for Annabelle, but it's because she trusts me that I can't be seen to collaborate with you. That's how she would interpret it, if I'm at the interview. You understand, don't you?'

'Yes,' said Haines. 'I wouldn't want to cut off her only avenue of retreat. Can you tell me, while we're here, who pays for her counselling?'

'I send my accounts to the school. Presumably they know who covers her expenses.'

'So the cheques are from Pastoral Enterprises and are signed by the executive director, Mr Fairweather?'

Ms Hestleton hesitated and flushed. 'No. The accounts are paid by personal cheque.'

'Whose personal cheques, Ms Hestleton? Mr Fairweather's?'

'No. Mr Radcliffe has been covering the costs. I assumed he was recovering it on his expenses . . . or something like that.'

'And if he wasn't? If he alone felt responsible for providing professional help for the girl, what happens to her now that he's dead? Does your professional concern extend to treating the girl without payment? I can imagine what will happen to her trust if you abandon her treatment due to lack of funds.'

'That isn't your concern, Sergeant. It's mine.'

'We'll leave it at that, then, Ms Hestleton,' said Haines. She closed the door after them with a resounding click and, as they descended the stairs, resumed clattering away on her Remington. Probably recording their visit, Fraser thought.

When they returned to the car, Haines instructed Fraser to head not for the highway but back to the station. There were, he said, a couple of phone calls he had to make before they paid a visit to Ms Delhunty. 'It'll give you a chance to ring Interpol, to see if they got that photo of Vandegaard. And by the way, I've left the other personnel records on your desk, and I'd like you to go through them, starting with Deitz. I can't put my finger on it, but I think Radcliffe was right – there's something strange about him. Maybe you should check with his other schools?'

'I'll bring the files with me. I can read them while you're driving.'

'What do you mean, while *I'm* driving?'

'It was worth a try,' said Fraser.

Finding Victoria Delhunty's address took them through several narrow streets to a quiet cul-de-sac about half a mile from the main thoroughfare of Glebe. They had, as was Haines's wont, dined on hamburgers and chips. 'Don't you ever eat salads or fruit?'

asked Fraser. 'If you've got high blood pressure, maybe you should lay off fatty foods.'

'Thank you for the diagnosis, Fraser. What did *you* just eat?'

'But I only eat it when . . . when I'm working.' Fraser had almost said, 'I only eat it when I'm with you.'

'So what do you eat when you're not working that's so healthy?'

'I eat grilled chicken, fish or lean steak, and I steam vegetables or I have a side salad. That's dinner. In the mornings I eat two pieces of fruit, an egg and some toast.'

'And who cooks it for you?'

'I do it myself.' Haines grunted and threw him a suspicious look. Healthy food was not a topic dear to his heart.

The house in which Ms Delhunty lived with her sister (or was it partner?) was an immaculately preserved Victorian terrace. Anything that had not been preserved had been painstakingly restored. The front garden, with its tiny sundial, was filled with lavender, box brush and daisies. There were leadlight panels in the front door, through which Fraser and Haines could see someone approaching. The door was opened by a diminutive woman, the opposite of what Haines expected from Amy's description. This would have to be the partner.

'Good afternoon. I'm Detective Sergeant Haines, and this is DC Fraser. We've come to see Ms Delhunty. She's expecting us.'

'Yes. She's in the back garden. If you wait inside for a minute, I'll get her for you.' She ushered them into a long hallway, at the end of which was a kitchen.

Ms Delhunty was exactly as Amy had described her – tall, with an Amazonian build and short, dark, closely cropped hair. What Amy had not described was her face. Her features were incongruously small – except for her eyes, which were large with heavily fringed lashes. She was uncommonly pretty. Fraser, who'd visited art galleries, told Haines later that he thought she looked like a Botticelli angel. This was a bit much for Haines.

Victoria Delhunty greeted them and asked if they would like coffee. Haines declined without giving Fraser a chance to reply. Fraser was too busy admiring their hostess's rich, soft voice, limpid eyes and flawless complexion. 'I won't beat about the bush, Ms Delhunty. I'm interviewing every staff member at Eldersley regarding the death of the headmaster and, given the nature of your . . . er . . . dispute, I have to include you in those interviews. Can you tell me where you were on the weekend of the twenty-first and twenty-second of May, and when you were last at Eldersley?'

'I haven't been to the school, Sergeant, since the dispute, as you call it. Just to make things difficult, I was in the area the weekend the headmaster died. I drove down to pick up some belongings from my flat, and I stayed there on Saturday night. And before you ask, I was alone. I neither saw anything of, nor heard anything from, Mr Radcliffe or any member of staff. I didn't want to. I had to force myself to drive there in the first place, and I was terrified of running into one of the girls.'

'Why?'

She hesitated. 'Do you know what it's like, Sergeant, to be accused and found guilty without ever being informed of the precise charges against you, or being given the chance to examine and explain the supposed evidence . . . or even being told who your accusers are? Don't think, Sergeant, that schoolgirls are sweet and innocent. They can be vicious, conniving little vixens. They nearly destroyed me.'

'So I understand. For what it's worth, Ms Delhunty, Amy Graham thinks very highly of you. She's been appointed temporary head until they find a suitable replacement for Horace Radcliffe, and she's asked me to say that she'd be happy to see you back at the school at any time.'

A flush spread over Victoria Delhunty's porcelain features. 'Pardon me for being cynical, Sergeant. Perhaps she means well, or perhaps she's just desperate for someone to fill the gap now that it's her responsibility. No one spoke up for me at the time, and no one made any effort to stop the whispering or the lies. It even went beyond the school. Mrs Graham must know that I can never go back.'

'Mrs Graham was an infrequent visitor to the school . . . board meetings and suchlike. Possibly she was unaware of what was happening, and once she discovered you'd left, it was too late. Given the chance, she would have told you what she told me – that you're a dedicated professional with the best interests of the girls at heart. I'm sure she's not the only staff member who thinks that way.'

Victoria Delhunty's eyes filled with tears. 'I'm sorry. Thank her for me.'

'I will. Now, Ms Delhunty . . .'

'Victoria, please.'

'Well then, Victoria, I'd like your candid opinion of the head-master, and any ideas you may have as to who murdered him and why. Take your time.'

She thought for several minutes. 'He was one of those right-wing, puritanical types . . . you know? . . . incapable of distinguishing between pornography and art? I think he felt he'd been chosen, and that it was his God-given duty to change society, starting with the school. He didn't like the staff he'd inherited, and I suspect, although I have no proof, that he set about getting rid of the ones he didn't approve of. He wanted staff who agreed with his ideals and his methods.'

'How do you think he planned to get rid of them?'

'By putting pressure on them to leave because he knew some-thing about them. I think he employed someone to pry into their backgrounds. He was spying on them.'

'What makes you think that?'

'It's what he did to me,' she said simply, 'and when some of the girls came up with the supposed "evidence", he threw it in my face with what I can only describe as malicious glee. It was nothing specific – just vague accusations about things he'd been told I had implied, or things he had reason to believe I had done. He would never say what things, or who had accused me of them. He made my life a misery, and I think he was doing it to other members of staff as well.'

'What was the evidence he threw in your face, Victoria?'

She hesitated, her embarrassment acute. 'Some of the girls claimed I'd been watching them undress . . . even that I'd been looking at them through keyholes! Sordid stuff. It makes me sick to think that people could believe it. I felt so betrayed.'

'Did anyone else ever suggest that the headmaster was doing to them what he did to you?'

She thought carefully. 'Madelaine Everhardt said something once that made me think he was putting pressure on her to leave. I think she was sorry afterwards that she'd let it slip, because she never mentioned it again. They didn't see eye to eye, and he frequently saw members of staff in his office after school. I may be wrong, but if there was little to criticise in their teaching or their results – and I don't believe any of the staff at Eldersley are poor teachers – perhaps it was personal. If he did it to me, why not to others?'

'Do you think this could have provided someone with a motive for murder?'

'Possibly, although I find it difficult to imagine any one of the people I worked with murdering anyone. They would have needed a much stronger motive than mine. I despised him, but I didn't hate him enough to kill him. In fact, I don't even know how he died. The papers are simply saying "suspicious circumstances" and "person or persons unknown". How did it happen?'

'I can't discuss that, but thank you for being so helpful. I'd already gained the impression that the headmaster was not universally liked, so what you've told me, although it's speculative, is feasible. If you feel like contacting Mrs Graham for a chat, she'll be in the headmaster's office next week. Have a think about it.'

Victoria accompanied them to the front door, where Fraser, who was only fractionally taller than she, snatched the opportunity to smile briefly into her dark eyes and experience the excruciating pleasure of seeing the corners of her delectable mouth turn upwards in response. 'Oh God,' he groaned as climbed into the car, 'she's got dimples!'

Instead of tackling the two-hour trip back to Bowral immediately, Haines and Fraser made their way to Circular Quay, where they bought sandwiches and sat on a bench to watch the ferries arrive and depart. Gulls squabbled for their scraps, and a lone busker played a medley of Scottish tunes. Sydney was full of eccentrics, said Fraser, and sooner or later they all made their way to the Quay.

'Speaking of eccentrics,' said Haines, 'did you know Deitz has been buying joints from Lily Thompson?'

'Spindles said she'd done a rego check on a car, and it turned out to be someone you knew. I take it that was Deitz?'

'Yes. Lily phoned it through.'

'Why did she cooperate?'

'Because I put the frighteners on her. She claimed there was only the one buyer. She was supposed to suss him out on alternative sources of supply, but Michael wasn't happy about her getting too nosy. When I rang her, she said she told Deitz she couldn't supply him any more and asked him whether he could get them somewhere else. She said he shrugged it off and mumbled something about Sydney. Not much joy there.'

'The Thompsons are small fry,' said Fraser. 'If the stuff's coming from around here, we should be looking at the ones with properties big enough to hide it. I suppose we could try aerial surveillance.'

'Would you know what to look for?'

'Not really,' said Fraser. 'I mean, I'd discount any areas supporting stock and look for signs of cultivation, but beyond that I wouldn't have a clue. It would be a start, though. If we found anything that looked promising, we could go in with a warrant.'

'And if it turned out to be cabbage, our cocky could go screaming to his local member, and Goulburn would be wanting to know what I was playing at.'

Fraser shrugged. 'There are always risks.'

'Okay. Get the names of the biggest landholders and see if there's a map in council showing property boundaries – and just in case I decide to send you into the blue with your box brownie, you might ring the airfield and find out what it costs to charter a plane and a pilot.'

It was two hours back to Bowral. When they were on the outskirts, Lockyer contacted them on the radio. Amy Graham had been trying to get in touch. It was important but not urgent. Could DS Haines telephone her at the school as soon as he returned?

'Thought she'd find something,' Haines said smugly. 'I asked her to have a poke around in that girl's room while she was with the counsellor. Amy doesn't miss much. I wonder what she's found?'

'Scissors, and magazines with holes in them?' Fraser speculated.

'If we can nail the little fruitcake for making death threats, we

can subpoena her shrink's records. Drive straight to the school –
I have a feeling this could be interesting. It's about time something
happened.'

They arrived at the school while the boarders were doing their
prep. Amy ushered them into the sitting room. The first thing they
saw was the crumpled, tragic figure of the bursar, who was sitting
at the table where Haines had conducted his interviews. Her eyes
were red and swollen, and there was a box of tissues and an empty
cup beside her. It looked like the calm after the storm. He suspected, from the bursar's dilated pupils, that Amy had given her
something with her tea.

'Laetitia, Detective Sergeant Haines and DC Fraser are here,
as you requested.'

She turned to Haines. 'Miss Hancock would like to confess to
the murder of Horace Radcliffe.'

TWENTY-TWO

Haines read Miss Hancock her rights and asked her whether she wanted a solicitor, but she shook her head. Fraser took out his notebook. 'Are you sure,' said Haines, 'that there's no one you would like to be present at this interview?'

'No. There's no one.'

'And you do not wish us to contact your solicitor or legal advisor?'

'I don't have one.'

'But if you wish, I could suspend the interview until you do contact one. I could even arrange for a solicitor to come to you.'

'No.' Her voice was flat.

'And you've come here of your own free will to volunteer information regarding the death of Mr Horace Radcliffe?'

'Yes.'

'In that case, Miss Hancock, tell me how you murdered the headmaster and why.'

'I poisoned him. I didn't do it deliberately . . . I mean, I did do it deliberately, but I didn't know it would kill him. I didn't intend to kill him . . . I loved him, you see.' Her ample bosom began to heave, and Haines was afraid she'd hyperventilate. He didn't want to be the one to have to resuscitate her. 'When I found him the next morning,' she continued, 'I took away his cup and washed it in the sink. But the cup is missing. Did you . . .? Did the police take it away to have it analysed?'

'We did remove some crockery from the sink on the day the headmaster's body was found,' said Haines. 'I'll have it returned. Tell me, Miss Hancock, what did you use to poison the headmaster?'

'It wasn't a deliberate poison – I told you – and I didn't know it would kill him. He must have been allergic. He was asthmatic, you know. I had a cousin once who died of an asthma attack, so I know it can happen. I just didn't think.'

'What sort of substance?' Haines insisted.

'It was a combination of herbs . . . you know . . . a sort of potion. There's this shop in Sydney that sells all kinds of medicine, and they make it up in the right proportions and grind it into a powder. They treat people, too, in cubicles with curtains. There didn't seem to be any harm in it, but now he's dead and I'm so very . . . very sorry.' She folded her arms on the table, rested her head on them and started sobbing once more. Haines pushed the tissue box towards her until it touched one of her hands. She dragged herself upright and removed a substantial number of tissues in rapid succession.

'Was it a herbal remedy, Miss Hancock? Was it supposed to cure his asthma?'

'No. It was . . . it was . . . to make him . . . you know. I just wanted to make him notice me. It was supposed to make him feel . . .'

'Sexually aroused?'

Miss Hancock went bright pink. 'Well . . . it was a love potion. I'm not sure how it was supposed to work.'

Fraser's mouth twitched, and Haines was nodding slowly at Miss Hancock. 'I see what might have happened,' he said, rubbing his chin. 'The potion must have begun working when there was no one around, and the headmaster just happened to be passing a mirror and . . . *whammo*! What do you think, Fraser?'

'Like Narcissus? He fell in love with his own reflection?'

'And then,' Haines continued, 'he went a bit peculiar and decorated himself with lipstick and flowers – that must be it! I don't know why we didn't think of it before. Perhaps you overdid the dose, Miss Hancock.'

Miss Hancock stared uncomprehendingly. The interview wasn't going quite the way she expected. Reluctantly, Haines decided to put her out of her misery. 'I'm happy to be able to reassure you, Miss Hancock, that you did not kill the headmaster. You are not responsible for his death. The cup of tea you made him on . . . Friday afternoon? . . .' She nodded. '. . . had no effect whatsoever. If I were you, I'd get my money back.'

'But . . . I . . . He wasn't . . .'

'He was deliberately murdered, Miss Hancock. It had nothing to do with anything he'd eaten or drunk.' As he said those words, Haines looked at Fraser, whose eyebrows indicated that he was thinking precisely the same thing. *Could* it have been something the headmaster ate or drank that rendered him relaxed enough for the murderer to deliver the fatal blow?

Haines found Amy in the kitchen talking to Mrs Watkins about how to ensure that mashed potato was lump free. Amy excused herself and followed him into the hall.

'A storm in a teacup,' said Haines, 'and I mean that literally.'

'It wasn't my place to question her, Edward, so I didn't even ask. Is she all right?'

'She should sleep better now that I've assured her she's not responsible for Radcliffe's death. Do you want me to run her home?'

'I can do that, Edward. It's no trouble. Her car is here, but I don't think she's in a fit state to drive. Might I ask what happened?'

'She's been putting Love Potion Number Nine into his tea, and she assumed he had an allergic reaction that carried him off.

When she realised the cup she'd been using was missing, she thought it was only a question of time before we caught up with her. Poor silly cow.'

'Edward!'

'Well, be fair, Amy. Feeding him powdered rhino horn or whatever? She's got to be a brick short of a load. I thought when I got your message that you had something to tell me about the little screamer, not that some loony had confessed to murdering Radcliffe. Did you get a chance to go through the girl's room?'

'Her name's Annabelle, Edward. And yes, I did find something interesting – a photograph of a woman, but not the sort of photograph you'd expect a teenage girl to have. Semi-naked . . . some sort of exotic dancer. It was done in a studio, so I think it may have been a publicity shot. I wrote down the name of the studio.'

'I think I'm missing something here, Amy. What's that got to do with Radcliffe's death?'

'I haven't told you everything yet, Edward. It's one of those black-and-white photographs that's been touched up . . . artificially coloured. She has bright-pink lipstick, and there's a flower behind her left ear.'

TWENTY-THREE

Harold Brand unscrewed the lid of his thermos and poured some of the scalding liquid into a plastic cup. He placed the cup on the dashboard and returned the thermos to the elasticised pocket in the driver's side door. The inside of his car was littered with chip packets and chocolate wrappings, testifying to many hours of boring surveillance. He switched on the radio, picked up his coffee and took a sip. Too hot. He warmed his hands around the cup and settled back to wait.

He was parked a couple of kilometres south of Goulburn, just off the highway. A few days before, he'd followed the truck north for about twenty kilometres after it picked up two blokes outside the gym. If he'd followed it further, they might have got suspicious. Anyway, he didn't have enough petrol and they were probably headed for Sydney. He was more interested in what was happening this end. Where was the truck coming *from*? What was in the back? Why did it always stop at the gym to pick up passengers before heading north? It was a large truck, yet it never dropped anything off or picked up anything else. He'd become aware of it while he was trailing the Delhunty woman, who often went to the gym late. He'd recorded its registration number and taken a few photographs of the guy who ran the place, Papandopoulos, talking to the driver. He'd also photographed the other two. There was no point in driving an empty truck between Goulburn and Sydney, so they had to be up to something.

He'd spent several hours parked at various points along the road before tracking it back to its source. It started from a property owned by Papandopoulos's father, a grazier, but it couldn't be carrying live animals because it was enclosed, and it couldn't be carrying carcasses because it wasn't refrigerated. What *was* it carrying? Harold had his own suspicions. He'd follow it, this time, all the way to Sydney . . . well, not follow it, exactly, but stay ahead of it. When it turned off to go to the gym, he'd drive straight through Goulburn without stopping. He'd drive slowly until it caught up. When he saw its headlights, he'd stay far enough in front to avoid suspicion. And if he lost it? A full tank of petrol wasn't cheap, so he'd have to get it right the first time.

At 1.00 a.m. the truck went past. He waited until it was out of sight and then pulled out. He caught up with it further along the road, travelling slowly . . . too slowly. Was there something wrong? The road ahead was empty, so he had no choice but to pass. He did so, feeling nervous. He kept glancing at its lights in his rear-vision mirror. It was travelling at normal speed again. He drove through the deserted main street and watched as the truck turned off. It would stop at the gym for five or ten minutes. He increased his speed. About three miles out of town there was a bend at the end of a long stretch of road. He pulled onto the verge, dowsing his lights but leaving his engine running. When he saw the truck coming, he'd pull back onto the road. Then, when he was around the bend, out of sight, he'd switch his headlights back on.

Harold Brand was a cautious man, but caution and economy are sometimes at odds. He'd dismissed the option of hiring a car because no one was covering his expenses. It was a decision he would regret. The truck not only caught up with him, but drove closely behind him, and blind Freddy could see that they were onto him. What could he do? He couldn't get far enough ahead to do a U-turn, and he couldn't outrun them. What he needed was half a dozen steep hills to slow them down. Where were the bloody hills when you needed them? For that matter, where were the bloody cops? They were both exceeding the speed limit.

There was a sickening jolt as the truck rammed into the back of him. Harold Brand started to sweat. They were trying to run him off the road! Fear took possession of him, and his gorge started rising. He couldn't see the road because the truck's headlights were flooding his cabin with light – a bright, hard, white light, like the light people claimed to see at the end of a tunnel after they'd had a near-death experience. That's what he was having – a near-death experience.

TWENTY-FOUR

It was two days before the annual Balmoral dance. The only topics of conversation were the degrees of attractiveness of the boys who would be there and what everyone would be wearing. There was a flurry of leg waxing and nail varnishing. The preceding weekend had seen last-minute shopping for perfume, stockings and clothes. Then there was the inevitable posturing and display.

Amy made it a rule to eat her evening meal with the boarders. She could not, therefore, avoid the incessant, twittering anticipation of the dance or the topics that were being discussed. But Annabelle Friedman appeared not to be taking part, so she took the girl aside. Was she was looking forward to the dance? Annabelle's response was negative: 'Gyrating around a dance floor with some pimply adolescent isn't my idea of fun.'

Amy laughed. 'Even in my day, Annabelle, there were toe treaders and arm pumpers and partners who couldn't take a step in time to the music to save themselves, but there's always the chance that Prince Charming might turn up.'

'There's a better chance of meeting the Tooth Fairy.'

Annabelle had twice been questioned by Haines, in Amy's presence. She admitted that she'd thrown one of her inhalers into the bushes, but denied that it came from the headmaster's study or that she knew anything about the headmaster's death. In the absence of hard evidence (the fingerprint and the photograph were inconclusive), there was nothing Haines could do.

At the second interview, Haines asked whether she was aware that the headmaster had been paying her school fees as well as the invoices from her counsellor. She said she knew someone was paying them but didn't know who; it had all been arranged by the headmistress at her old school. In the holidays she was fostered out to a family in Sydney with two teenage daughters. They gave her money to spend, and she had her own room.

Haines telephoned Mrs Mitchell, the headmistress at Annabelle's previous school, who referred him to a Mr Conway at the Department of Community Services. Mrs Mitchell didn't know the arrangements that had been made to support Annabelle, other than that a suitable foster home had been found and her education was to continue at a private school. She assumed that the foster parents were footing the bill.

Mr Conway, like Ms Hestleton, was uncooperative until Haines threatened to subpoena every record relating to Annabelle's case. He gained access to a file containing a search for next of kin from Annabelle's mother's earlier marriages. The Department had drawn a blank. Annabelle's stepfather, Friedman, was in prison, and her natural father had proved untraceable. The investigation did, however, turn up a solution to Annabelle's problem. Horace Radcliffe had, for a short time, been married to the deceased, and the dissolution of the marriage had revolved around Annabelle's paternity. There were results of blood tests confirming that Horace Radcliffe was not Annabelle's biological father. Radcliffe did, however, offer to subsidise the remainder of Annabelle's education, provided she attended Eldersley and was *not* informed that he was her benefactor. He was adamant on the issue of anonymity.

The file contained photocopies of pages from what appeared

to be diary entries in a round, childish hand. Haines's eyebrows shot up as he read them. He handed the pages to Fraser. Fraser's expression was grim.

Saturday, 1st September

Mum's still confused. They keep telling me it will take time, but I need to do something now. I can't do anything when he's there all the time. There's nowhere to go and if I tell Mum . . . But I can't tell Mum. I can't tell anyone. He said if I tell anyone they won't believe me and they'll keep me there and throw away the key and there'll be no one to look after Mum when she comes out. He says I'm a slut and a nutter, just like Mum.

Wednesday, 5th September

I hate him. If I get the chance I'll kill him. I told him if he touched me again I'd kill myself, but before I did I'd write to somebody to tell them why. I said I wouldn't care what people said about me if I was dead. I said I'd tell them everything. He said he'd lock me up and tell the hospital to come and get me. He said they lock people up who try to kill themselves.

Wednesday, 12th September

He's been searching my room but he didn't find anything. I use my locker.

Thursday, 13th September

Mrs Mitchell wanted to know if there was a problem. I told her Mum was in hospital and she asked who was looking after me at home. I had to tell her where Mum was. I told

*her my stepfather was looking after me. She said she was
sure Mum would recover. She said I could come to her if
anything was worrying me. Her eyes were boring into me
and I started having an attack. She kept asking me where
my inhaler was. She shouted at someone and then the
ambulance came.*

Monday, 17th September

*Mrs Mitchell rang. I heard him say he was aware of my
condition. He kept saying 'yes, I know that' and 'I am fully
aware of that'. He was just as nasty as ever when he finished
talking to her, but he hasn't touched me since.*

There was a typewritten report, dated 21st February, 1975, headed
'Report to the Board of Ellalong High School by Mrs Elaine
Mitchell, Headmistress'. Haines skimmed it as well, before hand-
ing it on to Fraser. It read:

> I wish to confirm that I have arranged with
> Community Services for one of our Year 9 pupils
> to be removed from parental custody and placed
> in care, pending criminal proceedings against
> her stepfather. The child's mother committed
> suicide whilst undergoing psychiatric treatment
> for depression and schizophrenia.
>
> The child's abuse was revealed to me only after she
> suffered a severe asthma attack during which I had
> cause to open her locker. I found a diary, the contents
> of which I immediately made known to the police.
>
> Investigations into next of kin are proceeding on the
> assumption that the girl's natural father is an earlier
> husband of the deceased.

The child's school fees will be temporarily waived.
In the absence of a natural parent or responsible
relative, we owe her a duty of care. She is currently
undergoing counselling and will be released into
a suitable foster home as soon as one can be found.

When Haines returned to the school, he relayed the substance of this to Amy, who decided to continue paying for Annabelle's education. She was, Haines knew, a wealthy woman.

On the morning of the dance, Amy decided that Annabelle must go to the ball, and she could think of only one way of getting her there. She rang Haines and then drove into Bowral. From the conversations she'd overheard at the dinner table, she knew that long skirts made from Indian cotton with a fine metallic thread were much coveted. They had drawstring waists, so size wasn't important. She purchased one of these in black and silver, together with a plain, black cotton top. 'A bit of last-minute buying for the dance, Mildred. What do you think? I thought I might be able to persuade Annabelle to go if she had something to wear that was like the things the others are wearing. This stuff seems to be all the rage.'

'She says she won't go,' said Matron dubiously. 'I don't know that you'll be able to change her mind.'

'We'll see. I may have something else up my sleeve.'

Fraser had spent the last hour going over the résumés, including Radcliffe's. It read like a construction manual, so much emphasis had been placed on 'building' this and 'designing' that. For five years Radcliffe had taught mathematics at junior level in a depressed area of Sydney's inner west. His previous positions had been clerical-administrative. There was an entire page devoted to short courses, each with a pompously worded précis, and a list of teaching diplomas from colleges all over the state, many of which the headmaster had completed by correspondence. In Haines's words, the résumé was 'a bit of a wank'.

He'd moved on to Victoria Delhunty's résumé, straightforward and unadorned, like its beautiful owner, when Haines came out of his office with the look of a man preparing to do battle. He looked at the résumés on Fraser's desk. 'Find anything?'

'There could be something . . . small gaps in Deitz's résumé. He's avoided giving precise dates, which means that he could easily have overlooked a couple of jobs that lasted one or two terms. I'm checking on it.'

'Anything from Interpol?'

'Nothing. I'll put in another call.'

'How would you like a bit of undercover work in the meantime?'

There was a look on Haines's face that Fraser didn't like. 'What sort of undercover work?'

'The sort you're not going to enjoy. I've just had a call from Amy Graham. There's no nice way of putting this. She wants you to escort the little screamer to the school dance at Balmoral Boys'. She needs someone to keep an eye on her, and she thought that you could keep your ear to the ground. What you do with the rest of your anatomy is up to you.'

'You're kidding! She's a child. What am I? A baby sitter? No bloody way.'

'Weren't you telling me you owed her one? The restaurant? Remember?' Fraser groaned. 'The headmaster of Balmoral has been complaining about boys smoking pot on school premises. He rang me a couple of weeks ago. I told him we were working on it, so it's not such a bad idea to do some follow-up, is it?'

'What if the girl construes it as serious interest? What then?'

'Amy will explain to the girl that we want a discreet police presence and that she can help us by allowing us to provide her with a plainclothes escort. You never know, she might tell you something about that photograph . . . or she might let something slip about Radcliffe. You do have a way with the female of the species.' He chuckled. 'Why don't you find out what all the groovy adolescent boys are wearing?'

'Do I *have* to?'

'I reckon you owe it to Amy. She wants you there about six-thirty. A bus has been hired to transport them there and back.'

'Oh no!' said Fraser vehemently. 'No you don't. That's where I draw the line. I'm not travelling on a bus with the whole bloody bunch of them. If I have to escort the screamer, she can come in the Cortina or not at all.'

'Suit yourself,' said Haines. 'I just thought there might be safety in numbers.'

Although dreading the main event, Fraser continued to work on the résumés, alert to the possibility of discrepancies and unexplained gaps. It was about two-thirty when he received a call from the deputy of one of the schools at which Deitz had taught. Yes, said Mr Quinlan, he remembered Dr Deitz. What did the police wish to know, and how could he be sure that it was the police who were telephoning?

Mr Quinlan had seen the reports of the headmaster's death in the newspaper, but he wasn't aware that Dr Deitz had taken a post at the college. It didn't surprise him, because Dr Deitz appeared not to stay very long in one place. He'd left them in 1972, after only eighteen months, to take up a position with a school that was, in Mr Quinlan's opinion, less prestigious. Dr Deitz had given no reason for the change. He was unpopular to say the least, leaving as he did halfway through the academic year.

'Can you give me the name of the school to which Dr Deitz went when he left?'

'Certainly. He went to Berkeley Boys' in the far west. I believe it's somewhere around Dubbo. I suppose he didn't stay there long?'

'It appears not,' said Fraser. 'Can you think of any reason for that? Did you have any reason to be unhappy with him?'

It was Mr Quinlan's turn to be evasive. 'We received no complaints from pupils or parents, and I was confident that Dr Deitz was covering the curriculum. He wasn't with us long enough for me to form an opinion, Constable.'

'Thank you, Mr Quinlan. You've been very helpful. I don't think we'll need to trouble you again.' Fraser hung up and flung his pen into the air. 'Got you,' he crowed. He dialled trunk information for the number of Berkeley Boys'.

'The headmaster's teaching at the moment,' said the woman who answered the phone. 'Can I take your number and have him call you back?'

It was three-quarters of an hour before Mr Bumford (God knows what the boys called him) rang. This time the conversation went a little differently. Yes, he remembered Dr Deitz, and yes, Dr Deitz had only been with the school a short time. No, he had not been happy with Dr Deitz and had asked him to leave. He preferred not to give a reason; nor was he prepared to put anything in writing.

'That makes it difficult for us, Mr Bumford. We're conducting a criminal investigation. Would you feel happier talking to the police in Dubbo? Anything you say to them can be relayed to us in strictest confidence.'

'Can you tell me why you're investigating Dr Deitz?'

'We're not, Mr Bumford. We're investigating a murder at the college where Dr Deitz is employed, and we're taking a routine look at the backgrounds of the academic staff, that's all. Your reasons for asking Dr Deitz to leave may be entirely irrelevant. Would you like to think about it and call me back?'

There was a momentary hesitation. 'My reasons for asking Dr Deitz to leave are based on something I witnessed. Dr Deitz, I'm sure, would deny everything and I have no evidence, other than what I saw, upon which to base a formal complaint. It would be his word against mine, you understand.'

'I understand, Mr Bumford. Please go on.'

'I believe I witnessed Dr Deitz handling . . . fondling one of the boys. He denied it, of course . . . said I'd misconstrued. He claimed he'd done no more than pat the boy on the back. I know what I saw, but I could hardly interrogate the child. I thought it best to ask Dr Deitz to leave. I told him if he refused, I'd report the matter to the Department.'

'Is there anything else you wish to tell me, Mr Bumford?'

'No. And I'm not prepared to take this any further or put anything in writing.'

'I understand. That won't be necessary. We probably won't need to contact you again. Thank you for your time and your comments.'

Fraser knocked on Haines's door, his ordeal by teenage dance for the moment forgotten. Haines was on the phone. He looked up and pointed at a seat. From the little that Fraser could hear, he wasn't a happy man. When he rang off, he stared at Fraser like the proverbial stunned mullet. 'You first,' he said.

'Deitz was asked to leave a school near Dubbo. The headmaster suspected him of touching up one of the boys.'

It deflected Haines's interest away from his phone call. 'Well, now. A pædophile, eh? And Amy had the feeling he didn't like children.'

'It's very much hearsay, because Bumford won't commit himself.

He doesn't have any evidence, other than what he saw – or thinks he saw – and he won't put anything in writing.'

'I wonder whether Radcliffe managed to dig up the same information? Being asked to leave a second time might have pushed Deitz over the edge. When you get a chance, ring the bod back and ask him whether there have been any other enquiries about Deitz, would you?'

'Okay. But that won't tell us if Radcliffe knew anything.'

'No. But if Radcliffe did dig it up and recorded it, someone else at that school has the information now. I'm convinced of that. Someone else knows about Deitz if Radcliffe knew, not to mention any other stray dirt he'd managed to collect about the others. I wonder if he had anything on Vandegaard? Highly likely, I'd say, under the circumstances.'

'What circumstances?'

'That was Amy on the blower. Vandegaard's done a runner.'

TWENTY-FIVE

Fraser's arrival at Eldersley caused a stir. There were a number of girls on the verandah. He smiled and said, 'Good evening,' before entering the hallway, where he was met by Amy and Matron. 'Constable Fraser, I can't thank you enough for coming,' said Amy Graham. He could tell that she thought she may have gone too far. 'I should have asked *you*, shouldn't I, instead of doing it through Sergeant Haines?'

'It isn't a problem, Mrs Graham,' he replied gallantly.

'Annabelle will be downstairs in a few minutes. Do you know where to go? If you don't, you could wait and follow the bus.'

'It's the school I attended, Mrs Graham. I could find my way there blindfolded.'

'Fancy that! You must have been to some dances there in your time, then?'

'Quite a few. Does Annabelle . . .?'

'She knows you're on duty,' said Amy with a knowing smile. 'I wouldn't embarrass you by suggesting otherwise. Here she comes now.'

Annabelle was a credit to Matron and Amy. Her hair had been puffed up behind her ears, and make-up made a huge difference to her appearance. It was a very different Annabelle who stunned the other boarders when she stepped onto the verandah.

'I didn't know you were coming, Annabelle.'

'I thought you said you weren't going?'

'When did you get that skirt?'

Fraser reappeared to collect the new-look Annabelle and shepherd her, in front of the awaiting girls, to his car. This he did with confidence and grace, ensuring that she was comfortably seated, her new skirt tucked within the confines of the passenger seat, before closing her door and climbing into the driver's seat. As he pulled away, he gave the girls on the verandah a cheery wave. And that, thought Amy, will make every boy they dance with tonight seem clumsy and immature. And that, thought Matron with equal satisfaction, will do Annabelle more good than all the psychologists in the world.

In the grounds of Balmoral Boys', Fraser and his charge could hear the pounding of music and see the flash of coloured lights. Outside the hall were clusters of boys awaiting the arrival of the talent. One boy was bragging of his ability to single-handedly undo a bra strap, while another was expounding the pleasures of French kissing. Several were awaiting the arrival of the bus from Eldersley, in particular of Josie St John. She was, they said, 'a fox', an analogy with which some female contemporaries might have agreed, if for slightly different reasons.

'If you don't mind, Annabelle, we'll sit here until they start moving into the hall. It's always better to arrive a little late.' Annabelle, who was having qualms about walking past all those boys, wholeheartedly agreed. She'd rather have sat with Fraser all night than go to the dance at all. While they were waiting, Fraser sounded her out on the subject of the day girl whose brother owned the Goulburn gym.

'Oh, that must be Philippa Papandopoulos,' said Annabelle. 'I didn't know her brother owned a gym. Her father's got a sheep property. He's one of the wool barons. Everyone calls them that because they're disgustingly wealthy. When we had our last open day he came in a limousine, and he had a gold medallion around his neck.'

'I suppose a lot of the girls have wealthy parents?'

Annabelle nodded. 'Some of them have parents with businesses in the city, but others come from farms and properties that their families have owned for years. When the daughters get married, they hyphenate their names and haunt the society pages – having a pedigree is very important.'

'Not to everyone, Annabelle. Some people make it without any help from their families at all. If *you* know who you are, it doesn't matter what sort of label society puts on you.'

'That's easy for you. You've probably got a family.'

'A large one, as it happens – aunts and uncles all over the place, and cousins I've hardly met. But no pedigree.'

When the action moved inside the hall, Fraser and Annabelle did too. Annabelle was the envy of every girl and stole a satisfactory proportion of Josie St John's limelight. She danced with partners other than Fraser. 'All you have to do is smile, Annabelle,' was his advice. 'I can assure you that most of these boys are terrified that you're going to say no. If you see one of them hovering, a little encouraging smile will do his ego the world of good. Besides, you're pretty when you smile.' It was sound advice. She tried it and it worked. She was even approached by the tall boy who'd been dancing with Josie St John.

It was during Annabelle's dance with Josie St John's partner that Fraser, patrolling the grounds at the back of the hall, saw what might have been an exchange. The boys attempted to wander off. He collared one of them, but the other melted into the darkness. He ordered the lad to empty his pockets.

'Who the fuck are you to tell me what to do? Mind your own bloody business.'

'This *is* my business and this is my ID. Now empty your pockets.'

The bluster turned to pleading. 'Look, it's only a couple of joints. If my parents find out, I'm in deep shit. For Christ's sake, it's just a measly couple of smokes. I could get expelled. What are you going to do?'

'I'm going to record your name in my little black book, when I can be sure I have your correct name. We're going to see someone in the hall right now, so I can identify you. Then, I'm going to expect a little cooperation from you about where this stuff is coming from and how it's getting into the school. Savvy?'

'I don't know where it's coming from! I just heard that someone had a few joints, that's all. I don't know nothing about where he gets it.'

'Perhaps I can ask him?'

'He'll kill me.'

'You have a choice – a little displeasure from your supplier, or a great deal more displeasure from your parents and the headmaster. What's it to be?'

After the dance, Fraser drove Annabelle down the main street of Bowral and bought milkshakes, which they drank in the car. Apart from the fact that he was hungry, he wanted to ensure that Annabelle arrived back at the school after the other girls. Might as well do the job properly.

There were several pairs of eyes peering out of dimly lit upstairs windows when he dropped Annabelle off. He parked conspicuously, handed her out and escorted her to the front door. Before she went inside, he gave her a folded slip of paper with his telephone number at the station. 'If you need to talk about anything, Annabelle – anything at all – please call me. If I'm not there, leave a message and I'll call you back. Okay?'

'Thank you,' said Annabelle. She knew it hadn't been his idea to take her to the dance, but she'd enjoyed herself. She took the paper he handed her and went upstairs.

Vandegaard had indeed done a runner. He departed only hours before the arrival of an Interpol report stating that someone answering his description, but using a different name, was wanted by the UK police. Haines circulated a description and details of Vandegaard's vehicle, and asked police in Sydney, Melbourne and Brisbane to check airport departure lists. He also sent Vandegaard's prints to Scotland Yard.

'Unless he's got several passports, we'll get him if he tries to leave the country. Bad bastard, by all accounts . . . Read that.' He slid the Interpol report across the desk to Fraser.

In view of the fact that Fraser normally occupied his time between traffic infringements, pub brawls and petty thefts, it seemed incredible that in the course of so many weeks he'd helped investigate a murder and was now involved in the search for an international criminal. 'Hans Vilmeister, alias Hans Vilheim, alias Hans Vanderholm,' he read. 'He seems to like the name "Hans". Maybe that bit's for real.'

Vandegaard belonged to a terrorist group suspected of carrying out bombings in central London between 1972 and 1974. He was believed to be an agent of the apartheid government of South Africa, and was credited with membership of a government-funded organisation conducting research into chemical and biological warfare, as part of the struggle to maintain white supremacy. According to reports, this organisation had experimented with the use of cholera and anthrax germs. Vandegaard was also believed to have been involved in the murders of several anti-apartheid activists, and the attempted murder of an African National Congress leader during a visit to London in 1973.

'Bumping off Radcliffe would have been child's play to this bloke,' said Fraser. 'If only we'd got the report earlier. Imagine being able to contact Scotland Yard and tell them we had their bomber under lock and key!'

'Yes, well, maybe we'll get him yet,' grumbled Haines. 'What puzzles me, though, is why he would want to draw attention to himself by killing Radcliffe – unless, of course, Radcliffe really had sprung him, which I find hard to believe. I don't see how he could have gained access to an Interpol report, and there's nothing in Vandegaard's résumé that looks even remotely suspicious. That rumour floating around that he had to get out of South Africa in a hurry would place him squarely in the anti-apartheid camp, wouldn't it?'

'Perhaps he started the rumour himself,' said Fraser, 'as a blind. You know – painted himself as the anti-apartheid hero escaping a regime with which the rest of the world was at odds.'

Haines nodded. 'You're probably right. He's the only one who could have suggested it. It must have amused him to see Radcliffe barking up the wrong tree.'

'And us,' said Fraser.

Shortly before lunch, Spinner came to Haines's office to report that the motor registry had come up with a match on the blue Vauxhall. 'It's DVF 823, Sarge, and its registered to a Harold Brand. I checked him out. He runs a business in Goulburn, and he seems to do a bit of everything – from conveyancing to bookkeeping and tax returns.

He also does a bit of snooping on the side . . . You know – dirty divorces, missing spouses and maintenance payments?'

'Where did you get this information?'

'I sniffed around . . . bought a few things in the shops near his office and chatted to the staff. Then I waited until I saw him go out and had a girly conversation with his secretary. Don't worry. She thinks I want to check up on my boyfriend. I told her I'd have to think about the fees.'

Haines was stunned by Spinner's audacity, not so much in approaching Brand's secretary, but in assuming that she could do so without clearing it through him. He was on the brink of chewing her out, but he had to admit that he would have applauded similar behaviour in Fraser. But Fraser was ranks ahead of Spinner and had years more experience. A little voice in his head said 'and Fraser's a bloke', but he pushed the thought away as politically unsound.

'As it turns out, Spinner,' he said, adopting what he believed to be a mildly admonitory tone, 'there's no harm done. But in future I don't want you to assume that you can conduct your own investigation. You should have told me what you planned to do. From now on, everything goes through me. Okay?'

'Yes, Sarge,' said Spinner despondently.

As she was about to leave his office, he added, 'The information you got is very useful. It's saved us quite a bit of leg work.'

TWENTY-SIX

At two that afternoon, Fraser received a call from Annabelle. She'd caught the bus into Bowral and was ringing from a public phone. 'There's something you ought to know that I haven't told anyone. I started thinking it might be important after all.'

'Are you happy to tell me over the phone?'

'Yes. It'll only take a minute, but I couldn't call from the school. One of the girls has been leaving the boarding house at night. I know because I'm often awake and my bedroom overlooks the back of the building. If I can't sleep, I sometimes sit at the window. I don't know who it is. She goes out through the kitchen door about midnight, sometimes two or three times a week. She goes up the stairs to the quad, then I lose sight of her. She's usually only gone for a few minutes, and I think someone lets her back into the kitchen, because she wouldn't be able to open the door from the outside – unless she leaves it open. I just thought you might want to know.'

'Thanks, Annabelle. I'm very grateful. When we find out who the night prowler is, and what she's doing, I'll make sure no one knows where the information came from.'

In passing this titbit to Haines, Fraser was surprised to learn that the latter already knew about the girl's nocturnal ramblings. 'I spotted her a few days after the murder, when I was doing a bit of prowling myself. I assumed it was a teenage prank and didn't follow it up. You never know, though. If it's a regular thing, we should get to the bottom of it. I'll leave that in your capable hands, shall I? Don't forget to take your thermals. It can get chilly up there at night.'

'Thanks,' said Fraser with feigned enthusiasm. He'd been trying to pluck up courage to call Victoria Delhunty, and he'd promised himself that tonight would be the night. Still, the fact that he had to spend a few hours at the school shouldn't stop him from making one phone call. He had a couple of days off and wanted to ask her to dinner. She could only say no.

His few hours at the school stretched into several. He waited for four hours that night, and the same the next night, Sunday. On Monday he'd almost convinced himself to pack it in when, like Haines, he saw a sliver of light at the kitchen door. A figure slipped through. It was one-fifteen. He'd stationed himself between two of the classrooms, a narrow gap that was completely in darkness. The girlish figure glided past, her features obscured by a head covering. She was making for the laboratory, which he knew was locked. She pushed something under the door and then retraced her steps. He was at a loss. If he challenged her she'd scream and wake the whole place, but if he let her go he wouldn't know who she was.

An owl hooted behind him, causing the girl to turn. The moon emerged from behind a cloud, allowing him to catch a glimpse of her face. All that remained was to discover what she was up to. When she was back inside Edwards House, he approached the lab and shone his torch through the glass panel. It illuminated an envelope. He had no way of getting it unless . . .

There was a wire coat hanger in the boot of his car, from which he fashioned a device with a hook at one end. This he inserted beneath the door. He could feel the envelope, but was he getting it closer or pushing it away? He shone his torch through the glass and cursed. It was further away than ever. He went back to his car for some masking tape that he kept in the glove box in case his radiator hose sprang a leak. He tore off a small section and wound it around the hook. Then he bent the wire at the end furthest from the hook, so that when he inserted the horizontal section and pulled back, the hooked end tilted up and could be placed over the envelope. When he got it out, he shone his torch on it. It was sealed and addressed to Dr Deitz.

Bernard Deitz stared at the envelope Haines held in his hand.

'How long have you been receiving these, Dr Deitz?' asked Haines.

'A few months . . . I don't know. What does it matter?'

'Do you know who's been sending them?'

'One of the bitches in the boarding house. I've got no idea which one. You're the policeman – *you* find out!'

'I have, Dr Deitz, and we'll be questioning her later. Why have you never reported this?'

'I would have thought that was obvious.'

'The girl is in possession of information you don't wish to be revealed?'

'Got it in one.'

'And you feared it would cost you your job?'

'Congratulations to the man in the blue suit and the funny tie.'

'And would this information be related to the reason you were asked to leave Berkeley Boys', Dr Deitz?'

'Ah, so we've been doing our homework, have we? That, Sergeant, was nothing. Were it not for . . . Well, anyway, I could have taken them to court for unfair dismissal if I'd wanted to force the issue. Nothing happened.'

'Were there other occasions when something *did* happen? What did this girl know about you? Blackmail is a serious offence. You might just as well tell us, because we'll get it out of her anyway.'

'One of the boys from Balmoral recognised me when he came here for a debate. Many years ago, I taught his brother at a school in Sydney. He . . . the brother . . . was a consenting partner in a relationship, but because he wasn't legally an adult, when it came out his parents wanted my guts.'

'If it was a consenting relationship, how did they find out?'

'We were seen, in my car. His father threatened to kill me, even after the boy explained that he'd been willing. That means nothing. I was a depraved monster and the kid was an angel of light.'

'So where does the girl come in?'

'How do I know? Maybe she's the kid's girlfriend.'

'How much have you paid her so far?'

Bernard Deitz snorted. 'What do you mean? She gets paid in kind.'

It was Haines's turn to look puzzled. 'In this note she's asked for twenty. I assumed that was twenty dollars?'

Deitz laughed insanely. 'She's asking for twenty joints . . . twenty bloody joints! The bitch has been bleeding me. I had a couple of plants for my own use, but now I have to buy it. It's costing me a lot more than twenty bloody dollars, I can tell you.'

'This girl's been blackmailing you for pot?'

'She, or whoever put her up to it. She can't be smoking it herself, or that human sniffer dog at the boarding house would be on to her. She's either selling it or giving it to someone else to sell.'

'But how do you get it to her if you don't know who she is?'

'I leave it under the bench outside the hall.'

'How can she be sure it's you who picks up the envelopes and not someone else?'

'Because I've got the lab keys, Sergeant, and I'm always in early.'

'Didn't the headmaster have keys?'

Deitz shrugged. 'He must have had a master, I suppose.'

'I was told he used to prowl around at night. Let's speculate that one night he saw what DS Fraser saw and let himself into the lab to recover one of these little notes. Did he challenge you with it, Dr Deitz?'

'That's pure speculation.'

'Which you refuse to either deny or confirm?'

'Which I am not *obliged* to deny or confirm.'

'Suit yourself, Dr Deitz.' Haines stood up. 'You can return to the school, but don't leave the area. You do realise I'll have to report this to Mrs Graham and the school board?'

'I am aware of that, Sergeant. You do your duty and I'll go back and write my letter of resignation. Anyway,' he added bitterly, 'why are you wasting your time trying to pin a motive for murdering bloody Radcliffe on me? Hasn't the Kaffir pissed off? Don't tell me doing a flit is no longer viewed as suspicious?'

'We like to keep our options open, Dr Deitz.'

Vandegaard's car was found at a railway station near Campsie. It was unlocked and all personal effects had been removed. There were no reports of any other cars being taken from the area. 'My bet,' said Haines, 'is that he's hopped a train for Sydney. From there he'll hire a car and drive to either Melbourne or Brisbane to get an international flight.'

'Why not Sydney airport?' Fraser asked.

'Too easy. We could be there in a couple of hours, and we know him by sight. I reckon he's decided to put some distance between himself and us and take his chances with the interstate police.

I've informed Scotland Yard that their bomber is on the move, and given them contacts in Melbourne, Brisbane and Sydney. The big cheeses are more likely to jump for Scotland Yard than they are for me. I've asked the feds and Immigration for passport checks at all airports. I'll wipe the smile off that bastard's face.'

'What're we going to do about the girl?'

'We, Fraser – by which I mean you – will wait for Miss Muppet tonight when she comes to pick up her parcel of pot.'

'Can you say that fast? Five times?'

'And,' Haines continued, 'when you have collected all of the pieces of pickled pot, you will bring them back to Radcliffe's office, where Amy and Matron and I will be eating cake and drinking tea.'

'Isn't this the last week of term?'

'Yes . . . works in rather nicely. The parents usually turn up on Saturday morning to take their darlings home, so Amy can enlighten them about their daughter's after-school activities.'

'Will we be charging her?'

'That's not the way it works, Fraser, when it comes to the children of the rich. I doubt Deitz will press charges, and Amy won't want adverse publicity. They'll come to a mutually satisfying arrangement, and if they can't, or if they give Amy any trouble, I'll step in and put the frighteners on them. The girl's committed two criminal offences.'

'We don't know for sure what she's been doing with the joints, but it would explain how they're getting into Balmoral. She probably took some with her to the dance.'

'It doesn't matter whether she's been giving them away or selling them,' said Haines. 'It's still supply. Who's at the receiving end will come out at interview, but we can't interview her without a responsible adult. I'd prefer that to be one of her parents. After we nab her, she'll put in a call to mummy and daddy, who will hotfoot it down here tomorrow. If she doesn't, Amy will do it for her. Amy won't want to spring it on them on Saturday.'

'What if the girl goes ballistic when I nab her?'

'A good thought. I don't want you accused of manhandling the minx. Take PC Spinner with you. The feminine touch, eh?'

'Spindles will love that.'

'I've always meant to ask,' said Haines, 'why you and Lockyer call that girl Spindles.'

'Have you ever seen her legs?'

It was a precaution worth taking. PC Spinner was delighted to share a little of the action. Being a woman in the police force was like being a one-legged man in an arse-kicking competition, she said. Fraser suggested that she should be the one to make the arrest and read the girl her rights. 'Cuff her, if you feel's it's necessary,' he said. 'The Sarge doesn't want me to lay a finger on her.'

'Quite right, too,' said Spindles. 'You never know where she's been.'

They settled down to wait in the shadows beneath the hall steps. Mercifully it wasn't a long wait (it was torture for PC Spinner to stand with another human being for any length of time without uttering a word). Eventually they were rewarded as the shadowy figure padded past. PC Spinner was seconds behind her, leaving only sufficient time for the girl to pick up the parcel they'd planted in the appointed place.

'Ms St John,' she said, shining her torch at the terrified girl, 'there's no need to be frightened. I'm a police officer, and I'm arresting you on suspicion of dealing in illegal drugs. You don't have to say anything, but anything you do say may be used in evidence. Do you understand?' Josie St John burst into tears. To Fraser's immense relief, she didn't struggle but came quietly with them back to the cottage, where she was ushered through the front door by Amy.

Amy rang Josie's parents then and there, regardless of the time. She hastened to reassure them that Josie was safe and well. When she outlined the trouble Josie was in, Mr St John refused to believe her. He insisted on speaking with Josie, whose tearful 'Daddy, I'm sorry . . . What will I do?' was enough to convince him that whatever his baby had done, she needed him. He rallied to the call. He and his wife would drive down in the morning, he told Amy brusquely.

The ordeal over, Josie St John's tears dried. She glanced around defiantly. 'Daddy will be ringing his solicitor by now,' she said with a laugh. 'Poor Andrew! I suppose Daddy will make him drop whatever he's doing and come down here tomorrow. But then, we pay him enough.' She yawned and stretched. 'Can I go to bed now?'

TWENTY-SEVEN

When Lucy Schumaker arrived for work on Wednesday, she found the contents of her boss's filing cabinet scattered over the floor. Harry was untidy, but he wouldn't have done this. And where *was* he? She dialled her boss's home number, but there was no answer. She bit her thumbnail. Once before, when the office had been ransacked, she'd called the police, and Harry had told her never to do that again. Anyway, there were no signs of forced entry.

She began picking up photographs and files. Many weren't labelled, so what she couldn't file she'd leave on Harry's desk. She'd just collected an armful of papers when she heard someone behind her. There were two of them.

'Don't be alarmed, Lucy,' said Haines. 'It is Lucy, isn't it?'

'Yeah. Who are you?'

'Detective Sergeant Haines, and this is DC Fraser.' He flashed his ID. 'Has Mr Brand had unwanted visitors?'

'No idea,' said Lucy warily. 'Talk to Harry. Maybe he was looking for something.'

'We'd *like* to talk to him. Do you know where he is?'

'No. He goes out a lot, and half the time I don't know what he's doing.'

'When did you last see him?'

'Friday. I only work Wednesdays, Thursdays and Fridays.'

'If he calls, Miss . . .?'

'Schumaker.'

'If he calls, Miss Schumaker, would you ask him to call DS Haines or DC Fraser at Bowral Police?'

'Do you think something's happened to him?'

'Do *you* think so, Miss Schumaker? Do you want to report him missing, or report a break-in?'

'No. I'll just tell him to call.'

In the car, it was Fraser who spoke: 'Someone looking for evidence he had on them?'

'Ten out of ten. Coincidence, do you think?'

'I eyeballed as many of those photographs as I could, and I didn't see anyone from the school. But if it was our murderer, and he found what he was looking for, there wouldn't be one of him – would there?'

'Or *her*,' said Haines. 'Male murderers don't use lipstick.'

'Not the macho ones. Do you think Radcliffe was . . .?'

Haines shook his head. 'According to Amy and the Delhunty woman, Radcliffe was into militant piety, not sex, straight *or* bent. I'm inclined to agree. Why would he pursue other people's indiscretions if he had peccadillos of his own?'

'We could get a warrant and go through Brand's files.'

Haines grunted. 'I will, when he contacts us.'

'*If* he contacts us,' said Fraser. 'His secretary made it fairly obvious her boss wouldn't want to cooperate with the police.'

'Pull him in, then. Spinner's got his details. If he was digging up dirt for our murder victim, he might have a good idea who the murderer is.'

'Why wouldn't he come to us?'

'Maybe there was something in it for him.'

'Blackmail, do you mean?'

'It's possible.'

Fraser raised his eyebrows. 'Not a very smart thing to do.'

At four they learned that a blue Vauxhall had been sighted by a local pig farmer at the bottom of a ravine. It was the second time, said the angry pig farmer, that a stolen vehicle had been dumped on his property. The first one he'd been able to tow back to the road, but this one was in thick scrub – and he wanted it removed. The police should do something about abandoned cars, since they obviously didn't know how to stop them being stolen in the first place.

Spindles delivered the message, and she had another: 'Molly Doherty's neighbour rang, Sarge. Doherty's at it again. Neighbour heard Molly screaming. I'm going around now, if that's okay.'

Haines was thoughtful. 'Take the cage, Spinner. I'll leave you to cuff Doherty. I know you've been dying to do it. Fraser and I will follow in the car, then we'll head out to McBain's to check this Vauxhall.' Spindles smiled broadly . . . too broadly. 'And no rough stuff,' he added.

'Okay. But who'd believe him if I *did* put the boot in? Look at the size of me and the size of him.'

'By the book, please, Spinner! And send Fraser in before you leave.'

'Reckon he's with the car?' said Fraser.

'McBain didn't say. Scrub's too thick. He thinks it's been abandoned.'

'If Brand went off the road on Friday, he's been there five days.'

'Don't jump to conclusions. He might have done a bunk if he

knew someone was after him.' He peered into the road. 'Put your foot down. I don't want Spinner getting to Doherty's too far ahead of us. I told her she could cuff him, by the way.' Fraser switched on the siren. When they pulled into Doherty's street, the driver's door of the cage was open, as were the doors of the ambulance. There was the usual gallery of neighbours. Two stretcher-bearers were coming out of the front door, but there was no sign of Spindles. Haines and Fraser waited at the ambulance.

'How bad is it?' said Haines to one of the ambulance men.

'Pretty bad. He's unconscious. I think maybe his skull's fractured.'

'He?'

'Christ!' said Fraser, staring at the body on the stretcher. 'It's Doherty!' At that moment, two people appeared in the doorway of the house. One of them was Spindles, who was looking foolish and dangling a pair of handcuffs. The other was Molly Doherty, clutching a frying pan. When she saw the policemen at the gate, her face lit up. She waved the pan. 'I did what you said, Sergeant 'Aines,' she bawled, loud enough for half of Bowral to hear. 'I give 'im one, just like you told me.'

'Let's get out of here,' mumbled Haines.

'What about Spindles?'

'She needs the experience.'

The ravine on McBain's property was steep, and only the top half of the Vauxhall was visible. The rest was buried in a sea of lantana. Although the driver's side door was open, it was impossible to see inside from the roadway. Fraser didn't fancy doing a Br'er Rabbit. Flynn and Lockyer were standing in the access road, arguing with McBain, who was gesticulating. He was wearing gumboots and overalls, and his tractor was idling a short distance away.

'Tow truck organised, Flynn?' yelled Haines.

Flynn looked sheepish. 'Just about to call one, Sarge.' He headed back to the car. Lockyer was holding a length of rope. He'd been trying to persuade McBain to attach it to the Vauxhall and pull it out with the tractor.

'Not planning on hanging yourself with that?' said Haines hopefully.

'No, Sarge. I just thought Mr McBain might be able to get the thing out.'

'And Mr McBain naturally prefers not to risk his tractor because he needs it to earn his living. Right?' Lockyer nodded, and Andy McBain smiled.

Haines extended his hand. 'Haven't seen you for a while, Andy. How's the Missus?'

'She's okay.'

'This is DC Fraser, and you've met Constable Lockyer.' Fraser shook hands with McBain while Haines turned to Lockyer, pointing at the rope. 'Put that back in the car, Lockyer, and think about why it isn't advisable to ask members of the public to consort with Joe Blakes.'

'He's the one with the gumboots,' grumbled Lockyer, as he turned to follow Flynn.

'Just a minute! That was well spotted.' He turned to McBain. 'I wonder, Andy, if you'd mind lending us your gumboots. Lockyer will return them as soon as he's been down to take a look at that car.' He turned to Lockyer. 'You won't, of course, touch the handle or the edges of the door, will you?'

'No, Sarge. Do you want me to attach the rope?'

'That would be helpful, provided we don't find your pinkies all over the bumper bar.'

Lockyer removed his boots and waited until McBain did

likewise. McBain kicked his gumboots in Lockyer's direction. 'Most of the pig shit's on the outside.'

Lockyer stepped gingerly into the boots and, with a martyred expression, began scrabbling down the ravine. It took him several minutes to reach the car. A couple of times he disappeared beneath a canopy of lantana. He skidded the last few feet, the car breaking his fall, and as he thumped against it a cloud of flies rose from the interior.

'Shit,' said Fraser.

'You think there's someone in there, don't you?' said McBain.

'It's possible,' said Haines.

Attention was focused on Lockyer who, clutching the roof of the car, made his way to the driver's side door. An exclamation escaped him.

'Jesus! There's a bloody body in there, isn't there?' said McBain.

Haines didn't answer. Lockyer kicked shut the driver's door, one hand covering his nose. Then he threw up.

'He'd better not get any of that on my gumboots,' said McBain.

Lockyer got to the top of the ravine just as the tow truck arrived. He was spitting and wiping his mouth.

'I knew you had guts, Lockyer,' said Fraser, 'but did you have to leave them down there?'

'Animals have been snacking.'

'Call Jamieson,' said Haines. 'I'm going to enjoy handing him this one. Oh, and ask the Schumaker girl about Brand's next of kin. If there isn't one, she'll have to do the ID.' A sudden thought struck him. He turned to Lockyer. 'There *is* enough face left to ID, isn't there?' Lockyer nodded. 'Good. Now, give Mr McBain back his gumboots, Lockyer, and help the truckies get the car out of the infernal pit.'

TWENTY-EIGHT

For Mervyn Jamieson, it was all part of the territory. He wore a mask, protective clothing and rubber gloves, and asked everyone to stand well back (not that anyone wanted to crowd him). It was difficult to gauge his reactions, because afterwards he sounded as chirpy as ever, leaving Haines to conclude that he was from another planet. 'How long do you think he's been dead?' he asked, when the body was zipped and in the back of the ambulance.

Jamieson peeled off his gloves. 'Several days. Can't be precise until the autopsy, but the smell was a dead giveaway.'

'Cause of death?'

'Can't be definite about that either, but I can tell you his neck was broken. It could have occurred as a result of plunging into the ravine. Possibly he had a heart attack and veered off the road? Who knows? We shall see what we shall see.'

'I need to know if there are any similarities with Radcliffe's death,' said Haines, following Jamieson to his car. 'It would be handy to know whether his neck was broken before he went into that ravine.'

'You want to know whether he was murdered?'

'Yes. When could you let me know?'

Jamieson was thoughtful. 'The body's a mess. Foxes . . . or wild dogs. Apart from that, there's not a mark. I'll have a look at him tonight and let you know first thing. Best I can do.'

'Thanks,' said Haines, surprised that Jamieson was being cooperative.

As the car pulled away, Fraser joined him. 'Any luck?'

'Broken neck. Jamieson's going to let me know whether it happened before or after the car went over the edge. I got the feeling he *thought* it was similar to Radcliffe's. He said there wasn't a mark on the body, apart from those made by animals.'

'Was he married?'

'No idea. When you pop back to Goulburn, get a home address from his secretary. There weren't any keys, because I got Jamieson to check. If he lived alone and there are no spares, you'll have to break in.'

'I might take Spindles,' said Fraser, 'in case the girl gets upset. They might have been . . .'

Haines snorted. 'Bollocks. He was old enough to be her father.'

'So?'

'Okay, so he might have got lucky, but does he strike you as lucky? Take Spinner, provided she isn't arresting Molly Doherty.'

'Spindles wouldn't do that. Want me to drop you back at the station?'

'No. I need the car. Tell Lockyer to follow us. When we get back, you can take the one he's driving. Hope he hasn't thrown up in it.'

There was something about coming face to face with death that made Haines think about the life he didn't have. Peggy was right. He was married to his job and another divorce was inevitable. What would he do? What *could* he do? He drove into the school grounds and parked. Once inside the office, he waved dismissively at Brenda Stokes to indicate that he didn't wish to be announced. Amy's office door was open, so he stuck his head around and knocked.

She looked up and smiled. 'Come in, Edward, and take a seat.'

Then she stood up, shut the office door and sat next to him. 'I can't talk to you from the other side of a desk.'

'I suppose the last people to sit in these chairs were Mr and Mrs St John. How did it go? I take it you didn't need us?'

She shook her head. 'We needed a third chair for the family solicitor. He was a sensible man, but Josie's father did most of the talking . . . bullying really. I don't like Mr St John. He said that the college had knowingly employed a pædophile, and that if any action were taken against his daughter, he'd sue us for exposing her to moral danger.'

Haines chuckled. 'I bet that didn't go down well.'

'It did not! I told him that it was his daughter who had brought disgrace upon the school. I said that in defending her rather than correcting her, he was encouraging her to become a moral vacuum. I *may* have indicated that I thought she was one already. I said I would not be bullied or threatened, nor would I tolerate a student who blackmailed staff to obtain drugs, then supplied those drugs to children at another school for a share in the profits. I told him how instantly Josie's crocodile tears had evaporated. I said I found her lack of contrition appalling, and that if she believed she could get away with anything because of her family's wealth and influence, she was wrong. She was not above the law. I told him that although she may be too young to prosecute, she wasn't too young to be expelled.'

'Did that take the wind out of his sails?'

'Enormously. He didn't fancy having his daughter expelled.'

'So the girl's coming back?'

'Not unless she writes a letter of apology to me, and one to Dr Deitz and the headmaster of Balmoral. She must indicate that she truly regrets her actions and is aware of the enormity of what she's done. I think Mr St John understands that some of the responsibility rests with him. No letters of apology, no acceptance next term.'

'Good one, Amy. You have to stand up to these people.'

Amy looked at him fondly. 'Thank you, Edward, but you didn't come here to applaud my dealings with the St John family. Has something else happened?'

Haines nodded. 'I don't know if I told you that Radcliffe hired a private detective to dig up dirt on staff?' Amy shook her head. 'It was your Mr O'Flaherty that alerted me to his existence. O'Flaherty noticed him paying regular visits to the office, and even remembered part of his registration number. We tracked him down to an office in Goulburn. Unfortunately, someone got to him before we did, because his office had been ransacked and this afternoon we found him dead. Don't know if it's murder, but if it is, we can rule out the Flying Dutchman, so it could still be another member of staff.'

'Are you saying Hans Vandegaard may *not* have murdered the headmaster?'

'That's what I'm beginning to think.'

'How can you be sure the two deaths are connected?'

Haines shrugged. 'I can't. The thing is, we haven't found any of the reports the bloke gave to Radcliffe. They were probably taken from the cottage on the night of the murder, but Brand would have kept copies. That's possibly why his office was ransacked.'

'It does seem coincidental. Is there anything I can do?'

'You could resign. That way I'd be sure you were safe.'

Amy flushed. 'I most certainly will *not*. I've made a commitment to see the college through this crisis, and that's what I intend to do.'

Haines shrugged. 'I thought you'd say something like that. It was worth a try.'

'There are only two days left before end of term, Edward. You're worrying unnecessarily. If we *are* harbouring a murderer, he or she has absolutely no motive for attacking me.'

Edwards House was alive with activity: bags were being packed, rooms tidied and phone calls made. The chatter in the common room turned from boys to who was going where and doing what; there was talk of villas in Italy, haciendas in Spain, skiing in Switzerland, yachts to Monte Carlo and flights to the Bahamas. Most of the girls were being picked up by car, but a few, including Annabelle, would be travelling to Sydney by coach.

The two days passed uneventfully, until the only thing between the excited boarders and their holidays was the end-of-term party. The party was a tradition, held in the common room in lieu of the usual Friday-night dinner. It included not only the boarders, but teachers and administrative staff. Even Mr O'Flaherty was invited. He was one of the first to arrive, scrubbed and brilliantined, to what was undoubtedly the highlight of his social calendar. Ira had been bathed and forced to wear a tartan bow tie, but he made up for this by being allowed into the common room to perform his I'm-sitting-on-my-haunches-and-being-cute act in return for food.

Mr O'Flaherty had also taught him a new trick. 'W'd jer like ter see 'im do 'is dead act?' he asked the girls. Enough did, so Mr O'Flaherty, in a booming voice that brought the rest of the room to attention, called the dog from beneath the table where he was trawling for food. Ira (he pronounced it 'ear-ah') squatted at his master's feet, and Mr O'Flaherty pointed at him with the index and first fingers of his right hand. 'Bang!' he shouted, and several of the girls jumped. Ira dropped to the floor, rolled onto his back, kicked his legs a couple of times and was still. There was thunderous applause and Ira was suitably rewarded. He 'died' many times over the next half hour, spoiling the effect only slightly by rolling his eyes to determine where his next reward was coming from.

There were, of course, staff who couldn't attend. Amy thanked those present for their hard work, and apologised that Mr Vandegaard, Dr Deitz and Ms Delhunty could not be with them. Dennis Hinds, who was watching events from the far corner of the room, gave a knowing smirk. It had not, Amy suggested, been a happy time (here he sniggered), but she hoped the worst was over and that Eldersley would not be subjected, in second term, to the tragedy and disruption that had marked the first.

Mrs Westham applauded and said, 'Hear, hear.' Amy wished everyone, including the girls, a relaxing and happy holiday break. When she'd finished, she rejoined Matron, Chauntel Worsley and Miss Hancock, who were discussing the virtues of boiled fruit cake. As she joined them, Miss Hancock tore her attention away from matters culinary. 'You didn't mention Madelaine. Shouldn't she be here by now? I haven't seen her anywhere.'

'She did say she'd be a little late,' said Amy, 'and I didn't want to embarrass her by drawing attention to her absence. But when another half an hour passed and Madelaine Everhardt had still not appeared, even Amy thought it strange.

'Perhaps she's ill,' said Matron. 'I'd better go and check. Shan't be long.' She collected the key from the kitchen and left by the back door. The evening was chill. She shivered, covering the ground between Edwards House and the art room quickly. She was puzzled that there were no lights. There were always lights; even when Madelaine wasn't working late, she'd leave a lamp burning. As she stood outside the darkened building, Matron's first impulse was to go back to the party and tell Mrs Graham that Madelaine had gone home, but then she went to the front of the building and let herself in. She felt for the light switch in the hallway. It was a dim, low-wattage globe.

'Madelaine? Are you there?'

She listened. Nothing. She walked to the end of the hallway and stopped at the door to Madelaine's classroom, reaching around the corner of the door jamb, feeling for the light. Before her hand found the switch, her foot touched something. In the meagre light from the hallway she could see that it was a walking stick, the one Madelaine kept inside the door. Beyond it was a blackness, like spilled ink, and a pale arm resting in that blackness, palm upwards, fingers slightly curved as if they'd just released something precious. The distance to the front door seemed immense and the darkness overpowering. There was another door behind her, into the storage room. What if the attacker was in there? She managed to force her fingers onto the switch, flooding the room with light.

Madelaine Everhardt was lying in a pool of blood, her eyes open. There were no visible bloodstains on her dark clothing; nor were there any marks on her face. Blood had soaked into the wooden boards. It was going to be hard to get out, Matron thought mechanically. She began to shiver, and then, like a night nurse, she turned off the light and retraced her steps. She walked slowly, listening to the sounds of revelry coming from the common room, and Ira's excited barks. They seemed to be coming from a distance. She went to the front door, opening it with her key.

Amy rushed to her side as she appeared in the doorway, turning her around and leading her into the kitchen. Matron was shivering. There was a coat on the back of the kitchen door that belonged to Mrs Watkins. Amy wrapped it around Matron's shoulders. Miss Hancock, who'd followed them out of the common room, was standing at the kitchen doorway.

'Is it bad, Mildred?'

'She's dead.'

'Laetitia,' said Amy, 'stay with Mildred and make her a cup

of tea. Don't go back into the common room, and please don't tell anyone who comes into the kitchen that anything is wrong. Will you do that?'

'What's happened?'

'Just look after Mildred for the moment and don't let anyone in through the kitchen door.'

Miss Hancock placed the old black kettle on the stove and thought of the time Amy had made her a cup of hot, sweet tea after the death of the headmaster. Something equally terrible must have happened.

Haines was just settling down to watch the football when the phone rang. 'Tell Fraser to drop whatever he's doing and go straight there. I'm leaving now.'

Amy, who'd been listening for his car, met him on the verandah. By now, everyone in the common room knew that something was wrong; one of the girls had seen Amy leading Matron into the kitchen and had told the others. Amy thought it best to say something, so she told them there had been an accident and asked them to remain in the common room until the arrival of the police. On no account, she said, must anyone walk in the grounds.

Dennis Hinds, his face pale, tried to push past her. 'That goes for staff too, Mr Hinds. Stay with the girls, please.'

'It's Madelaine! Something's happened to Madelaine!' She put a restraining hand on his arm, but he shook it off. 'There might be something I can do.'

'There's nothing anyone can do,' she said quietly, and his face contorted.

Haines entered the common room and asked everyone to remain in the building. Fraser, who arrived shortly afterwards, did the rounds to ensure that all of the windows and doors were locked. Amy handed Haines the art room key. 'I won't come with you,' she said wearily. 'I have no desire to . . . I'll stay here, where I might do some good.'

'I'm sorry, Amy. It's my fault you've ended up in all this. I suggested you to that slimeball, Fairweather. I had no right, and I didn't even have the courtesy to tell you I'd dropped you in it. I should have kept my mouth shut – it was his problem, not yours.'

'I know you recommended me to Gilbert Fairweather, Edward, because he told me. I don't mind, and for what it's worth, it wasn't you or Fairweather who prompted me to take the job. It was Matron. I could see the problem she was having with Annabelle, and I wanted to help. I've kept things going for a while, but now . . .'

'Talk to them. Better coming from you, eh? Or would you rather I . . .?'

'No, Edward. I'd rather do it myself. Word's got around anyway, and some of the girls are in tears. I'll just be making official what they already suspect. I think I might stay in the boarding house tonight, so Matron's not alone. Could you . . .?'

'There's a settee. I'll bunk on that.'

'Thank you, Edward.'

Amy returned to the kitchen, where Matron and Miss Hancock were still sitting, the latter chatting nervously, the former morbidly silent.

'Do you think you're up to coming back to the common room, Mildred?' asked Amy. 'We'd better make some sort of announcement.' Matron nodded. 'And I was wondering, Mildred, if you had any . . . alcohol. It probably sounds peculiar, but Madelaine loved to toast absent friends. I thought we could remember her the way she would have wanted to be remembered.'

'There's a bottle of brandy in my room and some dry ginger in

the refrigerator. That's all I've got. The glasses are above the sink.'
Amy and Miss Hancock set about putting glasses on a tray and
waited with it at the bottom of the stairs. When Matron returned
and the three women re-entered the common room, they presented
a strange sight. Amy put the tray on the table and Matron poured
medicinal proportions of brandy into glasses, which Miss Hancock
handed out.

'Some of you will by now have guessed that Ms Everhardt has
met with an accident and is . . . no longer with us.' There was
a little scream, but Amy held up her hand. 'There's no point in
getting hysterical. I think it's more fitting to salute her, and I'm
asking you to drink a toast to her charm and vivacity, her apprecia-
tion of beauty and her love of life. For those of you who can't drink
brandy neat, there's dry ginger ale on the table.' She held up her
glass. 'To Ms Everhardt.'

'To Ms Everhardt.'

TWENTY-NINE

Mervyn Jamieson arrived at the school at eleven, long after the distraught boarders had gone to bed. He pronounced life extinct, donned his surgical gloves and began his examination of the body. 'No damage to her hands or fingernails, so nothing to suggest that she put up a fight.'

'She used the walking stick as protection,' said Haines, remembering the evening he and Fraser let themselves into the art room. At the time he'd thought she was posturing, but perhaps she had reason to be frightened. 'Maybe she was taken by surprise.' It could only, he thought, be someone she'd let into the art room, or someone with a key . . . someone she didn't expect to attack her.

Jamieson lifted Madelaine's head, only to discover that her voluminous hair had matted into the congealed blood. He cursed. 'Need to get her onto the slab, but it looks as though her neck's broken, probably the result of a heavy blow to the back of the skull in the vicinity of the left ear. Ruptured a few blood vessels. You can take your holiday snaps now, and I'll make a start on her after lunch.' He pulled off his gloves and got up, slowly and painfully. 'Arthritis,' he explained. He looked at his watch. 'Won't be much traffic at this time. I'll be in touch.' He snapped his bag shut and headed for the door, pausing only to say to Fraser, who'd just entered, 'You'll need water, Constable . . . or scissors. She's stuck to the floor.'

It was a subdued party of boarders that assembled on the verandah to await their holiday transportation. Missing was Josie St John, whose parents had picked her up the day before. Mary Grimes, in the same seat she'd occupied the morning the headmaster's body was discovered, couldn't help thinking that it was the second time her friend Josie had missed the excitement. She was itching to telephone her, and would do so as soon as she got back to Sydney.

Annabelle Friedman was more subdued than the rest. The people with whom she was fostered were kind, but she felt their lack of kinship and she had little in common with their daughters. She was fighting an inner battle, one that Mrs Graham had initiated with her announcement that Madelaine Everhardt, with whom Annabelle had a good relationship, was dead.

Cars began to enter the driveway under the watchful eyes of Mr O'Flaherty and Ira, but not just ordinary cars: there were BMWs, Mercedes and Rollers – the *crème de la crème* of motors. One by one, girls in jeans and sneakers disappeared into their lavishly appointed interiors, amidst shouts of 'Call me you when we get back!' and 'Don't forget to send me a postcard!' and various other injunctions that would probably never be carried out. As the numbers dwindled, Annabelle's anxiety increased. Soon the bus would arrive, and then it would be her turn and it would be too late. She ran back into Edwards House in search of Matron.

'You want me to ring the police, Annabelle? Why?'

'There's something I have to tell them . . . well, Fraser . . . the one that took me to the dance. It's important, Matron. It's about Mr Radcliffe. If I don't do it now, I'll probably never be able to make myself do it. Please, Matron.'

'You'd better come to my room. I'll get the number for you.'

'I've got the number, Matron. He gave it to me. I've got it right here.' Annabelle's sense of urgency was acute. When they reached the door, Matron pointed to the phone by her bed.

'I can't be too long, Annabelle. I have to be there when the parents arrive. There are probably more of them coming up the driveway this minute.'

'He'll come, Matron. I know he will. If you want to go, I'll be straight back down. I promise.'

Fraser had just stepped out of the shower when Lockyer called. 'Sorry, mate. I just took a call from a chick called Annabelle. Ring any bells? She wants you real bad. Says it's urgent. I told her you weren't starting till this afternoon, but she wouldn't take no for an answer. Made me promise to ring you at home and tell you that she was leaving soon and had to see you before the bus came. She didn't say what bus.'

'I'm on my way,' said Fraser. 'Ring Haines at home and tell him the little screamer is about to spill the beans. Say I've gone to the school to catch her before she leaves. I think he'll want to be there.' He rang off before Lockyer could complain, pulled on his jeans and a clean T-shirt, ran a comb through his hair and a toothbrush over his teeth, grabbed his car keys and left.

Annabelle was waiting on the verandah. She stood up, agitated and pale, when Fraser approached. Matron motioned them to the sitting room and shut the door after them. Annabelle tried to get everything out at once, but her teeth were chattering. 'I couldn't tell anyone. I thought I'd be locked up, but I heard her . . . I heard her voice, and if I'd said something maybe she wouldn't be dead. I should have told you . . . and now she's . . .' Tears trickled down her face and her breathing was raspy.

'Hold it, Annabelle. I don't want you to say anything just yet. I just want you to stay calm. Don't worry about the bus. We'll make sure you get to Sydney. Just relax. I'm going to go and see Matron and ask her to ring your parents . . . your foster parents, and tell them you'll be arriving by car. Then I'm going to get you something to drink. What would you like?'

'I'm not thirsty. My bags are out there. If the bus comes, they'll probably put them on board.'

'I'll get them. Just sit tight and don't get uptight. All right?'

Annabelle managed a weak smile. She hoped he would still be this pleasant after he found out what she'd done.

Fraser found Matron and explained that Haines would be arriving soon and that they'd need speak to the girl without the added pressure of holding up the bus. They would undertake to get her safely to her foster parents. Would it be possible to get something to settle her nerves?

'I'll make some cocoa,' said Matron. 'Cocoa is best.'

Haines took longer than Fraser expected. It gave him an opportunity to explain to Annabelle that his sergeant would be present, and that he wanted Matron to be present, too. To his relief, Annabelle agreed. By the time Haines arrived, everything was ready to go.

'You do the questioning,' said Haines, 'since she's specifically asked for you. Read her her rights. Hope that doesn't frighten her off.'

Fraser began by asking Annabelle whether the things she wished to tell him could incriminate her. 'The police are under an obligation to follow certain rules. One of these is to warn you that what you tell us could constitute evidence against you . . . that it could be used against you, in court. I'm not saying this to frighten you. It's something I have to do. Is what I've told you clear?'

Annabelle nodded, but she'd gone white. Matron patted her reassuringly and Fraser started again: 'You said when I arrived that you had something to tell me, and you thought it might have a bearing on Ms Everhardt's death. Is that right?'

'Yes.'

'Take your time. Tell us what it is that's been worrying you. Start from the beginning.'

Annabelle took from her pocket a photograph and placed it on the table. It was the photograph Amy had found in her room. She moved it around the table so they could all see it, but it was clear that she alone was allowed to touch it.

'It's my mum. She was beautiful, and she could sing and dance. She used to tell me about how my dad left her . . . left both of us . . . and she had to work nights in this club to earn enough money to keep us and send me to school. He never came back to see if we were alive or dead. He just walked away.

'When Mum got sick, I asked her to tell me who he was. She promised that one day she'd tell me, but she died before that happened. It was horrible when she was in hospital. I was so lonely I thought about killing myself, but he said if I tried it they'd lock me up and throw away the key, but they locked him up instead.' She gave a triumphant little laugh. 'And then I came here. But I'd started to hate him . . . my real father . . . for not being there.

'When I got here, they'd arranged for me to see a counsellor and I've been seeing her once a month. She's okay. I go because it's someone to talk to who knows. One day she gave me a letter to give to Mr Radcliffe, and I steamed it open. It was an invoice, with his name on it. I had no idea it cost so much. I couldn't understand why he should pay, so I . . . got into the office one weekend, when I knew he'd gone out, and tried to find out. I even spoke to that girl who works in the office . . . Brenda . . . but she couldn't tell me anything. Then, last time I was on holidays, Anita – she's one of the daughters of my foster parents – made a crack about me going to an exclusive school where they couldn't afford to go, and I realised that someone else must be paying my fees.

'I got back into the cottage, and this time I searched upstairs. I found a folder in his wardrobe. There were letters in it from the Department of Community Services about me, and a copy of one from him saying that I wasn't to be told he was paying. I knew he must be my father, and I decided to punish him.

'It was so easy to get into the cottage, that I started leaving notes. I'd leave them just inside the front door, so he'd think they'd been pushed underneath. I didn't want him to know I could get in. I wanted to make him feel frightened, like I had.'

'What did you write in these notes, Annabelle?'

'Horrible things,' she said, matter-of-factly. 'I told him he was a hypocrite and a liar, and that I wanted to kill him. I said he didn't deserve to live.'

'You didn't write anything specific? About you and your mother?'

'Why? Then he would have known who was sending the notes. And I didn't write them. I cut the letters out of magazines.'

'What happened the night the headmaster died?'

'It was Saturday, two days before they found him. I hadn't seen him around, so I went up to the art room after dinner and poked a long bit of wire through a crack in the garage door to see if his car was there. It wasn't. I looked outside, in the streets, but it wasn't there either, so I thought he was away. I waited until everyone had gone to bed and went to the cottage. I'd just climbed in when I heard voices.'

'Where did you climb in, Annabelle?' asked Matron who, in her anxiety, had forgotten that she wasn't supposed to ask questions.

'Through the bathroom window. I'll show you if you like. It's easy. Anyway, I was terrified. They were in the bedroom. One of the voices was Ms Everhardt's, but I didn't recognise the other. It was a man's voice, and he was talking softly. They were looking for something. I heard her say, "There might be more in his office," and "Don't be so bloody squeamish," and then they went downstairs. I heard her scream – not very loud, but it was a scream – and then I heard him shooshing her. They were either in the headmaster's study or the main office – I'm not sure which – for about another ten or fifteen minutes. I thought they'd never go. They must have had a key, because they left by the back door. I looked out of the window, but I couldn't see either of them. It was dark.'

'Then what did you do, Annabelle?'

'I went downstairs to leave the note inside the front door. I don't know what made me look into his study. I shone the torch through the door and it went straight onto his face. It was like when you shine the torch on a tarantula. His eyes shone. I screamed then, but when he didn't move I knew he must be dead. It felt funny, standing there with a letter saying I wanted him to die and he already had. I didn't feel sorry. I felt angry that I couldn't punish him any more. I couldn't even make him understand how much I hated him.'

'Where did you get the flower?' said Haines quietly.

'I climbed back out of the window and went up the street. At the top of the hill there's a house with a big garden. I got the flower from there and took it back.'

'And the lipstick?' Annabelle drew from around her neck a silver cylinder on a chain. She opened it and shook a lipstick into her palm.

'She always used the same colour. I used to watch her put it on when she was going to work . . . before she went into hospital.'

'So you decided to get even? For her death?'

'If he'd stayed with us she might have been alive, and I wouldn't have . . .' She was struggling to use the right word for something she'd probably still not come to terms with, something so ugly she'd tried to deny it ever happened. Using clinical terminology was a way of facing the reality and dealing with it, thought Haines. As it was, she came up with not one word but three: 'I wouldn't have been molested, and abused, and . . . raped.' After she said the word, tears coursed down her cheeks and her small frame convulsed with sobs. 'I felt so dirty. And there was no one there. He should have been there.'

Matron, who had for some time been holding Annabelle's hand, was crying. Caught up in the general catharsis, Fraser's eyes and even those of Haines were more than a little moist.

'Why didn't you tell me, Annabelle?' said Matron, putting her arm around the girl's heaving shoulders.

'I thought all of the staff knew.'

'No, Annabelle. I knew you were having counselling, but I wasn't told why. You poor, dear girl. Dirty indeed!' She brushed Annabelle's hair back from her face.

'What about the headmaster's inhaler?' said Haines, anxious to reach the end of the story.

'I started having an attack. I thought I was going to die. There was an inhaler in his hand, but I had to get his fingers open to get it out. I knew I couldn't climb back out of the window with-out . . . I couldn't breathe. I used it. Afterwards, when I got outside, I vomited. I couldn't bear the thought that I'd used something that had been in his mouth. Every time I thought about what I'd done I wanted to be sick.

'And your nightmares?'

'Always the same,' said Annabelle, shuddering. 'I'd be in his office, searching for the inhaler. His fingers were curled around it and I could feel them getting tighter, not wanting to give it up. I had to pull them, uncurl them. And then, when I almost had it, he would grab my wrist and look at me. He was alive, not dead. I'd scream and scream and scream.'

'What kind of woman was your mother, Annabelle?' asked Haines, changing the subject.

'She used to laugh a lot, before she got sick. She liked parties. She was kind. She had lots of friends.'

'Was she narrow-minded? The sort person who would condemn people for lapses of morality or making mistakes?'

'No. She either liked people or she didn't. It had nothing to do with . . . She didn't judge people.'

'She sounds nice. I wonder what made you think that a beautiful, broad-minded, fun-loving woman like your mother could have fallen in love with a narrow-minded, pudding-faced puritan like the headmaster?' Matron looked disapprovingly at Haines.

'She married him, didn't she?' Annabelle responded.

'Indeed, but for what reason? We all make mistakes, and I suspect your mum came to appreciate hers very soon after the marriage. It lasted less than twelve months. In fact, I think it was hastened to a conclusion when your mother met someone she could really care about and you were conceived. Or maybe you were already conceived before she became Mrs Radcliffe. I'm only guessing, but the facts suggest it.'

'What facts? How do you know so much?'

'I'm a policeman. I know that Horace Radcliffe wasn't your biological father. There are documents to prove that. Who your real father was, I don't know – nor do I know why he left you. Only your mother knew that. I'm sorry.'

'Why did he pay for me, then?'

'He walked out on your mother when she was nursing you, simply because he believed – had taken great pains to prove – that you were not his child. He was an unforgiving man. He made no attempt to provide for you or your mother because he was the kind of person who believed that lapses of morality shouldn't be rewarded. Perhaps, when he found out what had happened to you, he felt guilty and saw things in a different light. He might have felt responsible, you being the innocent victim.'

'What's going to happen to me now?'

'Nothing, if I have anything to say about it,' said Matron.

'If you mean, are there any charges against you, the answer is no,' said Haines, ignoring Matron's interjection. 'You've simply joined the long line of people who had a motive for killing the headmaster. If you mean, what's going to happen to you in terms of your schooling, I think you'll find that Mrs Graham has some ideas about that. And for what it's worth, Annabelle, I don't think that telling us sooner would have altered the course of events. There's nothing you could have done to prevent Ms Everhardt's death.'

THIRTY

The administrative staff remained at the school for several more days, but the academic staff had gone. Haines was left with no suspects and no further clues. His interviews with the staff after the end-of-term party proved fruitless, and his superiors, apprised of the third murder, were considering taking matters out of his hands. The thought that some 'jumped-up ponce' might take over his office and his investigation incensed Haines to the point where he became almost unbearable. Lockyer was glad that Fraser bore the brunt of it.

Within an hour of Madelaine Everhardt's body being discovered, Haines had taken the precaution of stationing an officer outside her house. It was an old house (*circa* 1915), with an all-round verandah and a garden that was wild and overgrown. A weather-beaten wicker chair and wooden coffee table were against the eastern wall, where Madelaine had undoubtedly combined her morning coffee with the morning sun. Haines and Fraser let themselves in through the front door and were greeted by a black cat that assumed their sole purpose in coming was to feed her. Fraser found an opened tin in the refrigerator and spooned some into a plate.

Fraser could see Madelaine's touch everywhere, from the paintings on the walls to the books on the shelves. The mis-matched pieces of furniture in her bedroom were functional and beautiful. There were no frills, dolls or lace cushions – just a heavy, white damask quilt to complement the richness of the surrounding wood. There was nothing in the way of paperwork in the wardrobe, drawers or dressing table, he told Haines when he joined him in the living room. The latter was more of a studio, with an old upright piano at one end and an artist's easel at the other. On the easel was a half-completed canvas, at which Haines was staring.

'Don't tell me,' said Fraser. 'You don't know much about art, but you know what you like.'

'And it isn't that. What do you make of it?'

Fraser couldn't make anything of it, but he wasn't going to admit that to Haines. 'It's the back yard, of course. There's the jacaranda and the shed, and that little black bit there is the cat. It isn't finished, otherwise it'd be a lot clearer.'

'Has anyone ever told you you're full of shit?'

They searched every room. In a canister in the kitchen they found letters that confirmed Madelaine's next of kin, stated on her résumé as her daughter who lived in Western Australia. Next to the canister was a flowery greeting card of the sort Madelaine would probably not have chosen for herself. Haines read the inscription: 'To my darling Maddy from *the Menace*. Love you always.'

'That would be Dennis Hinds,' said Fraser. 'I thought he looked green around the gills last night. Mind you, everyone was looking stunned, but even Mrs Graham thought Hinds was taking it hard. "Dennis looks shattered," she said.'

'What makes you think this card's from Dennis Hinds?'

'Dennis the Menace . . . the comic strip character. Don't you read the Sunday papers? Come to think of it, Mr Wilson could be modelled on you.'

'Hinds lives locally, doesn't he? Did he go away for the holidays?'

'Yes to the first, and no to the second. He said he'd be con-tactable at home most of the time. I'll check.' He took out his notebook. 'Yep. You want him in for another interview?'

'The sooner the better. I'm running out of leads.'

It was Fraser who turned up the manila folder of handwritten and typewritten documents hidden beneath several pieces of music in the piano stool. 'I think,' he said slowly, 'these are the records that went missing from the cottage. They're reports, and they're signed by Brand. Listen to this: "My investigation reveals an earlier incident involving a fifteen-year-old boy, an incident over which Dr Deitz narrowly escaped criminal charges. Only the desire of the parents to protect the boy from publicity prevented the matter from going to court. Dr Deitz agreed to resign his post and seek psychiatric treatment, provided the headmaster agreed not to reveal what he knew to subsequent employers."' He pushed the document towards Haines. 'Look what Radcliffe has written at the top: "Not the first time Dr Deitz has transgressed!"'

'Who uses a word like transgressed nowadays, this side of the pulpit?' said Haines. 'The guy was definitely OT.'

'Don't you mean OTT?'

'No, I mean Old Testament. But he was OTT as well.'

'What about this!' Fraser read from another report: '"I have searched Mr Vandegaard's flat. He has a number of passports in different names, but apart from this I found no evidence of crimi-nal activity. My investigations have been hampered by the difficulty of obtaining information from the South African police, but I'm hoping for a breakthrough soon via a contact in Johannesburg." It doesn't seem to have occurred to either of them that his activities may have been political.'

'And this,' said Haines, picking up another: '"Ms Delhunty has been active in the women's movement for many years and is a supporter of equal pay for equal work, as well as the right of women to work *and* bring up children. At university, she edited a newsletter, the purpose of which was to expose instances of discrimination in the workplace and the professions. She reported, in this newsletter, instances of harassment against women. She is a professed champion of women's rights."'

'Here's one on Madelaine,' said Fraser. 'It says she was sent down from university and didn't ever graduate, and it claims she lied about her age. The guy here says he has a copy of her birth certificate that shows she was born in . . . Bloody hell! That would make her over sixty!'

'So? Some women are attractive at sixty, and others are dogs at twenty-five.'

'There's a whole page here,' said Fraser, 'that lists the age of every member of staff. It's in his handwriting. He's ranked them from the oldest to the youngest. Guess who's at the top?'

'Unless there's a prize, Fraser, just spit it out.'

'Mr O'Flaherty. He's seventy-two. Doesn't give the age of his dog. Then there's the librarian, Mrs Westham – she's sixty-four. Then there's the cook, Mrs Watkins – she's sixty-two. Then he's listed Madelaine. He's got fifty-four, but there's a question mark next to it.'

'And how old is Matron?'

'Forty-six, according to this. Not a young staff, is it?

Haines began rummaging through the reports. 'Must be something on Dennis Hinds. Did you see a report on Hinds?'

'No, but there should be one,' said Fraser. 'Why would Radcliffe leave him out? Unless, of course, he was Mr Clean.' Haines and Fraser searched the contents of the folder in vain. Dennis Hinds was mentioned on the age list as being thirty-nine, but that was all.

Fraser couldn't accept that Hinds had been having an affair with Madelaine Everhardt. 'She was more than twenty years older than him! When she was in her early twenties, he was being born. She was old enough to be his mother!'

'There's no substitute for experience,' said Haines. 'You were in with a chance there, too. She fancied you.'

'Don't be disgusting.'

'Careful, now. You're beginning to sound like Radcliffe.'

On Sunday morning, Amy drew up a substantial list of repairs for Mr O'Flaherty and suggested he make some changes to the garden. And there were, she told him, some pigeons nesting in the roof, because Matron could hear them rustling and chirping early in the morning. Mr O'Flaherty had several times cleared them out by crawling through the manhole in the kitchen ceiling, but he could only do this when the girls were away and Mrs Watkins wasn't cooking, 'on account o' the lice'.

Annabelle Friedman, Amy told Edward, would be returning to the school next term, as her foster parents had accepted Amy's offer to pay her fees. And, she added with satisfaction, she'd offered Victoria Delhunty the position Madelaine's death had made vacant. 'Victoria has a fine arts degree, Edward. I don't know why she'd want to do sport when she's qualified to teach something in which she excels. She's promised to think it over. I've inserted an advertisement for Vandegaard's replacement in the Sydney papers, and I've told Bernard Deitz he can stay until the end of the year and that we'll reassess his position then.'

'What about your position?'

'I'll stay on until we have a full complement of staff. I can't leave now, Edward – not with things the way they are. How's your investigation going?'

'It's going nowhere. The post-mortem results on Brand confirm that he was murdered. The results on Madelaine Everhardt should come in tomorrow, and we'll be interviewing Dennis Hinds again – when we can find him. Apart from that, I'm no closer to discovering who killed Radcliffe *or* Brand *or* Madelaine Everhardt. If I don't get a break soon, they'll send in the big guns and I'll be relieved. Not a state of affairs I relish.'

'I'm so sorry, Edward. I hope something happens soon.'

At ten the next morning, Haines received a call from Jamieson. 'I can confirm that her neck was broken by a massive blow to the head with the proverbial blunt instrument,' he said. 'Death probably occurred after the first blow.'

'And the weapon?'

'Well, I assume you're looking closely at that walking stick, but my feeling is that she was killed with something heavier. There were no shards or splinters in the wound, so whatever it is must be solid – maybe metal or some kind of heavy, smooth, solid wood. That's it. The written report is on its way.'

At eleven, he and Fraser were sitting opposite Dennis Hinds, who looked as if he hadn't slept for twenty-four hours. He was unkempt, unshaven, and smelled of stale sweat and alcohol. 'I'll get straight to the point, Mr Hinds. I believe that you were having an affair with Madelaine Everhardt. Is that correct?'

'Yes. I don't see the point in denying it.'

'And I believe that in the early hours of Sunday, 22nd May, you and she entered the headmaster's cottage to search for reports on members of staff, including yourselves. Is that also correct?'

Dennis Hinds looked at Haines in astonishment. 'How can you say that?'

'There was someone else in the cottage that night, Mr Hinds,

237

who overheard the two of you talking. You commenced your search in the bedroom upstairs. When you went downstairs, Ms Everhardt was heard to tell you not to be so bloody squeamish. Your voices were recognised. Our witness says you had a key to the back door. Is this correct?'

'Yes. I don't know where Madelaine got it. She may have had one for years.'

'Did you and Madelaine Everhardt conspire to kill Horace Radcliffe, Mr Hinds? Did you murder him in the early hours of Saturday morning and then return the following morning to search for records or to remove evidence that might incriminate you?'

'No. We were there on Saturday night . . . the early hours of Sunday morning. He was in his chair, dead. We didn't kill him. We only went there because we thought he was out. I panicked, but Madelaine stayed calm. She wiped everything clean – everything we'd touched. She said the police would be crawling all over the building, and she was right.'

'What time was this, Mr Hinds?'

'About two-thirty. Who was there? Who heard us?'

'I can't tell you that. You found a folder containing reports that the headmaster had been compiling. We know there was one on Ms Everhardt. Was there also one on you, Mr Hinds? What did it say?'

'He was having me followed. There's no other way he could have found out about Maddy and me. When he did find out, he used it against her. He was trying to make her leave.'

'I'll ask you again. Did you conspire with Madelaine Everhardt to kill the headmaster?'

'No! I can't abide the thought of killing. I couldn't kill anyone.'

'How can you be sure Madelaine Everhardt didn't kill him?'

'Because I know she didn't give a damn what Radcliffe knew.

238

She wasn't about to cave in. She told him that if she lost her position because of him, she'd make damned sure he was charged with blackmail. That's why she wanted the records. She wanted evidence. Said she'd fight fire with fire – that was how she put it.'

'Quite a woman,' said Haines. Hinds gave a bitter, almost hysterical laugh. He was on the edge. Haines and Fraser knew he was the key to some, if not all of it. They were so close, and if they pushed the right buttons it might come tumbling out. Dennis Hinds sat like a rag doll, his head bowed and his hands loose. He looked more like a little boy than a man of forty. Haines spoke quietly to him again.

'Women who don't let men push them around are rare – *real* women, the ones who haven't traded in their stilettos for a set of balls. She was tough, but she only had to snap her fingers and she could have had any man she wanted. You must have felt lucky.'

Dennis Hinds raised his head and focused his bloodshot eyes on Haines. 'Lucky? I've lost everything.'

'And do you feel she was to blame for this? Did she lure you onto the rocks?'

'No . . . I . . . I did that myself. She was always the sane one – practical and rational and sensible. I was the romantic. It was always "Be reasonable, Dennis," and "You know I can't do that, Dennis," or "Why do you want to spoil it, Dennis." I was besotted. I wanted to live with her, marry her, go away with her. I didn't want a sordid little affair, I wanted *her*.'

'But she rejected you. She didn't care enough about you to take you on full time. Was this on Friday afternoon? Did she tell you then that it was all over?'

'I told her I'd asked for a divorce. She couldn't believe that I'd been so stupid. That was the word she used. She said she didn't want to be responsible for inflicting misery on my family. She said

I was trying to force her to be the "other woman" . . . turn her into what she'd made it clear she could never be. She said we'd have to end it, and that the best thing I could do was go back to my wife and promise her it wouldn't happen again. She said that as far as she was concerned, it wouldn't.'

'You must have been devastated . . . and angry,' said Haines. 'What did you do?'

'Nothing. I didn't do anything.'

'You were angry, and yet you tell me that you just walked out?'

'Yes. I sat in the classroom for a couple of hours, and then I went to the common room. It wasn't until Mrs Graham said there'd been an accident that I realised something was wrong. I didn't hurt Maddy. I loved her.'

Haines groaned inwardly and Fraser's spirits sank. Possibly Hinds didn't kill Madelaine Everhardt, but they both felt certain he knew more about her death and getting it out of him wasn't going to be easy.

Haines decided on a tougher approach: 'I know there's something you're not telling me, Mr Hinds. Either you're lying, or you're not telling me the whole truth. If *you* didn't kill Madelaine Everhardt, then I think you might be able to tell me who did. The last person to see her alive, Mr Hinds, was her murderer, so if that wasn't you, who else would she have let into the art room? Who else had a key?'

'She was alive when I left her. I'd like to talk to a solicitor.'

Haines stared balefully at Hinds. 'For Christ's sake, give him a phone book and then lock him up.'

When Fraser returned, Haines had been on the phone. He was just replacing the receiver. 'According to Amy Graham, Hinds's wife's a Pommie, and she's the twin-set-and-pearls type. Was she about when you picked him up?'

'No. He appeared to be alone.'

'What about his car? Was that out front? He drives an HD Holden.'

'Not that I recall, and it wasn't in the garage, either, because the door was open when I arrived. He shut it before he came to the station.'

'Get his house keys and see if she's done a flit. In the meantime, I'll get Lockyer to broadcast the registration. I'm going to check on her passport, then I'll get onto Immigration. If she's taken the kids, it isn't going to be easy for her to get onto a plane.'

'You think *she* did it?'

'Why else would he clam up? He's the self-sacrificing type. He'll wait until she's in the air and then put up his hand for the murder. Her parents are in the UK, so that's where she's headed.'

Haines was right. Empty wardrobes and drawers told their own story, and there was evidence that Mrs Hinds had packed for three. What could not be packed had been left scattered around the floor of the girls' bedroom, including books, shoes, sporting equipment and stuffed toys. Fraser radioed in and then headed back to the station.

THIRTY-ONE

At three that afternoon, Hans Vandegaard was picked up by the Melbourne police while attempting to board a flight to the Middle East.

'I'd like to have seen his face when they fingered him,' said Haines. 'I've told them he's a suspect in a murder inquiry and that he's not to be extradited before we've had a crack at him.'

'Do you think he murdered Radcliffe?'

'It was a professional job and Vandegaard's a professional killer. We know now that Radcliffe was onto him, because we've got the evidence in that report – on top of which, he tried to do a runner. In a looking-guilty competition, he'd win first prize.'

'That's not what I asked.'

'Okay. I have a nagging doubt,' said Haines irritably, 'because I know he couldn't have killed Brand, but it's going to get the big guns off my back – and it means I won't be invaded by some upwardly mobile prick who'll take the credit for all of our leg work. I'm reporting in right now. I'll be suggesting to the inspector that we're very close to bringing both murder investigations to a close. Got any better suggestions?'

'No. Just doubts, like you. Do you mind if I nick off? There's a couple of things I'd like to do.'

'Such as?'

'Feed Madelaine Everhardt's cat. Her daughter will be here tomorrow, so she'll work out what to do with it then.'

'And?'

'I want to talk to Mrs Graham and Matron about security. Put it down to those nagging doubts.'

Amy rose from her chair and greeted Fraser warmly. 'I haven't had a chance to thank you for helping us with Annabelle. I can't tell you how much it was appreciated. And I understand it was you who cleaned the art room floor, for which I'm also grateful. I was going to do it myself, because I didn't feel I could ask Mr O'Flaherty, and Mrs Watkins would have been hysterical.'

'I didn't want you to end up with either a shrine or a horror museum on your hands. Maybe the floor could be sanded and polished? It wouldn't have to be a professional job. I could hire a sander and have a go at it myself, and then it would only be a matter of a couple of coats of varnish.'

'Would you really be prepared to help? According to the executive director, the school isn't flush with money. Mr O'Flaherty does his best to hold things together, but the buildings aren't getting any younger and there are some jobs for which we can't avoid using tradesmen.'

'No plumbers and electricians amongst the parents?'

'I'm thinking along those lines,' said Amy. 'It's what the Church did – call on parents with expertise. I don't see why it should be different now. The less we spend on maintenance, the more we can spend on equipment for their daughters.'

Fraser nodded. 'Anyway, what I really came to discuss, Mrs Graham, is security. When the administrative staff go, there'll be no one here, and we've got three unsolved murders. I'd like to go over the boarding house again. There's also the question of the back door to the cottage. Madelaine had a key, but nothing's turned up at her house or in the art room. I'd like you to change the lock. I'm not a locksmith, otherwise I'd do it.'

'I'm grateful for your concern,' said Amy. 'I do worry that Matron's here by herself at night. I've offered to stay, but she won't hear of it. During the day, Mr O'Flaherty is always around – and Ira, of course.'

'Mr O'Flaherty's seventy-two, and that dog of his is only good for doing medium-sized rodents and left-over lamb bones to death.'

Amy laughed. 'You might be right about Ira, but don't underestimate Mr O'Flaherty. He's as strong as an ox and very agile. I had no idea he was over seventy. I've seen him shinny up ladders like a monkey when there's been storm damage to the roof. He's in the ceiling above the kitchen now, getting rid of unwanted pigeons.'

'I hope he doesn't give them to the dog.'

'I wouldn't allow that, Constable Fraser, but I have to be realistic.' She hesitated. 'He wrings their necks, which is at least quick, then he burns the nests. Tomorrow, when he's finished, Matron and I will don rubber gloves and plastic shower caps and vacuum every horizontal surface for lice – after he's gone for the day, that is, because we can't be too sure the lice haven't transferred to him.'

Fraser double-checked all the windows and doors of Edwards House. The windows in the common room and the girls' bedrooms were as secure as they could possibly be. Both the front and back doors were locked at night, according to Matron, and couldn't be opened from the outside without a key. Mrs Watkins had keys to both doors, and Matron herself had two sets that she kept in a drawer in her room. Mr O'Flaherty didn't need keys because there was always someone at the school when he arrived.

The headmaster had owned a set, which Matron thought he'd kept on his keyring, together with his car keys.

'Would you mind very much, Matron, if I borrowed your spare set? I'll return them when all this is over.' Matron sniffed, as if to say she thought it was all a bit pointless, but she gave him the keys. As he rolled down the driveway, he caught sight of Ira sitting on what appeared to be Mr O'Flaherty's coat, on the lawn that sloped away from the wall of the kitchen. He was waiting, patiently, for his master to finish for the day.

That evening, Haines and Fraser learned that Mrs Hinds and her daughters had been taken into custody at Sydney Airport and were on their way back to Bowral. Vandegaard, who was being questioned by Melbourne police, was still denying that he had anything to do with Radcliffe's murder.

'By the way,' said Fraser, 'where are Radcliffe's keys? I want to check something.'

'In the glove box. Why?'

'Matron said Radcliffe had keys to Edwards House, and she thinks he kept them with his car keys. I've got a spare set that I borrowed from her this afternoon. I wanted to match them up and make sure nobody else has got them.' But the keys Fraser took from the glove box did not include any matching those borrowed from Matron. He mentioned his concern to Haines.

'You think the murderer took them off the keyring after he murdered Radcliffe, pocketed them, and put the remaining keys into the drawer of Radcliffe's desk?' His tone indicated that he thought this unlikely.

'All I'm saying is that there's a set of keys to Edwards House missing, and there's a possibility that whoever killed Radcliffe has got them. I don't think it's something we can afford to overlook. Haines still didn't look convinced, so Fraser decided to go all the way. 'When I first came here, you gave me some advice. You said always use a process of elimination, and don't accept what appears to be either obvious or trivial. It was good advice, but I don't think we've been following it.'

Haines's eyebrows shot up, but he respected Fraser's views. The lad had a nose like a ferret, and with a murderer on the loose, now wasn't the time to discourage him. 'Okay. Where do you think we should start?'

'I've been looking at that staff list. I went through them all again about an hour ago and re-checked their motives. We concentrated mainly on the academic staff and didn't look as closely at the administrative staff, or the kitchen staff, or Mr O'Flaherty. That one in particular has been worrying me. We know nothing about the man, and there are little things floating around in my head . . .'

'Such as?'

'According to Radcliffe's list, he's seventy-two years old, yet Mrs Graham says he's as strong as an ox and nimble as a monkey.'

'Not to mention twice as fucking pretty.'

'That's the trouble,' Fraser continued. 'We've accepted him for what he appears to be – a funny, eccentric old man. We've never tried to eliminate him in the same way as we did the academic staff. Why should we assume he didn't have a motive for killing Radcliffe?'

'There was no report on him.'

'No, but he was at the top of Radcliffe's age list. He's the oldest member of staff. Radcliffe was concerned about age, otherwise he wouldn't have had a list. He had a question mark next to Madelaine Everhardt's age. It was one of the things about her he'd investigated, so there's your common denominator. If Radcliffe was hassling Madelaine Everhardt about her age, why not Mr O'Flaherty?'

Haines leaned forward, his cynicism having evaporated. 'Deitz called him a dinosaur . . . said he was a survivor from the era of *noblesse oblige*. He said the school was O'Flaherty's *raison d'être*. Why don't we ring the dean?'

Fraser nodded. 'Before you do, there's something else. On the morning of the murder I was in the yard most of the time, but Mr O'Flaherty was in the street, sweeping the footpath. It was where he was when Lockyer and I arrived, and it was where he stayed. He didn't stop doing whatever it is he does out there every morning, even after the ambulance arrived. Why didn't he come up to the cottage? He's an acknowledged stickybeak . . . likes to be in the thick of things. I can recall someone saying that he was always hovering in the background if there was a drama.'

'But this time he wasn't because . . .'

'. . . he already knew?'

Haines stuck his head out of his office door and bellowed to the duty constable to get Dean Blessinham on the phone. 'Now! Immediately! Urgently!' They sat in silence for what seemed an eternity but was in reality less than three minutes. Haines's telephone shrilled. He snatched it from its cradle.

THIRTY-TWO

The phone made Matron jump. Who would be calling after nine? She was in bed, leafing through the latest edition of *Vogue*. There was a cup of hot cocoa on her bedside table. Reading in bed was a luxury she allowed herself once the boarders had gone. She picked up the receiver. 'Eldersley College.'

'It's Amy, Mildred. I hope I didn't startle you. I just wanted to make sure you were all right. Everything's locked up, is it?'

'I locked every door myself,' said Matron, 'and I'm tucked up in bed with a magazine and a hot drink. There's absolutely no need for you to worry about me, Mrs Graham.'

'Please call me Amy. We shouldn't be so formal when the students aren't around.'

'Amy it is, then,' said Matron, eying her cocoa. Mrs Graham was fussing.

'Mildred ... I ... the police think it may not have been Hans Vandegaard who killed Mr Radcliffe. I really should have told you, especially since you're there alone. I don't want to alarm you, but you should be aware that the murderer could be anyone, so please be careful. You mustn't trust people because you think you know them, and don't let anyone in ... *any-one.*' Matron was silent, her cocoa forgotten. Something was nagging at her, something she'd been trying not to dwell upon.

Amy's insistent warning had brought it to the surface. 'Are you still there, Mildred?'

'Yes, I'm still here. There *is* something I suppose I ought to have told you . . . and the police. It's probably unimportant, but . . .'

'You know something that you didn't tell the police?'

'I remembered it later,' said Matron. 'I'm sure it's nothing.'

'What is it, Mildred?'

'Perhaps you could come around for breakfast?' said Matron. 'I could discuss it with you then, and you could tell me whether you think it's worth mentioning.'

'I'll be with you first thing.'

Matron replaced the receiver and sank back into her pillows. Perhaps she *ought* to have said something. She reached for her cocoa. It was then she heard it – the floor in the corridor outside her room creaked. Matron knew every sound the old building made, and there was a particular spot in the corridor that creaked when someone walked on it. She picked up the receiver, her hand shaking. What was Mrs Graham's number? No. That was no good. She needed the police. If only she'd kept the number that Annabelle used. She'd have to dial emergency. Her finger was dragging around the zero for the second time when the handle of her bedroom door began to turn.

'Well?' said Fraser, as he and Haines were speeding towards the address given to them by Dean Blessingham. 'What did he say?'

'His predecessor employed O'Flaherty. He told Blessingham that O'Flaherty was ex-army . . . worked for the British in Northern Ireland. Blessingham couldn't remember anything else. He said he was under the impression his predecessor had been asked to do someone a favour by finding O'Flaherty a job. Everyone assumes

Mr O'Flaherty was some kind of charity case, but it may have been more than that.'

Mr O'Flaherty lived in a nondescript brick house in one of the less desirable streets of Bowral. Their knock was answered by a woman in her sixties. 'He lives out the back,' she said. 'Rents our granny flat. Don't think he's in, though.' She peered beyond them, her eyes roving up and down the street. 'Van's not there, and there's no light in the flat. He sometimes takes his dog for a walk, but if he'd done that his van would be here, wouldn't it? Did you want to go out back?'

Haines and Fraser knocked briefly on the door to the flat and peered half-heartedly through the window. 'The dog would have barked,' said Fraser, as they retraced their steps. 'You don't think he's still at the school, do you? He was there when I left this afternoon – at least, the dog was.'

'Why would he be there after dark?'

Fraser had a sinking feeling in his stomach. He remembered Matron's peculiar look the morning he'd collected the headmaster's inhaler. He could hear Ira's excited barking, and he could also hear Amy Graham saying, 'He's in the ceiling above the kitchen now, getting rid of unwanted pigeons.' There'd been an extension ladder in the kitchen when he'd checked the back door and kitchen windows, but the trapdoor in the ceiling had been shut. There weren't any noises in the roof, so he'd assumed . . . But Mr O'Flaherty couldn't have finished for the day, because his dog was waiting for him outside.

When Fraser finally spoke, what he said sent a chill through Haines. 'He was in the roof this afternoon, clearing out pigeon nests. It's possible he stayed. There was a ladder.'

They drove on in silence. When they reached the school, Haines gestured towards a battered panel van. Fraser pulled up behind it, killing the engine. They moved quickly up the driveway on the grass verge. There was a light upstairs, but the downstairs rooms were in darkness. Fraser opened the door with Matron's keys, making as little noise as possible. Haines followed him into the kitchen, where he shone his torch at the ceiling. There was a gaping hole where, in the afternoon, a manhole cover had been.

The two men went back into the hallway and began mounting the stairs. When Fraser reached the first landing, he heard heavy, slow footsteps coming down the hall, and gestured for Haines to stop. His hand went to his ankle, and he slid his police revolver from its holster. They stood there, hardly breathing, for what seemed forever. It was a cold night, but there were beads of sweat on Fraser's forehead, and his fingers, cradling the grip of his revolver, were wet.

The footsteps came nearer. Fraser saw him before he saw them, and in that brief instant, illuminated by the light from further down the hall, he looked like an advertisement for a monster movie. Fraser could imagine him swatting at planes with his free hand while he cradled the heroine's body in the other. At that moment, Mr O'Flaherty looked up and stopped, Matron's limp form dangling from his arms. Her hair, in a single plait, hung down underneath her head, and her bare feet protruded from beneath the hem of her nightie.

'Why don't you put Matron down on the floor, gently, Mr O'Flaherty, and then we can all go downstairs.' Mr O'Flaherty stared but didn't move. Fraser, climbing slowly to the top of the stairs, raised his revolver and aimed. 'Put her down, please, and then I want you to move away from her, face the wall and put your hands behind your head.' To his immense relief, Mr O'Flaherty did as he was told. While Haines bent over the prostrate form of Matron, Fraser cuffed Mr O'Flaherty and read him his rights – or rather, he gabbled them. His voice was shaking, and all he could think of was that Mr O'Flaherty had hands like plates of meat.

Matron had blacked out, but she was alive. Haines's fingers were resting on her neck, feeling for her pulse. As he removed them, she groaned and came to, saw him bending over her and lashed out, catching him on the bridge of his nose, which bled profusely. It took him several seconds to make her understand that she was no longer in any danger – a more difficult task, he complained, than Fraser had faced in subduing O'Flaherty.

They went into the common room, where Haines, his head held back and a handkerchief at his nose, manœuvred Matron to a chair. Fraser retrieved a second pair of handcuffs from the car and secured Mr O'Flaherty to the handrail of the stairs. Then Haines called the station and asked them to send the cage, after which he rang Amy Graham and asked her to come and stay with Matron.

The cage arrived first. Mr O'Flaherty was detached from the handrail and bundled inside. He was agitated in the extreme, and expressing remorse. By far his greatest concern was his dog. 'Ira's out 'dere,' he said with tears in his eyes, 'and 'e needs me ter look a'ter 'im. What's ter become o' me dog?' Fraser promised to make sure Ira was secured and fed for the night.

When the cage had gone, Fraser left Haines with Matron, who was apologising over and over for having bloodied his nose, and went in search of Ira. He found the little dog still sitting on Mr O'Flaherty's coat on the grass outside the kitchen. When he approached, Ira growled protectively, his lips curling to expose his teeth.

'Have to get in a dog handler,' Fraser told Haines. 'O'Flaherty's left his coat and the dog's guarding it. Can't get near him.'

Haines was derisive. 'Don't tell me you're frightened of that microscopic excuse for a dog? Have you got a rope, Matron?'

'There's string in one of the kitchen cupboards, and there might be some rope in the laundry. Mrs Watkins uses it as a clothes line.'

Haines, his nose perceptibly swollen, headed for the kitchen. What followed sounded more like the baiting of a bear than the capturing of one small dog: there was barking, snarling, yapping, yelling and cursing, and finally, an ominous silence. Fraser looked at Matron. 'Are you a betting woman, Matron?' Haines reappeared with his hand wrapped in a tea towel, through which blood was beginning to seep.

'Have you had a tetanus shot recently?' asked Fraser.

'It'll be all right,' Haines growled.

'I'll take you to the hospital as soon as Mrs Graham arrives. You know what you always say. Never overlook the bleeding obvious.'

THIRTY-THREE

'What were you thinking of, Mildred!' Amy exclaimed at breakfast. 'Why didn't you tell someone? Why didn't you tell *me*?'

'I didn't think . . . I mean, I knew that he'd been here that night, because I remembered when I heard Ira bark at that young detective. It came to me in a flash. I woke hearing Ira bark the night the headmaster died. He . . . Mr O'Flaherty . . . he could see that I remembered. He read my mind, but somehow I couldn't believe, even though I knew that he'd been here, that he could have killed the headmaster. It's too incredible. He's been with us for years. I didn't say anything, because I didn't want to believe . . . How could he have tried to . . .? I've known him so long! How *could* he?' Matron was shaking, whether with anger or delayed shock or both, Amy wasn't sure.

'Don't talk about it, Mildred. Perhaps you should take another of those sedatives.'

'No. I don't want sedatives. I just keep thinking that if the police hadn't . . . What was he going to do?'

Amy, who had in her mind a picture of Matron at the bottom of the stairs, her neck apparently broken in a fall, shuddered. 'When the police question him, we'll know more.'

'I told him I wouldn't say anything, but it didn't do any good. I tried to get away from him, but he was too strong. Everyone had gone and there was no one . . .' She began to weep. 'He had his hands on my neck and he smelled *terrible*. I don't remember what happened. I must have fainted. He killed Madelaine, and he was going to kill me. Why? I mean, I know why he wanted to kill me, but why did he kill poor Madelaine?'

Amy put her arm around Matron's shoulders. 'We don't know yet that he did. We'll leave that to the police. Why don't I make us both a nice hot cup of cocoa?'

But there are some things, as Amy once remarked, that cocoa can't fix. Matron did dwell upon the night she narrowly escaped death. She was so grateful to her rescuers that she visited Haines in hospital, where he was recovering from an allergic reaction to his tetanus injection, bringing him chocolates (which his doctor advised him not to eat) and flowers that made him sneeze. She and Mrs Watkins baked an enormous boiled fruitcake for Fraser and Haines with 'Thank You' emblazoned across it in blue icing that everyone in the station helped them eat. She informed Fraser that he and Sergeant Haines were welcome to have dinner at the school at any time. She particularly recommended Mrs Watkins' baked dinners.

In an effort to forget, Matron needed a hobby, and an opportunity presented itself when Gilbert Fairweather next visited the school. The executive director, fearing that he'd face bankruptcy if bad publicity prompted parents to remove their offspring, mentioned to Amy that he'd decided to sell some of his shares. To his surprise, he found a willing buyer in Matron, who'd saved a tidy sum as a result of living and working at the school. She commenced her investment with no knowledge of business, and every appearance of being happy to leave financial matters in Mr Fairweather's hands.

She soon discovered, however, that managing her investment

in Pastoral Enterprises was far more rewarding, particularly after a discussion with Detective Constable Fraser on the subject of shareholder's rights. She became the shareholder from hell, insisting on regular meetings, offering to purchase Gilbert Fairweather's brother's holding, and demanding that the company produce annual reports. She made it her business to know how much money was coming in, and where and how it was being spent, paying particular attention to the executive director's salary and personal expenses.

During his incarceration in the local hospital, Haines did some soul searching about his professional and private life (if he could be said to have one). He revisited his conversations with Mr O'Flaherty, anguishing about his failure to investigate the man's past, and groaning every time he recalled Mr O'Flaherty's grubby hand raised to his forehead in military salute. If it hadn't been for Fraser, Matron would now be dead. Maybe he should pack it in and make way for a younger, smarter man.

Fraser could see that Haines was depressed. 'If it's any consolation,' he said, 'I've been doing the same thing. I was the one who saw Matron staring at O'Flaherty, and I didn't question her about it. To top it off, I saw the dog waiting for O'Flaherty outside the kitchen, and Mrs Graham told me he was clearing pigeons out of the roof. If anything had happened, it would have been my fault.'

'You put two and two together in the end. But for you she wouldn't be alive. The bugger saluted me twice, and still I didn't tumble. He didn't look like someone who was trained in unarmed combat.'

'Did Goulburn say why he did it?'

'Radcliffe told him he had to retire. The school was his life, so he followed Radcliffe to the restaurant and disabled the car. He wore gloves so there wouldn't be prints. He parked up the highway and watched the restaurant car park until he saw Radcliffe opening the bonnet. Then he pulled in as if he just happened to be driving past, and offered Radcliffe a lift back to the school. He pleaded with Radcliffe for his job but it had no effect, so when Radcliffe got out of the car he followed him and killed him. He took the keys from Radcliffe's pocket, carried him into the office and arranged him in the chair. When he was putting the keys in the drawer, he saw the inhaler and thought it might bamboozle us into thinking Radcliffe had died during an attack. He wound Radcliffe's fingers around the thing and pressed. Rigor mortis did the rest.'

'What about Hinds's wife?'

'Hinds told her he was leaving her for another woman, and she knew it was Madelaine Everhardt. When she picked up her daughters from hockey practice, she went to the art room to have it out. She took the girls with her, but things got heated and Madelaine refused to talk in front of the girls. They went back to the car, but she kept one of the hockey sticks with her. It was the fact that for Madelaine it was only a casual affair that incensed her – even more so, she said, than if her husband's love had been returned. When Madelaine laughed at the idea of cohabiting with her darling Dennis, she belted her with the hockey stick and followed up with the lethal blow while she was semi-conscious.

Amy, who was also curious to discover what details had emerged following the arrests, invited Haines to dinner when he was released from hospital. Because he'd required hospitalisation, the case had been removed to Goulburn. Haines, although he normally wouldn't discuss police matters with anyone outside the job, gave her a brief précis of events leading up to Madelaine Everhardt's death.

'And what about the private detective?'

'Ah. We think that might be a drugs killing. Brand must have stumbled onto something while he was sleuthing for Radcliffe, and thought he'd cash in. That's my theory. We're working on it. Mum's the word.'

'Of course,' said Amy. 'And Mr O'Flaherty? What did he have to say for himself?'

'He was a trained killer, Amy. He belonged to a division of the SAS that was stationed in Northern Ireland about 1950. His mission, if you can call it that, was to infiltrate the IRA. During a patrol, two members of his troop were ambushed and murdered, and he became obsessed with finding the men responsible. When he did, he despatched them, like your pigeons – broke their necks. He was spirited out of Ireland and sent to Australia, in time-honoured fashion. Why is it that when the Brits have a problem, they transport it to us?'

THIRTY-FOUR

Ira grieved for Mr O'Flaherty, but was eventually persuaded that a bed in the laundry at Eldersley and regular lamb bones from Mrs Watkins went part of the way towards compensating him for his loss. He was promoted to watchdog and, without Mr O'Flaherty to follow around the grounds, transferred his affections to the girls.

Amy, in a campaign to counter the avalanche of adverse publicity that followed in the wake of Madelaine's murder, made use of Ira's cutesy canine qualities in a series of professionally taken stills to accompany articles she'd submitted to chosen magazines and newspapers. Her aim, she said, was to present the human face of education. These articles proved so popular that enrolments increased. Gilbert Fairweather was forced to admit that a strong-minded, eloquent woman could be every bit as much a drawcard as a male anglophile.

Media publicity after the murders was inevitable, but Amy fought fire with fire. If Eldersley was to be in the spotlight, she'd make sure that people liked what they saw. In a ten-minute segment for commercial TV, she allowed herself to be interviewed in the office where Horace Radcliffe died. She expounded her views on educating women and the importance of bringing women into politics and the professions, and she countered, with agility and grace, any negative comments.

'Quite the contrary,' she replied to the young journalist who suggested that the stigma of two murders would linger. 'At Eldersley we rise above tragedy. Mr Radcliffe's legacy to this school will not be forgotten, and we will preserve, in the Girls' Service Training Unit, the ideals of loyalty and discipline that he so strongly upheld. We will also cherish the ideal of intellectual freedom that Madelaine Everhardt held dear. In education, nothing is mutually exclusive.'

'But surely,' the journalist insisted, steering the conversation back to the murders, 'these killings will make every parent wonder about the safety . . .'

Amy cut him short with a patronising smile. 'Mr Newly . . . the only way we lose *our* pupils is through successful completion of the Higher School Certificate. They go on to complete their university education and take up positions and roles in business and the professions, for which the staff at Eldersley help them prepare.'

After the interview with Amy, the segment continued with some well-chosen clips of girls conducting experiments in the laboratory, girls painting and sculpting in the art room, girls performing Shakespeare in the hall and, inevitably, girls dressed in khaki, marching around the playing field. The musical backing for the last of these clips was a song by Helen Reddy that Amy had particularly requested. As the camera followed, for the final fifteen seconds, the precision marching of the girls in their slouch hats, and captured in close-up their fresh faces and hands held up in united salute, the words of the song seemed peculiarly apt:

> *If I had to, I could do anything*
> *I am strong*
> *I am invincible*
> *I am woman . . .*

Gilbert Fairweather, when the segment went to air, called Amy 'a class act'. She'd not only demonstrated her ability to handle the media, but she looked fantastic on TV. Haines agreed with him, but then he thought Amy looked fantastic all the time.

Haines and Fraser received commendations and congratulatory messages from the chief inspector in Sydney, for saving Matron's life. Their success was compounded, in the months that followed, by the discovery of a marijuana plantation on a sixty-acre property owned by Mr Georgiou Papandopoulos, who was arrested together with his son. The gymnasium, thanks to Fraser's suspicions, Haines had placed under surveillance long enough for the Bowral patrol to establish the routine whereby the plants were leaving the farm and being transported to Sydney. Only when he'd collated the evidence did Haines present it to the inspector and relinquish control of the operation, although he insisted that he and his men be allowed to participate in the raid. He also acknowledged his indebtedness to the suspicions of Detective Constable Fraser.

Encouraged by a second invitation to dinner with Amy, Haines plucked up enough courage to invite her to the highlight of the Southern Highlands winter social season, the Bong Bong Race-course Ball. To his amazement she accepted, initiating his resolve to go on a diet and get some exercise.

The ball was patronised by the cream of Southern Highlands society, as well as the Sydney social set. Haines, who managed to lose a stone and a half, felt like a million dollars. This wasn't surprising, if one considers that the attractive woman on his arm was probably worth considerably more than that. Their picture appeared in the social pages, as did the photograph of Fraser and Victoria Delhunty – the latter wearing a black, off-the-shoulder gown, and the former a hired dinner suit and an infatuated smile. There was, as far as Fraser was concerned, not another woman in the universe.

Children's books by Wendy Milton

Zach's Story series

Paperback and eBook editions available for sale at www.wendymilton.com